LOVING
THE
Storm

THE DELANEYS OF CAMBRIA, BOOK 3

Linda Seed

LINDA SEED

The author is available for book signings, book club discussions, conferences, and other appearances.

Linda Seed may be contacted via e-mail at lindaseed24@gmail.com or on Facebook at www.facebook.com/LindaSeedAuthor. Visit Linda Seed's website at www.lindaseed.com.

ISBN-13: 978-1983753718
ISBN-10: 1983753718

First Trade Paperback Printing: February 2018

Cover design by Tara Mayberry, Teaberry Creative

BY LINDA SEED

THE MAIN STREET MERCHANTS
MOONSTONE BEACH
CAMBRIA SKY
NEARLY WILD
FIRE AND GLASS

THE DELANEYS OF CAMBRIA
A LONG, COOL RAIN
THE PROMISE OF LIGHTNING
LOVING THE STORM
SEARCHING FOR SUNSHINE

THE RUSSO SISTERS
SAVING SOFIA
FIRST CRUSH

LOVING
THE
Storm

For Condee, with love, for bringing sunshine into my life every day.

Chapter One

Liam Delaney had a reputation as a temperamental asshole, but that didn't mean he actually was one. For instance, he didn't especially *want* to fire the poor bastard standing in front of him in the Delaney Ranch stables.

But Liam's father was retired now, and his brother Ryan was too damned nice for his own good. So, that left Liam to do what had to be done.

"We're gonna have to let you go, Kev." Liam leaned his butt against the metal railing of one of the horse stalls, his arms crossed over his chest. A light rain drummed onto the roof.

Kevin, an annoyingly cocky guy in his early twenties, reacted first with surprise and then with belligerence. "Don't give me that 'let you go' bullshit. What you mean is, you're firing me."

Liam nodded. "That's what I mean."

"This is crap." Kevin's face was turning red, and he was starting to puff up a little the way men did when they wanted to scare each other. "What the hell, man?"

"Look." Liam pushed off from where he was leaning against the stall and let his hands fall to his sides, unconsciously preparing for a potential fight. "You've been here, what, six weeks? You're not catching on the way we'd hoped you would. Don't take it personally. This work isn't for everybody."

And that was God's honest truth. Not everybody could spend a whole day from sunrise to sunset dealing with the stink of cow shit, let alone the messier parts of ranching, like delivering calves. The first time this guy had to castrate a bull, he was going to pass out like a 12-year-old girl at a dogfight. Not that Liam had ever been to a dogfight.

"You didn't give me a chance," Kevin said. The guy was shorter than Liam, maybe only five-foot-ten, and he had a kind of permanent pout that made Liam want to punch him. "You didn't give me time to learn. I could—"

"You've had time." Liam kept his tone mild. "I've been doing this long enough to know when it's not a good fit. We'll give you two weeks severance—that'll help you get settled somewhere else."

In fact, he hadn't needed six weeks to know Kevin wasn't going to work out—he knew the first day. The guy showed up late, left early, and was about as comfortable with a herd of cattle as Liam was performing classical ballet.

"Aw, fuck you." Kevin took a step closer to Liam. "You and your brother think you're so much better than everyone else. He's a pussy, and you're a goddamned gimp."

Liam knew what he was supposed to do at this point, according to the rules of what it meant to be Liam Delaney. He was supposed to shove this dickhead up against the wall, his forearm crushing the asshole's windpipe. But his heart wasn't in it, so instead, he stood his ground and glared at the guy.

"You'd better think about it before you say anything else about me or my brother."

Liam was vaguely aware of someone coming into the stables, and then he heard Ryan speak. "What's he saying about us?"

"That you're a pussy and I'm a gimp." Liam didn't take his

eyes off Kevin.

Ryan looked from Liam to Kevin and then back again.

"You doing okay?" Ryan asked Liam. The real question—the one left unsaid—was, *Am I going to have to stop you from knocking this guy's teeth out?*

"I'm good," Liam said. "But I think Kevin here had better leave."

Ryan nodded. "Go on, now," he said to Kevin.

Kevin glared at both of them, spat a big wad of saliva onto the ground between them, and walked out of the barn and into the drizzling rain.

When he was gone, Ryan clapped Liam once on the back.

"You okay?" he asked.

"Yeah."

"You sure?"

"Yeah." Liam nodded.

"Huh. I'm just asking because a year ago—hell, even six months ago—you'd have had ol' Kevin on his ass before he'd even gotten out the *g* sound in the word *gimp*."

Liam glared at Ryan, his hands on his hips. "You give me shit if I fight, now you're giving me shit when I don't."

Ryan scratched the back of his head. "Well … you just don't seem like yourself, is all."

Gray morning light streamed in through the stable's big doors. The place smelled like fresh hay, dirt, and horse piss.

Instead of answering his brother directly, Liam said, "I can't fuckin' stand that guy."

"Well, I don't much like him, either, but that's not my main concern right now," Ryan said. He put a hand on Liam's shoulder and gave it a quick squeeze. "You want to talk, I'm here."

"Talk about what? I don't need to talk."

"All right." Ryan nodded. "It's just … it's gotta be hard,

man, knowing it's really over. That she's not coming back."

"Ah, hell," Liam said.

The *she* in question was Megan, Liam's ex-girlfriend. Liam had thought he was doing okay with the breakup. That was, until she'd moved to British Columbia to be with her new guy—who also happened to be Liam's cousin.

He should be over it by now. The breakup had happened almost a year and a half ago. That should have been enough time for Liam to get his head out of his ass and move on.

But the news that she was moving in with Drew had been a gut punch. Liam had acted like it was no big deal, like it didn't mean anything to him. But he wasn't feeling like himself anymore. Normally, he would have handed Kevin his ass, but right now, he couldn't seem to care enough to do it.

Ryan had read that one like one of the damned billboards out on Highway 1.

She's not coming back.

Liam wasn't mad at Megan. Hell, he wasn't even mad at Drew. He knew things hadn't been right between himself and Megan, and he knew she was happy now. He wanted her to be happy.

But it didn't change the fact that he'd loved her, and she loved someone else. That made a man feel a lot of things, and none of them were good.

A guy like Kevin didn't seem to matter much amid all that.

You're a goddamned gimp.

Well, it was true, wasn't it?

Two summers before, Liam had been in a bad accident involving a horse and a shattered leg. He'd had surgery, and that had been a success—to a point. When the cast had come off and Liam had started walking again, his doctors had said it was normal that he didn't have full range of motion. But here it was sixteen months after the fact, and he still walked with a noticeable limp.

Physical therapy had helped, but not enough.

He didn't have pain anymore, and he could do all the things he used to do, so that was good. But every day as he went about his work, he was reminded that he was a broken man. His brothers didn't get it, and neither did his dad. They thought he should be glad he was walking at all, and hell, he *was* glad.

But being glad was one thing. Glad or not, he still felt the loss, still mourned what once had been.

You didn't stop mourning overnight—not if you'd lost something that mattered. Liam was still grieving over the leg just like he was still grieving over his uncle Redmond.

Redmond had been gone almost four years now, but for Liam, the pain of it was still as raw as if it had happened last week.

He didn't understand how the rest of his family had moved on so easily—how everyone had simply adjusted and gotten on with their lives. But then, none of them had been as close to Redmond as Liam was. Redmond had been like a second father to him when his real father had been too busy with his other children to notice his middle boy.

Only one other person in the family seemed to be as affected by Redmond's death as Liam was. Drew McCray—Redmond's son, and the guy who'd just moved in with Liam's girl—seemed pretty screwed up about the man's death, and Drew had never even met Redmond.

At least Drew and Liam had something in common, other than the woman who used to love one of them and currently loved the other.

Liam knew he needed to stop feeling sorry for himself. He

was alive. He was healthy. He could still walk, which hadn't been a foregone conclusion after his accident. He was still himself. He could still work.

Liam took a moment to calm his mind, then followed Ryan out into the wet, dreary day.

Aria Howard wondered whether it made more sense to fashion the door of the yurt she was building out of discarded water bottles or used sandwich bags. The bags would be easier to work with, no question, but the bottles were so much more abundant on the beaches of California's Central Coast.

The yurt, a ten-foot-diameter dwelling that would eventually have a bottle-cap floor and a mosaic skylight of broken glass, was to be made entirely of trash she'd scavenged from the local coastline—or the semi-local coastline, anyway. The beaches of Cambria tended to be admirably clean, so she sometimes had to venture south to Cayucos and Pismo Beach to gather materials. If that failed, then Santa Barbara was a treasure trove.

She hadn't considered the relative tidiness of Cambria when she'd accepted Genevieve Porter's offer of an artist's residency. If she had considered it, she still would have accepted. But she'd have brought more of her own trash.

So far, the yurt was no more than a set of sketches and the beginnings of a basic frame. As she stood back and looked it over in the cavernous barn she was using as a studio, it wasn't the yurt's skylight that was causing her problems. It was the one above her in the barn.

Rain pattered on the barn's roof, and some of that rain was coming in through the skylight, plunking down wetly onto the first pieces of her yurt.

True, most of her materials had been in the ocean or out in the elements for God knew how long and probably wouldn't suffer much. But still.

She moved the pieces of her yurt out of the line of fire and considered the skylight. The question of why there was a skylight in this old, retired barn in the first place was a mystery. But here it was, and it did provide lovely natural light on her work space. When it wasn't leaking.

Aria dug a five-gallon bucket out of the supplies she had stacked in a corner of the barn and placed it under the skylight. Drops fell into the bucket in a rhythmic *plink-plink-plink*.

She stretched her neck, which was stiff after a morning of work piecing cigarette butts, drinking straws, and plastic cutlery together to form part of the yurt's frame. Then she breathed in deeply the scents coming through the big, open doors: earth, hay, wet grass, pine trees, and the vast, churning ocean less than a half mile away.

She crossed over to where the doors opened onto the world and peered outside from her relatively dry spot under the barn's roof. The earth was green and fragrant, and the music of the rain on the grass soothed her mind.

Accepting the residency had been a good idea. She'd needed a break from her routine, from the day-to-day demands that always seemed to call her away from her work. And it wasn't as though she had anything to keep her close to home.

She had no family, no real friends, no man in her life. Most of the time, she managed to stave off the loneliness by throwing herself into her work. But lately, that strategy hadn't been working as well as it used to. She'd needed a distraction.

And she could hardly imagine a more picturesque spot than the Delaney Ranch to provide it.

From where she was standing, she could see a few black and brown cows dotting the rolling green hills in the distance. Above the patter of the rain, she heard a mournful moo.

Aria was thinking about the cows and what they might or might not be saying to each other when she heard the squish of shoes on a wet path. She looked up to find Gen Porter, in a slicker and rubber boots, waddling toward the barn. A red umbrella protected her curly, copper-colored hair from the rain.

"Hey!" Gen gave Aria a friendly wave.

"I thought you'd be at the gallery," Aria said. Gen owned an art gallery on Main Street in town, and at just before noon in the middle of the week, she should have been showing paintings and sculptures and scenic watercolors to whatever tourists were out braving the weather.

"Lunch break," Gen said. "I'm meeting Ryan. I never get much foot traffic when it rains, anyway." Ryan Delaney, Gen's husband, was one of the owners of the ranch where Aria's temporary studio space sat, as well as the guest cottage where she was staying. The barn she was using as a studio had been taken out of use some years ago when the Delaney family had built a bigger, state-of-the-art facility elsewhere on the property. Now, it was used as a work space for the artists in Gen's residency program.

Gen came into the shelter of the barn and lowered her umbrella. "I just thought I'd pop in and see how you're getting by." Aria had constructed numerous long rods, roughly the size of two-by-fours, out of trash. Gen looked at the rods, which were waiting to be assembled into the skeleton of the yurt. "Well, that's coming along."

"It is," Aria agreed. "I had to move it a little while ago. It was getting dripped on."

Gen went to where the bucket was catching the rainwater from the skylight. She peered up at the roof, where the rain was making a *rat-a-tat* rhythm on plexiglass. They could see the gray of the cloudy sky beyond.

"Well, crap," Gen said.

They stood side by side, staring up at the skylight. Gen, in the unconscious way of pregnant women everywhere, laid one hand affectionately atop the generous bump of her belly.

"I'll see if I can get Ryan to come out here and take a look at it," Gen said. "Though I don't think he can go up on the roof until it dries out."

"No, I wouldn't expect him to," Aria agreed. "And there's no rush. I can work in another area until it's fixed or until the rain stops. But I hate to, because it's really nice light."

Gen told her the story of the skylight and how Ryan had installed it for Gordon Kendrick, the first artist Gen had brought to the ranch for the residency.

"Ryan thought it was stupid. But he put it in anyway because he was trying to get into my pants."

"Well, that must have worked out for him," Aria observed.

"It really did." Gen was due in about a month, and she fondly rubbed her large, round middle. "But that doesn't mean he's a genius at installing skylights. I'm pretty sure this was his first one."

Aria looked up and considered how high the barn's roof was. "You sure it's okay for him to go up there? It's a really high roof. I don't want to be the cause of him falling on his head and leaving your baby fatherless."

"Now that you mention it, he almost fell on his head when he put the thing in," Gen remarked.

"Really? Jeez."

"He got distracted because he was trying to look at my ass," Gen said.

"Well, he's already seen it," Aria answered. "So that's one less danger to think about."

Chapter Two

By the time Liam got back to the house for lunch, he was cold, soaked, and grumpy as hell. Ryan was already there, settled in at the big kitchen table across from his wife. Ryan and Liam's mother bustled around the table with a pot of food in her hands, fussing over Gen.

"Now, you eat," Sandra said as she spooned hot, steaming stew into Gen's bowl. "That baby needs nourishment, and so do you. *Hmph*. A woman can't be expected to grow a human being eating nothing but those salads you like so much."

Sandra moved on to Ryan. "I've got beans and cornbread for you. Though I don't know how you expect me to keep making all these special vegetarian meals just for one person. My God. Nobody would think you live on a damned cattle ranch."

"I don't expect you to make special meals," Ryan said. "I've told you that. I can cook. I can—"

"Now, you can stop right there, boy," Sandra scolded him. "You know as well as I do that you're not going to cook a hot lunch after you've been doing hard work since dawn. And I won't have you going without. Not in this house."

Nobody considered it odd that Sandra was complaining about doing something she actually wanted to do and wouldn't have stopped doing even with a gun to her head. They were all pretty much used to it.

"Liam, don't you sit on down yet," she told him as he came into the room. "Go and see what's keeping your father."

Liam went into the living room to look for his dad. Orin wasn't out there, but Liam found him upstairs in his office, frowning over a stack of papers in front of him on his desk.

"Mom wanted me to call you for lunch," Liam said.

Orin looked up, distracted. He scratched his nearly bald head and looked mournfully at the papers. "Tell her I'll be down directly."

"Everything okay?" Liam asked.

"Oh … I suppose it is. But I've got these papers from your sister's Realtor, and I can't make heads or tails of 'em."

Liam blinked a few times in surprise. "Breanna's got a Realtor? What for?"

"Well, so she can buy a house, son. What else do people have Realtors for?"

Liam rubbed his face with one hand. "Wait. Back up. Breanna's moving?" His sister had been living in the Delaney house with her two boys since her husband, a Marine officer, had been killed in combat when their youngest was just two years old. When had she decided to leave? And why? And how had he missed it?

"Well, she's been talking about it awhile now. You mean to tell me you didn't notice?"

He *hadn't* noticed, but he was too embarrassed to admit it.

"So, what are the papers?" he asked instead.

"It's a draft of an offer she wants to make on a place in town." Orin looked as though he were suffering from a bout of constipation. Which, at his age, he might have been. "She wanted me to look it over, but …" He shoved the papers away. "I don't have much of a head for this kind of thing."

"Well, why isn't Colin doing it?" Colin, Liam's other brother, was the main steward of the family's substantial fortune. He was a lawyer, and he specialized in real estate. Liam couldn't fathom why his father was being given this task instead of the one Delaney who'd made his career out of that sort of thing.

"Colin's not here, son. Or maybe you didn't notice that, either."

Colin had been living on the family's other ranch property out in Montana for the past few years. Liam scowled at his father. "That doesn't mean—"

"What in the world are you two doing up there?" Sandra bellowed up the stairs. "I think I told you lunch was ready. Or do you expect me to walk up there and feed it to you?"

Orin raised his eyebrows. "I guess we'd best get down there."

As soon as he got downstairs, Liam started in on Breanna, who was just settling in at the table next to Gen.

"Since when are you moving?" He sat down across from his father and began spooning stew into his bowl.

"Where have you been?" Breanna said. "I've been looking for a place for months."

"Well, nobody said anything to me about it."

"Sorry to have kept you out of the loop." The *sorry* part might have been sarcasm. "I thought maybe when I discussed it right out in the open on several occasions while you were in the room, you might have caught wind of it. But I can see I should have put something in writing for you." She arched one eyebrow at him.

"Huh. I guess I might have been a little distracted lately," Liam said sheepishly.

"You think?"

"Yeah, yeah." He buttered a slice of bread and focused on her. "Why do you want to move in the first place? This is home. You got a problem with us?"

"She doesn't have to have a problem with anybody to want her own place," Ryan put in.

"Yeah, but if she wants her own place, she could have one built here on the property," Liam said, as though Breanna herself were not sitting just two chairs away. "If that was good enough for you and Gen, why isn't it good enough for her?"

"I'm right here," Breanna said, reaching around behind Gen to smack Liam lightly on the back of the head. "I can hear you."

"Now, you all settle down," Sandra said as she finally took her own seat at the table. "If a grown woman wants a place of her own, why, there's no reason she shouldn't have it. She's talking about moving across town, not to the moon."

To Liam's mind, Breanna's boys, Michael and Lucas, belonged here on the ranch, with the family. They didn't have a father anymore, but they did have a grandfather and a couple of uncles right here who could fill the gap, at least a little. If Breanna moved into town, what would her sons have in terms of male influence?

"Speaking of me moving, did you get a chance to look over that offer?" Breanna asked Orin.

Orin looked uncomfortable, and he rubbed the back of his neck with one hand. "Well, I tried to, but I can't say real estate is my strong point."

"You need to talk to Colin," Ryan said.

"I don't want to talk to Colin," Breanna said.

"Why not?" Gen asked.

Breanna dropped her fork onto her plate and gestured emphatically with both hands. "Because he'll tell me not to buy the house! He'll say it's priced too high, or it's in the wrong location, or … or it needs too much work."

"*Does* it need too much work?" Gen wanted to know.

"Yes!" Breanna's shoulders fell. "But I love it anyway. And I don't want to be talked out of it."

"On the topic of DIY," Gen said, turning to Ryan, "can I get you to look at the skylight in the old barn?"

"I've seen the skylight in the old barn," Ryan said. "I installed it."

"I know you did," Gen said in a soothing voice as she patted Ryan's hand. "And you did a great job. But there's a little problem."

"What kind of problem?"

"The kind where water pours in through the roof when it rains."

"Since when?" Ryan asked.

"Since today. I went out there to see how Aria's doing, and she was using a bucket to catch the rainwater."

"Who the hell's Aria?" Liam demanded.

"She's the new artist." Gen leaned across Breanna to see him better. "And I've talked about her several times, right in front of you."

Liam ignored the last part, where Gen had basically pointed out to him that he was a dumbass. He didn't think there was much in it for him to argue the point.

"You've got a girl artist out there?" he said.

"A woman, actually," Gen said.

Sandra stopped with her fork halfway to her mouth and gave Gen a look that meant she was up to something. "Liam can go on out there and look at that skylight."

"But Ryan—" Liam started to say.

"Ryan's got a lot on his plate," Sandra said, without giving any indication of what that might be. "You can do it, boy. Help out your sister-in-law."

"I'd appreciate it," Gen said hopefully. "Please?" She batted her eyelashes at him and grinned.

"Well, hell," Liam said.

Liam had other things to do besides looking at a damned skylight, especially when Ryan was the one who'd put it in. If a man didn't do something right the first time, he ought to be the one to fix the thing when it stopped working right.

But Sandra had gotten the idea that Liam was the one who should do it, and when Sandra got an idea, any effort to change her mind was a waste of time. Liam's mother was a stronger force of nature than the storm that was causing the skylight to leak in the first place.

He could have argued with his mother for the hell of it, but he'd known he was going to lose.

That was how he ended up standing in the barn after lunch, looking up at the roof and listening to the sound of rain dripping into a plastic bucket.

"Well, shit," he muttered, looking at the leak.

There in the barn, off to the side to keep them out of the water, lay some long, rod-shaped things he couldn't identify. At first he didn't know what the hell they were, but then, peering at them more closely, he saw that they were made of used cigarettes and sporks. Where did a person even get that many sporks?

"It doesn't much look like anything yet. I've really just started on it." A woman's voice came out of nowhere, and he jumped a little. He covered that up the best he could, because what man wanted to look anything but composed in front of a beautiful woman?

And she was beautiful, though maybe not in an obvious

way. Maybe not in the way most people would recognize.

The first thing he noticed as she came into the barn was the body, in skinny jeans and a clingy T-shirt under her rain jacket. The body, with its lush curves, almost struck him speechless.

The second thing he noticed were the eyes. Pale gray, like the clouds on a rainy day.

Add to that the thick, dark hair and lips so plush they were begging to be kissed, and Liam temporarily forgot what he was doing in the barn in the first place. Hell, he might have even forgotten his name.

He didn't realize he was staring at her until she said, "Are you here to fix the skylight?"

"Uh … yeah. I am," he said, recovering himself. "What are those things, anyway?" He gestured at the spork constructions.

She waved him over to a worktable set up against one wall of the barn, where she had more cigarette butts, more sporks, tubs of some kind of glue, and in the middle of all that, a sketchbook.

She flipped open the sketchbook and pointed at a page covered in drawings. "This," she said simply.

Liam peered at the drawings, trying to make sense of them. "Looks like some kind of tent … or maybe an igloo."

"It's a yurt," she said.

"A yurt."

"It's a kind of rudimentary dwelling that—"

"I know what a yurt is," he told her. "What I don't know is why you're building one out of sporks."

"It's not just sporks," she said. "And it's not just a yurt. It's art."

He guessed that was a matter of opinion, and his opinion was that it didn't look much like art to him.

"Gen said you were some kind of artist," he said, because

that seemed safe enough.

"Aria Howard," she said, holding out her hand.

He took it, only then realizing that his social skills were so lacking that he hadn't even bothered to introduce himself. "Liam Delaney."

"It's nice to meet you, Liam." She smiled at him with those sensual lips of hers. Then she tightened her grip on his hand just a little before letting go.

Looking back, he'd probably say he knew even then that he was screwed.

Chapter Three

Liam felt confident that he could safely get up on the roof and fix the skylight, even with his leg still giving him trouble. But he sure as shit wasn't going to do it on a rainy day. Hell, he wouldn't have tried that even if he were one hundred percent able-bodied.

Given the weather, there was nothing of any practical value he could do in the barn today. But he didn't seem to want to leave yet, either.

"So, why a spork yurt?" he asked. He tried to sound like he was interested and not mocking her project. Though he was mocking it, just a little, in his head.

"It's not just sporks," she said again.

"I can see that. It's cigarette butts, too."

"That, and other trash I've scavenged from the local beaches."

"You've found that many sporks on the beach?" he asked.

"You're fixating on the sporks," she pointed out. "But it's all kinds of beach trash. Water bottles, plastic bags, broken flip-flops, sand toys. The piece is about what we do to our environment, but it's also about consumerism. Consumption. The things we use and throw away."

He looked at the beginnings of the yurt with a skeptical

grimace. "There's a reason we throw that stuff away." He picked up a broken red plastic sand shovel from her worktable, turned it over in his hands, then put it back down. "What are you going to do with the thing when it's done?"

"I'm going to live in it," she said simply.

"You're gonna live in it," he repeated, as though he hadn't understood her. And he was pretty sure he hadn't.

"Well, temporarily. But, yes. I'm going to live in it, inside an art gallery, as a performance piece. For a period of time to be negotiated later, when I find a gallery that wants to show it."

Liam raised his eyebrows and assessed her. "What the hell for?"

"Expression," she said.

"Expression."

"Yes."

He rubbed the stubble on his chin. "Well, all right. Though I can't say what the hell it is you're trying to express."

"That's up to the viewer," Aria said. "My job is to create the art. It's your job to decide what to think about it."

"You didn't tell me your brother-in-law was so ... attractive," Aria told Gen later that afternoon at Gen's gallery. The rain was still coming down outside, and Aria was finished working for the day. She'd come downtown to check out the shops, and she'd stopped to say hello when she saw that Gen was alone in the gallery.

"Both of my brothers-in-law are attractive," Gen said. "It's a thing with the Delaney men, apparently." She wrinkled her nose. "Except Orin. Though I suppose he might have been good-looking too, back in the day."

Aria was sipping coffee she'd poured from a machine Gen kept in the back room of the gallery. Gen, who'd given up caffeine for the duration of her pregnancy, was making do with herbal tea.

"So, is Liam going to come back to fix the skylight?" Gen asked.

"He said he would."

Gen wiggled her eyebrows at Aria. "Do you want me to fix you up with him?"

"What? I ... no."

"You're single, right?" Gen asked. "And it's got to be kind of lonely in that guesthouse." She looked at Aria meaningfully.

It *was* lonely. As she sat there, she pondered it. *Did* she want Gen to fix her up with Liam? She didn't want a relationship—she didn't do relationships—but that didn't mean they couldn't have fun, did it? She hadn't had fun with a man in a long time. A very long time.

"What are you thinking?" Gen prodded her.

"I'm just ... considering my options," Aria said.

"I'm not trying to be pushy, really." Gen fidgeted a little with her teacup. "But it would be good for him to go out with someone. He needs to have a little fun."

The gallery was brightly lit, with gleaming, pale wood floors and white walls splashed with vibrantly colored art. In contrast to the riot of colors, Gen was dressed in a slim black dress that hugged her huge belly. Probably due to the rain, the foot traffic from the street was next to none. The sound of the rain on the sidewalk and the roof was pleasant and comforting inside the warm gallery.

"I probably shouldn't be saying anything," Gen went on. "It's not my business. But ... Liam's been hurt a couple of times. He's been burned pretty badly, and it's been hard for him to get back out there. He's a good guy, so I'd really like to see him bounce back a little ..." She blew a stray red curl off of her forehead. "Don't mind me. It's the estrogen. I want to mother everyone."

Aria thought of how Liam had favored his right leg earlier in the barn. If he was suffering from emotional wounds as well as physical ones, that was an indication she definitely shouldn't go there. She had enough issues of her own without dealing with someone else's.

"Liam didn't strike me as the emotionally vulnerable type," Aria told Gen after a while. "He seemed ... I don't know. More like the classic cocky bad boy."

"Yeah," Gen said. "He's got that act down."

They all had parts they played, didn't they? Everyone had a persona they presented to the world, whether it was real or not.

"So. Should I talk to him?" Gen asked.

"Oh ... no. No."

"Well, let me know if you change your mind," Gen said.

Liam absolutely did not want to get involved with the artist in the barn. Hell, no. Not a goddamned chance.

But getting involved was one thing. Sex was another.

He hadn't been with a woman since his breakup with Megan, and that was a long damned time ago. He wondered if Aria Howard might be amenable to a little no-strings fun.

Working in the barn later that afternoon—the barn they actually used, not the one with the spork thing in it—he kept thinking about her, about her body, and the eyes, and the hair, and that mouth. And the way she'd tightened her hold on his hand.

He wasn't one to use women just for sex. But would it hurt to ask her what she thought of the idea?

He hoped the rain would end soon, so the barn roof could dry and he'd have an excuse to go over there and see her again.

Liam just hoped he wouldn't fall off the damned roof. It was hard to impress a woman when you were screaming like a girl. At least, he assumed it would be.

It was dark by the time Aria got back to the Delaney guest cottage. She flipped on the lights in the sitting room, the kitchen, and the bedroom until the entire little house was aglow. Then she lit the gas fire in the fireplace, less because she was cold than because she needed more light, more life, inside the house.

After about ten days at the ranch, she was feeling the solitude and the loneliness of being out here in the middle of nowhere by herself.

Yes, the cottage was on the property of a large ranch where a lot of people lived and worked. But the guest cottage itself was away from all of that, off a little dirt road near a creek, far enough from the busy bustle of the ranch that Aria could imagine there was no one left in the world but her.

She'd stayed away from the house all afternoon for that reason. She'd thought the isolation would be peaceful, and it was— to a point. But she wouldn't have minded a little company, a little noise.

And the thought of company made her think of Liam Delaney.

She went to the kitchen and opened a bottle of wine from the fridge. She poured herself a glass and took it back to the sofa in front of the fireplace.

Would it be so bad to spend a little time with Liam? He was interested—she got that from the way he'd looked at her. If he was in a period of emotional turmoil, then it might not be a good idea, because she wasn't thinking long-term; she was thinking about one night during which she wouldn't have to feel the loneliness and isolation that were so much a part of her life.

Was Liam really as fragile as Gen had made him out to be? Really as vulnerable? He didn't seem that way to her, but she had nothing to go on but a first impression.

Lacking any other form of companionship, Aria turned on the TV, then turned up the volume. She didn't particularly want to watch anything, but at least the chatter of the television was better than nothing.

By morning, the rain had stopped and the sun was breaking through the clouds just above the horizon. Aria got up early and made coffee in the cottage's tiny kitchen. She drank it at the kitchen table, then showered and put on warm clothes for a walk at Fiscalini Ranch, a nature preserve with acres of trails and rugged land atop bluffs overlooking the Pacific Ocean.

This early on a Tuesday morning in November, there were a few people out on the trails, but not many. She passed an elderly man walking a cocker spaniel on a leash, and a couple of joggers, but she mostly had the place to herself. She could imagine that in the middle of summer, the preserve was probably thick with tourists. But right now, it was mostly her, the crash of the waves, and the barking of the sea lions lounging on the rocks below the bluffs.

Out here in the beauty of the morning, feeling her muscles grow pleasantly warm with exertion, it was hard to remember that she'd been unhappy the night before.

It was mostly the nights that got to her.

She thought too much at night, and it was hard to turn those thoughts off.

But in the mornings, she had her work to look forward to, and the beauty of the landscape here, and that was enough.

Almost.

As she walked, with the crunch of the dirt path beneath her

shoes, she reminded herself of everything she had.

She had good health, a rising art career, the opportunity Gen Porter had given her with this residency. She had the art itself, which was immensely satisfying when it was going well. And that was a lot. It didn't pay to think about all of the things she *didn't* have, like a family. Like the kind of happy childhood memories the Delaneys probably had.

Like a relationship with a man who loved her.

The childhood and the family were things she could do nothing about—they were what they were, and she was still here, still alive, still breathing.

And the relationship?

Aria had never had anyone in her life who hadn't eventually left. And she'd survived anyway—she'd gotten through hell and back out the other side.

Her own strength, her own will, her own *self* were the only things she'd ever been able to count on, and she wasn't naïve enough to think that was going to change.

But the idea of a fling with Liam? Well, that was undeniably appealing.

That train of thought made her think about the fact that the rain had passed and the sun was coming out. Sun that would dry the barn roof, allowing Liam to come and work on the sky-light.

If Liam wanted to spend some time with her—time that would chase all thoughts of loneliness out of her head, if only for a little while—then who was to say that was wrong?

Warm and loose from her walk, she hiked back to her car, drove up Highway 1 to the ranch, and got settled in with her piece in the barn, with its leaky skylight.

With a day of work and a possible visit from an attractive man in front of her, it seemed like she really did have all she needed.

Chapter Four

Liam was looking forward to going to the barn to inspect the skylight—and to seeing the woman who was out there building things out of sporks. But for some reason he didn't fully understand, he didn't want everyone to know he was looking forward to it.

So he found it happily convenient when Ryan started nagging him about it at the breakfast table that morning.

It was just before sunrise, with Sandra slapping platters of eggs and bacon and toast onto the big kitchen table, when Ryan started in about it.

"Gen wants to know if you're going to go out and look at that skylight," Ryan said as he started to dig into his oatmeal—his usual vegetarian alternative to the eggs and the bacon.

"Well, why doesn't Gen ask me about it, then?" Liam responded.

"Mainly because she doesn't get out of bed for another hour, like normal people," Ryan said. "She wanted me to ask you, so I'm asking."

Liam's usual mode was to be crusty about such things, and if he changed that now, people were likely to think there was something wrong with him. So instead of just saying yes, he was going to check the skylight, and in fact he didn't mind at all, he gave Ryan a ration of shit about it.

"I don't know why the hell that skylight is a priority when we've got a ranch to run," Liam grumbled. "It's not even raining anymore."

"Which is why today's a good day to look at it," Ryan pointed out. "But if you don't want to, I can go out there and—"

"I'll do it," Liam grumbled.

"Look, I don't mind," Ryan said. "It's my wife's deal, I guess I ought to be the one who—"

"I said I'll do it," Liam snapped at him.

"Well, whoever's going to do it is going to need some damned breakfast. So you two ought to shut your pie holes about it and eat," Sandra put in as she sat down at the table with her own plate of eggs.

"How are they supposed to shut their pie holes and eat at the same time?" Orin asked, suppressing a grin. "They've gotta open their pie holes if they're—"

"That's enough out of you," Sandra said.

Liam left the breakfast table that morning satisfied with how it had all turned out.

He showed up at the old barn later that morning with a ladder and a toolbox, knocking on the open door and peering into the cool depths inside.

"Anybody home?" he said. But he didn't say it right away. Because she was in there, all right, bending over the spork thing with her ass turned toward the door. The ass in question was covered by a tight-fitting pair of jeans, and it was almost unbearably round and luscious. There was no harm in enjoying the view for a minute before announcing himself.

When he did finally make his presence known, she straightened and turned. "Oh!" She had a bottle of glue in one hand and a used, crumpled drinking straw in the other, and her face turned just a little bit pink in a way that he found cute as hell.

"I thought I'd take a look at that skylight." He lifted the ladder and the toolbox a little to demonstrate his intentions.

"Great." She smiled, and he felt the smile in places on his body that were especially dear to a man's heart. She must have been at work for a while, because the knees of her jeans were dusty from the floor, she had spots of glue on her shirt, and her hair, which was up in some kind of bun, was starting to come loose a little at the edges.

"How's the … " He motioned vaguely at the pieces of trash sculpture on the floor.

"The yurt," she supplied.

"Yeah, the yurt. How's it coming?"

"It's coming." She pointed to the two-by-four-shaped structures on the floor. "When these pieces are done, I'm going to interlock them to make the basic frame."

He nodded as though this all seemed completely sensible. "Then what?"

"Then, I've got to cover it all up with a kind of skin. Most people use canvas, but I'm going to weave together some plastic grocery bags."

"Huh." He rubbed at his chin. "I guess there are a lot of those around."

"You have no idea. Globally, five trillion plastic grocery bags are produced every year. And they've got to go somewhere. Some people recycle them, and that's better than nothing, but most of them end up in landfills, where they don't even start to degrade for seven hundred years. Do you have any idea how many of them end up in the ocean? They—"

"You don't have to lecture me about the environment," he said, interrupting her.

"I wasn't trying—"

"You were. But that's okay. It's worth lecturing people about. I'm just saying, you're preaching to the choir." He'd already set his ladder and his toolbox down on the dirt floor of the barn, and now he was standing with his hands in his jeans pockets, just taking her in.

"Sorry. I get worked up."

"I can see that." He couldn't help grinning at her a little; she was just so fired up and full of energy, and so pretty out here with the sun from the skylight shining on her hair.

"You think it's dumb," she said, her head tilted slightly, peering at him. She wasn't being defensive; she was just stating an observation of fact.

"What? Worrying about plastic bags? I told you ..."

"No, the yurt."

She had him there. No sense trying to deny it. "Well ... sort of. I just kind of don't see the point."

"You don't see the point of art?"

He shrugged. "Paintings, stuff like that ... sure. But this? I don't know what this is. I guess I just don't get it."

Admitting that he didn't get it might set him back in any effort to get her out of those tight jeans, but he didn't see the point in lying, or in pretending to be someone he wasn't.

"That's all right," she said. "You don't have to get it."

"I don't?"

"No."

"Why not?"

She considered him. "Because if I do it right, you will."

Aria wasn't offended that Liam didn't get the point of her yurt. In fact, it would have been less fun if he had. When some-one immediately identified with her artistic vision, that was fine.

But it wasn't nearly as thrilling as starting with a doubter—or even a mocker—and converting him.

There were people who couldn't be converted. Some people simply didn't have the depth or the vision to appreciate anything that didn't present obvious beauty or utility. But she was willing to bet that Liam wasn't one of those people.

He had a certain arrogant tough-guy exterior that said he wasn't the kind who could see the potential in her work. But the exterior was wrong. She didn't know how she knew that, but she knew.

She had a knack for spotting such things, and she was rarely mistaken.

Liam wandered to her worktable, where she had an array of broken glass—pieces in green and blue, brown and red—laid out in a big circle.

"What's this for?" he asked.

"The skylight."

He peered up skeptically at the roof and at the leaky skylight he'd come to fix.

"Not that one," she told him. "It's for the yurt."

"The yurt's going to have a skylight?"

"It is." She came over to the worktable, flipped through some pages in her sketchbook, and showed him a sketch of a circular structure with a mosaic pattern of broken glass pieces in various colors. "See? I'm going to set up an overhead light just above it, so the colors will reflect inside the yurt."

For the first time since she'd shown him the project, he looked interested. "Huh. That could work."

"The skylight in the barn was what inspired me. For that part of it, anyway." She turned to him and looked up into his clear blue eyes. "Inspiration can come from anything. Or from anyone."

For a moment, he didn't move or speak, and the connection between them almost drew the air out of her lungs. Then he blinked once, stepped back, and headed toward his tools.

"I guess I'd better get up there, then." He didn't look at her, just picked up his ladder and his toolbox and headed toward the door. "Seeing as how the damned skylight is so inspiring and all."

Liam set up his ladder and began climbing toward the roof. He'd wanted to flirt with Aria—she'd seemed open to it—but instead, he'd hauled ass out of there. Because risking life and limb on a damned ladder was preferable to putting himself out there with a woman, apparently.

Was he that pathetic after what had happened with Megan? He hadn't thought so, but now he was beginning to wonder.

As he climbed the ladder, he reminded himself that he needed to focus. Going up onto a twenty-foot-high roof was dicey under the best of circumstances. It was dicier when one of your legs didn't work one hundred percent right. Add the memory of Aria's ass to the equation, and he was likely to find himself lying flat on his back on the ground with a team of paramedics over him.

Aria was standing on the ground looking up at him anxiously.

"Are you okay?" she said. "I mean, going up the ladder with your … your …"

"The leg's not a problem," he called down to her as he ascended. "I know what I'm doing."

It was true that the leg wasn't that big of a problem. He'd lost some of his range of motion, sure. But he had full strength in the leg, and he'd been doing all of his usual work—including climbing ladders—for months now.

The issue, in his mind, wasn't what he could or couldn't do. The issue was what a sexy woman on the ground *thought* he couldn't do.

Fuck his goddamned leg, and the accident. And fuck the goddamned crisis of confidence that had him up on this ladder instead of down on the ground making a move on a deliciously attractive woman.

He had to get his shit together, and soon.

Aria went back into the barn and wondered what kind of signals she should send to Liam—and whether she should send any at all.

She saw the looks he'd given her, and she knew he was attracted. The looks didn't lie.

She had hoped maybe he would make some kind of move, but he hadn't. Was he still too hung up on his ex to start anything with someone new?

Maybe. And even if he wasn't, there was a chance Liam was the kind of guy who wouldn't be interested in something casual with a woman he'd barely met.

Liam had a big, tight-knit family, so maybe he was traditional about relationships. On the surface, he seemed like the sort of man who might enjoy the occasional fling or one-night encounter. But Gen had suggested that Liam's surface didn't match what was going on underneath, and Aria had gotten that same sense herself.

If Liam Delaney was looking for someone to sip lemonade with on the front porch before taking her inside for dinner with Mom and Dad—well, that was a sweet and appealing thought, but she just couldn't do it. If that was what he wanted, she'd be better off steering clear now instead of later.

Chapter Five

The skylight wasn't going to take long to fix. A quick look at the thing showed that a couple of roof tiles needed to be replaced. That and some fresh sealant, and he'd be good to go.

He had some sealant in his toolbox, but he would need to go to the hardware store to get the roof tiles. He was pleased with how that was going to work out, because it would give him an excuse to come back out here and talk to the artist again once he had the necessary supplies.

He climbed down the ladder carefully, then folded it, leaned it against the side of the barn, and stood in the doorway with his thumbs hooked through his belt loops.

"Well, it looks like I'm going to have to put in some new roof tiles," he said, trying to sound like doing it would be a pain in the ass.

Aria was at the worktable with a pot of glue and a pile of trash, making one of the long rod-like things she was using for the frame of the yurt. She looked up at him with sunshine from the skylight shining on her face.

"Thanks for doing it," she told him. "It's supposed to rain again on the weekend."

He shrugged in a way that was supposed to say it was no

big deal, while at the same time communicating that he was putting himself out for her benefit. It was a lot to expect from a shrug.

"A man's got to maintain his property," he said. "Just part of my job."

"I suppose," she said. "Still, I appreciate it."

He stood there awkwardly, trying to think of ways to avoid leaving now that he'd stated the status of the skylight repair. Talking about the spork yurt seemed like a sure bet.

"Is your ... uh ... project coming along okay?"

"Not bad." She had a drinking straw in one hand and what looked like a used condom—but surely it had to be something else—in the other. "It's a slow process, though. I'll need about twenty of these supports before I can assemble the frame."

"Is that a used condom?"

She raised one eyebrow. "It is."

He grimaced.

"I washed it first. With bleach. While wearing rubber gloves."

"Well, that's something, I guess."

He didn't particularly want to talk about the condom, but he didn't want to leave, either. He wanted to be here with her, if only for a few minutes.

It wasn't just about how she looked. He'd been around sexy women before, on many happy occasions, but they didn't usually affect him like this one did. Usually when he saw a hot female, he was mainly interested in looking at her, with the future goal of maybe, with her consent, touching her. But this felt different. He just wanted to be in her presence for a little while because he had the sense that it would make him feel better.

He wasn't good at small talk—it wasn't a skill he'd managed to master in his thirty-three years of life—but he gave it a try.

"So, where are you from?" The question sounded lame, even to himself, like the kind of thing the shopkeepers on Main Street asked the tourists.

"Portland," she said. "The one in Oregon, not the one in Maine."

He nodded. "You got family there?"

It was an innocent question—anyone would say so—and yet something in her face changed. Her eyes went fractionally harder, her mouth just a hint firmer. "Just me," she said after a while.

"So, where do they live?" He had a sense that he was touching some kind of nerve, but he couldn't seem to help poking at it to see what happened.

"When do you think you'll come back to finish the skylight?" she asked. She kept her voice light.

Liam wasn't the most sensitive guy, or the most intuitive one, but he could tell when his question was getting the brush-off. He considered pursuing it to see where it would go, but instead, he let her change the subject.

"Well." He scratched the stubble on his chin. "I can get out to the hardware store this afternoon to get the tiles, then come back out here tomorrow to do the job."

He knew he should get the job out of the way today so he could get back to his real work on the ranch. But the more he dragged out the roof thing, the more he could look forward to seeing Aria. He figured he could make a one-day job into a two-day job, or even a three-day job, without much maneuvering.

But, since it felt like he'd pissed her off with the questions about her family, he wondered whether he should even bother with the maneuvering.

"I guess I should get going." He picked up his ladder and his toolbox and stood awkwardly in the doorway.

He was just about to turn around and go, when she said, "Liam?"

He waited.

"Where do people go around here for nightlife?"

"Nightlife?"

"Yeah." She cocked her head at him. "I know Cambria's a quiet town, but people must go somewhere in the evenings."

"Well, there's Ted's," he said.

Ted's was a dive bar just off Main Street that he and his brothers frequented when they wanted to blow off steam. It wasn't much—it was poorly maintained and it smelled bad—but they had darts and pool, and beer by the pitcher.

If they'd been talking about a nice restaurant or a swanky wine bar, Liam would have hesitated to ask her to go with him, because that would be a date, and he didn't think he was ready to date anyone. But this was Ted's, and taking a woman to Ted's couldn't possibly be interpreted as a date. It didn't say, *I want a relationship with you.* Instead, it said, *I might try to get in your pants later, but if not, at least there's beer.*

It was perfect.

"Ted's?" Aria asked, her eyebrows raised in question.

"A bar. It's pretty crappy, but all the locals end up there at one time or another." He put his hands into his jeans pockets and rocked back on his heels. "I'll probably be heading out there tonight, if you want to go."

"Is that right?"

The sexiness of her smile scared him so much that he panicked.

"Uh … yeah. Me and Ryan. My brother. And his wife. You know Gen." He had absolutely no plans to go to Ted's with Ryan and Gen, but he needed to communicate that this was not a date, and nothing said *not a date* like bringing your brother.

"That would be fun."

"Well, all right. Pick you up about eight?"

"I'll be ready."

She looked at him just a beat too long, and he felt the look in the center of his chest—and somewhere farther down.

Something told him he was in dangerous territory—that Aria Howard was going to be more than he knew how to handle, and much more than he was prepared for. But it was just Ted's, and besides, he was going to talk Ryan and Gen into going with him.

How much trouble could he possibly get into?

"I think we're just gonna stay in tonight."

Ryan was brushing down his horse, a big chestnut gelding, in the stables as the early evening sun streamed through the windows. Dust motes drifted through the wide beams of light, and the place smelled like leather, horse sweat, and manure.

"What the hell do you want to do that for? You want to waste a perfectly good Wednesday night when you could be over at Ted's having a good time?" Liam leaned against the side of the stall, scowling at Ryan.

"You know, as delightful as Ted's is, what with the spilled beer on the floor and the broken jukebox, I believe I'll make the sacrifice." He gave Liam that smartass smile he used when he thought he was being funny.

"Just because you've got a baby coming, you think you've got to act like an old man," Liam complained. "Maybe Gen wants to go. Have you thought of that?"

"Then the two of you can go while I stay home and relax." Ryan flexed his shoulder. "Maybe I am getting to be an old man. Seems like I never used to feel this sore at the end of the day."

Liam wasn't about to let Ryan distract him from his mission

with talk of things like soreness and age. "Look, just come for an hour. A half hour. One drink."

Ryan paused with the curry comb in his hand. "What's this about? Why are you suddenly so dead set on me going to Ted's? You got something you're not telling me?"

Ryan had that big brother thing going on where he could catch Liam in a lie like he was wearing a sign around his neck that said I'M BULLSHITTING YOU. So, Liam went with the truth.

"I need you to come because of Aria."

"The artist."

"Yeah." Liam straightened up from where he was leaning and pushed a hand through his hair. "I asked her to come to Ted's, but I told her you and Gen were coming, too, so it would seem … you know. Casual."

Ryan raised his eyebrows. "Because a bar where your feet stick to the floor isn't casual enough by itself?" He let out a low chuckle. "I need to teach you a few things about women. Like if you're going to ask one on a date, you don't choose Ted's."

"One, it's not a date. That's the whole point. That's why you have to come—to show that it's not a damned date. And two, the day you've got anything to teach me about women is the day I sprout a goddamned third arm."

Ryan continued combing the horse, unperturbed. "I got Gen, didn't I?"

Liam kicked at a clump of hay on the floor. "Yeah, well, I still think she's gonna regain her sanity one day and kick you out on your ass."

"By the time that happens, it'll be too late," Ryan said. "I've already knocked her up."

Liam shoved his hands into his pockets and scowled. "Look, just come. And bring Gen. I said you would, and if you don't, it's going to look like I lied to her."

"Which you did."

"Goddamn it. Would it kill you to just help me out? I'll buy the beer."

Ryan finished with the horse and came out of the stall, latching the door behind him. He walked across the room to put the comb away, then came back to stand in front of his brother.

"I'll ask Gen. And, listen: I think it's great that you're getting out there again. It's time."

"Ah, bite me," Liam said, embarrassed.

"But this *it's not a date* thing is silly. If you like her, just ask her on a real date. Like an adult." Ryan went on as though Liam hadn't spoken.

"Yeah, yeah. Are you coming or not?"

Ryan gave Liam a friendly smack on the shoulder. "I'll talk to the missus. Far be it from me to stand between you and a woman. Maybe if you get laid, you'll be in a better mood."

Privately, Liam thought the same thing. But he wasn't about to say so.

Chapter Six

Liam's assessment of Ted's wasn't wrong.

As Aria got settled at a table in the middle of the room with Liam, Ryan, and Gen, it occurred to her that she wouldn't consider hanging out at a place like this in any other town. In LA or New York or San Francisco, the atmosphere would have said trouble—possibly of the type that included police and the occasional gunfire. But here in Cambria, where crime was such a rarity that people barely even noticed there was no police force, the place seemed comfortable. Harmless. Even charming.

Everything seemed to be sticky—the floor, the tabletop, the chair. Eighties rock played over the speaker system, punctuated by the occasional shouts of a group of guys who were engaged in a game of pool, and a few more who were playing darts.

It wasn't much, Gen explained as they all got settled in at their seats, but at least it provided a break from the constant tourist traffic of Main Street.

Liam ordered a pitcher of beer and three mugs, and an iced tea for Gen. Ted, the bar's owner, brought it over with a couple of bowls of peanuts and pretzels that had likely been pawed over by other people's hands.

"Liam. Ryan. Gen." Ted, a middle-aged man with a sizable

belly that hung over the apron tied around his waist, greeted the Delaneys with a nod. Then he waggled his eyebrows at Aria. "And who do we have here?"

"Ted, this is Aria Howard," Ryan said. "Aria, this is Ted."

"Nice place," Aria said.

"Ah, bullshit." Ted cackled. "Enjoy your beer."

When he was gone, Liam poured a beer and placed it in front of her. Then he poured for himself and Ryan and leaned back in his battered wooden chair with his long legs stretched out in front of him, crossed at the ankles. He looked completely at ease, as though he'd poured himself into the chair in exactly the same way a thousand times before.

All at once, Aria got the sense of a careless grace she hadn't noticed before. It made her wonder how that grace might show itself under more private circumstances.

"So, your skylight all fixed up?" Ryan asked Aria as he hefted his mug.

"Not yet," she told him. "Liam says another couple of days."

Ryan, looking amused, raised his eyebrows at his brother. "A couple of days? To fix a little leak?"

"Ah, shut up," Liam said, without heat. "I'm getting it done. I've been busy. I'm a busy guy."

"You're not busy fixing the skylight, apparently," Ryan said.

The exchange felt like the kind of brotherly bickering that had to be utterly routine in a large family. Both of them seemed at ease with it, as though it were a simple and immutable part of their world.

Looking at the two of them—Liam with his rugged, manly magnetism and Ryan with a kind of dark-eyed deliciousness, Aria had to wonder about the other brother, the one who lived in Montana. If he was even half as attractive as these two, it seemed almost criminal that one family should be so genetically blessed.

"I told you I could do it if you didn't have time," Ryan went on, still talking about the skylight. "It's not that big a deal, I—"

"I said I'd do it," Liam snapped at him.

"I can wait," Aria put in. "It's not even raining anymore."

"Oh, it's not about the skylight," Gen said, sipping her iced tea. "It's about competition and sibling rivalry. And penis size, probably." She grinned, enjoying herself.

"Nah, it's not about that," Ryan said, smirking and giving Gen's forearm a squeeze. "He lost that competition when I hit puberty back in seventh grade."

"I'm only letting that go because you've got your woman here with you," Liam remarked. "It's better for your marriage if she doesn't know the truth."

"Are they always like this?" Aria asked Gen.

"Yes," Gen said. She got up from her seat, picked up her glass of tea, and gestured toward the pool tables, which had just been vacated. "Come on. Let's leave these two twelve-year-olds to it. I want to play pool."

Watching Gen play pool was unexpectedly amusing, mostly because her baby bump kept getting in the way every time she bent over to take a shot. If the cue ball was close to the edge of the table, she could get to it without much trouble. But when it was situated closer to the middle, her belly pressed awkwardly against the railing. It gave Aria an advantage, and she found herself wishing they'd played for money.

"So. That kind of … irritable thing Liam's got going on. Is that real, or part of the bad-boy act?" Aria asked as she stood near the wall, cue in hand, waiting for her turn.

Gen took a shot, missed, and then straightened to consider the question. "It's both, I think. He's always been kind of prickly. But it's gotten worse over the past few years."

"Why do you think that is?" Aria said it as though it were just idle conversation. But it was more than that, and they both knew it.

"Well … his girlfriend cheated on him. Then his uncle died. Then another girlfriend—a serious one—fell in love with his cousin. And then there was the accident."

Aria lined up her shot—nine ball in the side pocket—then leaned over the table. She glanced at Gen from where she stood poised to shoot. "Ouch. That's a lot."

"It is," Gen agreed. "He's taken it all pretty well, considering. But he hasn't been himself."

Aria made the shot, then walked around the table to line up the next one.

"Look," Gen said. "Liam's a good person. A genuinely good person. He'd give his life for any of us in the family. In a heartbeat. He wouldn't even think about it." She said it with such conviction in her voice, such emotion, that Aria didn't doubt it was true. "So, if you're thinking of going there …"

Aria waited for Gen to go on.

"It's just, if you start something with him and it doesn't work out, he's going to get hurt again. And if that happens …" She shook her head. "Well. It would just be a shame."

"I'm not really thinking of 'going there'," Aria said. "But I was kind of wondering about something light. You know, just … something fun."

Gen shrugged one shoulder, looking uneasy. "Well … just make sure both of you are having fun, that's all."

Aria was still thinking about Gen's warning when Liam came over and asked if she wanted to throw a round of darts. She was on her second mug of beer by then and was starting to feel pleasantly loose and relaxed.

She shot first, and was so disconcerted by the proximity of Liam's testosterone-fueled sexiness that she didn't get the darts anywhere near the bull's-eye.

"Huh. I think I can beat that," he said, gathering up the darts and going to stand behind the line of red tape on the floor.

"You think so?" Aria said. If she'd flubbed her turn because she was distracted by him, then that suggested a possible strategy she might use to her advantage. As Liam aimed to take his first shot, Aria made a production of bending over to tie her shoe, a posture that gave Liam a prime view of lush and abundant cleavage in the V-neck of her T-shirt.

Liam threw, and the dart missed the board entirely, landing with a thunk in the wood paneling six inches to the right.

Aria straightened and looked at the dart, a theatrical display of puzzlement on her features. "Oh. You must be out of practice."

He gave her a wry half smile. "You did that on purpose."

"Did what?" She widened her eyes in innocence.

"You know exactly what." He was grinning. The grin, the way his T-shirt hugged his body, the tattoo that was peeking out from beneath his sleeve, and the way his eyes crinkled a little at the edges when he smiled—it all combined to make her feel alarmingly melty inside.

"Well. It looks like it was a winning strategy." She nodded pointedly at the dart, so far away from the board that it looked like a castaway in a lonely sea.

"Not exactly safe for the bystanders, though."

Aria wasn't usually bold with men. She found that such things generally led to trouble. But Liam was so appealing, and her body buzzed with such happy excitement when she was around him, that she told herself it would be okay, just this once.

What harm was there in having a good time with an appealing man? Why shouldn't she give that to herself?

Having worked herself up to it, she took two long, slow steps toward him. She put her mouth near his ear and said softly, "Maybe we should take it somewhere else, then. Somewhere a little quieter. For the sake of the bystanders."

"I … uh …" He let out a shaky laugh. "I can't leave Gen and Ryan without a ride home. Let's go on back to the table, huh?" He turned, with the darts still in his hand, and headed back to where Ryan and Gen were sitting. Then he realized with a start that he was still holding the darts, hurried back to the area where the board was, put them down on a table, and went to sit next to Ryan, his limp a little more prominent than it had been just a few minutes ago.

Aria stood there and watched him go, her female ego stinging. Either she'd misread his attraction to her—which she hadn't—or Liam was seriously awkward with women.

Of course, there was a third possibility. Maybe he really was as emotionally fragile as Gen had said. And if so, maybe it really was the best thing to leave him alone and move on.

It was probably for the best. She was here in Cambria to focus on her work.

She sighed, put a *that never happened* smile on her face, and went back to the table.

Chapter Seven

Aria had decided that it wasn't going to happen between her and Liam. And that was fine. She tried to keep her mind on her work—mostly—the following day when Liam showed up to fix the skylight.

Her ego was a little bit hurt, sure, but not enough to matter. She was polite and friendly when he showed up with the roof tiles and the ladder—and then she went back to the painstaking task of piecing together her yurt.

"Uh … this shouldn't take too long," he said as he gathered his tools and prepared to go up on the roof.

"Okay." She was working with an unidentifiable piece of plastic that had washed up in Pismo Beach, attempting to re-shape it with a piece of sandpaper to make it fit better into the frame she was making.

"So … I'll just go on up there," Liam said.

"Great. Thanks." She looked up at him and smiled to show there were no hard feelings, then continued what she was doing.

"I … uh … had fun last night."

That made her stop, the piece of plastic and the sandpaper in her hands. He seemed nervous, and that was interesting.

"I did, too," she said. "It could have been more fun, though, if you'd wanted it to be." And now it was out there.

What was the point in dancing around it?

"Ah, hell." He was looking at his work boots, and not at her.

"Look, it's no big deal," she said. "You're not interested. I get it." She knew she sounded irritable and a little bit hostile. She hadn't intended to be that way, but maybe Liam's rejection of her had stung more than she'd thought.

"Look ... it's not that I'm not interested." He was still standing in the doorway of the barn, looking at his shoes.

"Okay."

"It's just ..."

"You don't have to explain. Really."

"Would you just be quiet and let me say what I want to say?" His voice held no heat; instead, he sounded embarrassed. He set down his things and came a few steps into the barn.

"Okay." She put her things on the worktable and turned to face him.

"You made me an offer last night," he said, coming closer until he was just a couple of feet away. "And it was a nice offer. A very nice offer."

"But?"

"But, maybe I want to take things slower."

She propped one hand on her hip and looked at him. "All right. I get that. And it's sweet. It really is. But dating? That's not ... I don't do that, Liam."

His eyes widened in surprise. "So, that's it, then?"

"Well ... yes."

He seemed to consider that. He nodded thoughtfully. "You think it's sweet."

"Yes. It really is."

He nodded again, his jaw flexing. Then he turned and headed toward the door.

About halfway there, he stopped and turned around.

"Fuck sweet." In two long strides, he reached her, grabbed her around the waist, pulled her to him, and kissed her.

Liam should have kept right on walking out the door. He knew he should have. It would have been so much smarter to go up on the roof, fix the skylight, and get the hell out of here like his ass was on fire.

But what kind of man could refuse an offer of no-strings sex from a woman as appealing as this one? Whatever kind of man that was, it wasn't Liam, and it wasn't anyone he particularly wanted to know.

He wasn't a coward, and he wasn't goddamned *sweet*. He wanted to put that thought—and every other thought she might be having—out of her mind with a kiss so thorough she'd forget she said it, or that she had the power of speech in the first place.

He wrapped himself around her and devoured her, his mouth on hers, his tongue claiming hers. His heart was beating faster, and his blood seemed to have heated up several degrees. The feel of her body against his made him so hard he thought he might explode.

And the way she responded to him—Christ. She was melting against him, giving everything back to him with a passion he'd only imagined she might be capable of. Her hands were in his hair, and he breathed her scent of good soap and warm, soft skin.

He broke the kiss after a long time because he had to take a moment to slow down, to catch his breath. He didn't let go of her, though, and she didn't pull away.

"Guesthouse?" she said, her voice barely above a whisper.

"You sure?"

She nodded.

Only then did he start to think about the logistics of the thing, the practical matters.

"I don't ... I mean, I didn't ..." Damn it, he was an adult man. Since when did he have such a hard time talking about safe sex?

"I have condoms," she said, as though she were reading his mind. "In my bedside drawer. I got them when you asked me to go to Ted's."

He grinned at her, already feeling the lightheaded giddiness that resulted from all of the blood rushing to other parts of his body.

"Well, then, let's go."

They hurried to the guesthouse, hand in hand. The cottage was only about a hundred yards away from the barn, so it didn't take them long to get there. Still, to Liam, it was too long. Now that he knew this thing was going to happen, he couldn't wait to get her out of her clothes, to feel those soft curves against him.

They weren't in the door more than a couple of seconds before they were on each other, kissing and touching and un-dressing themselves and each other.

Together, they fell onto the bed in a glorious tangle of limbs and bare skin. He ran his hands over every part of her, tasted her and touched her, unable to get enough of her.

Once the practical matter of the condom was dispensed with, he slid into the silky warmth of her with something like sweet relief.

For the moment, for right now, he wasn't thinking about his grief over Redmond, or his heartbreak, or his injury, or any of the other myriad things that plagued him.

For this moment, at least, he felt healed.

And then something horrifying happened: He felt himself

starting to get emotional, the hot sting of tears forming in his eyes.

He blinked hard and held her closer, his face buried in her shoulder, so she couldn't see.

When she sighed and shuddered with pleasure, he tried to think only of that—of the bliss of the moment. He gave himself over to her until he felt the power of his own body's release.

The thing about sex with Aria was, Liam felt so damned grateful. It had been a long time, and he felt like a weight had been lifted. He felt as though he'd put down a heavy burden and could now walk lightly, with a new energy and optimism that had, until now, been lost to him.

When it was over and they lay in each other's arms in Aria's bed, tangled up in the covers, he felt a buoyant good cheer he hadn't experienced in quite some time.

"That was pretty damned great," he told her, enjoying the feel of her naked body, the cool sheets, and the pure luxury of lying in bed in the middle of a work day.

"It wasn't bad," she said.

"Not bad?" He grinned. "Well, hell. If the best you can say is, 'It wasn't bad,' then I guess I didn't get it right. Nothing to do but take another go at it." He pulled her closer and moved in for a kiss.

She accepted the kiss, then gave him a friendly pat on the shoulder and got out of bed. "I would, but I have to get back to work."

"Work?" He scowled.

"Yes. That thing I do for money." She'd pulled the blanket off of the bed and was holding it around her body, leaving him with only the top sheet.

"It's not like you have a boss who's keeping an eye on you," he said. "It's not like you're punching a time clock." He reached out, grabbed a handful of her blanket, and pulled her toward him. On his knees on the bed, he hauled her in and wrapped an arm around her.

"Well, neither do you," she reminded him. "But that doesn't mean you can slack off in bed all afternoon." She unwound herself from his embrace and went toward the guesthouse's little bathroom. "Besides, you have to get up and fix the skylight."

"Well ... hell."

Even if she wasn't up for another round, he still felt pretty damned happy about how things had worked out. If he didn't feel entirely like a new man, he felt like the old one had gotten a much-needed tune-up. He got up, looked wistfully toward the closed bathroom door, and grabbed his jeans off the floor.

Aria stayed in the bathroom until Liam had left. He'd called to her through the door, wanting to say goodbye, or thank you, or whatever was on his mind. But it was better if they didn't talk. Especially if Gen was right and Liam was the type who'd want to have a relationship, maybe even—God forbid—an eventual commitment.

It wasn't that she didn't like him, because she did. And it wasn't that she didn't want to do this again, because that was a very appealing thought. But she wasn't up for any kind of emotional entanglement.

Lying in bed holding each other and talking, and maybe even having sex again, would send the wrong message, and she didn't want to do that. She didn't want to mislead him about what she was and was not capable of.

The sex, though—it was good. Good enough, in fact, that she was cautious not only about misleading Liam, but about misleading herself.

After all she'd been through, after all of the people she'd loved and needed who had left her, she wasn't about to let herself need anyone again. The space between having sex with someone and beginning to need them could be deceptively short, and the slope was notoriously slippery.

She knew the dangers, and she wasn't about to succumb to them.

When he was gone, she took a quick shower, dressed, and went back to the barn to work.

Chapter Eight

"So, did you and that artist have a good time?" Ryan asked, waggling his eyebrows. Liam had just come into the new barn, and Ryan had started in on him right away.

"What the hell are you talking about?" Liam asked, playing dumb.

"Oh. You mean you two didn't just have a quickie in the guesthouse?" Ryan gave him a wide-eyed, innocent look.

"How did you …?"

"I stopped by the old barn to see if you needed any help with the skylight. Didn't want you to fall off the roof and split your head open. Your tools were there, and the two of you weren't. Since I've been able to add two and two for quite some time now …"

"Ah, shut up." Liam said it without rancor. Actually, it would be nice to be able to talk things over with Ryan.

"So?" Ryan did the eyebrow thing again. "You two did get together, right? How are you feeling about it?"

If Liam were asking this same question to one of his friends, he'd likely ask it in terms far more crude than the way Ryan had phrased it. But this was Ryan, and he was too polite for that kind of thing. As a result, he sounded more like a therapist than like a guy shooting the shit with his brother about a woman.

"I feel just fine about it," Liam assured him.

"Well, good," Ryan said. "What about her?"

Liam's first instinct was to tell Ryan to mind his own damned business—mainly because that's what Ryan would expect him to say—but instead, he leaned against a stall door and scratched the back of his neck.

"You know … I'm not sure."

"Not sure about what?" Ryan asked. "She maybe having regrets?"

"Well, hell, it was her idea," Liam said. He ran a hand through his hair. "And it was fun. I mean … damned fun."

"So? What's the problem?" Ryan had just brought a sick calf into the barn, and now he got it settled in a stall and faced Liam.

"I don't know that there is one. She was just in a hurry to get me out of there, that's all."

"And you're worried that she was just using you for your body?" Ryan smirked.

"Ah, bite me." That was exactly what he was worried about, but it didn't seem manly to say so. Ryan must have known that, because he canned it with the teasing and smacked Liam once on the back in a brotherly kind of way.

"Look, don't overthink it. Just … let it go wherever it's going to go, okay? If you're having fun and she's having fun …"

"Yeah," Liam said, embarrassed.

"Meanwhile, while you were having personal time with the artist, I was out here working my ass off. You want to help, or you want to stand around talking about your fragile, fragile heart?"

The smart-ass remark lightened the mood, and Liam was

glad for that. Otherwise, next thing he knew, he'd be complaining about how Aria hadn't wanted to cuddle. And if it came to that, well, the humiliation would be such that he'd have to move to New Zealand without a forwarding address.

"Let's get in there and take care of that damned calf, since you can't seem to handle it yourself," Liam said, feeling as though their brotherly equilibrium had been restored nicely.

Aria spent the rest of the day working on the yurt, trying to keep her mind on her work and not on Liam Delaney.

After their encounter in the guesthouse, Liam had come back to the barn and had finished his work on the skylight. Which meant he had no reason to come back out here, unless it was to see Aria.

She wasn't sure how she felt about that. Part of her was glad that what had happened between them might be a one-time thing, because that made things so much neater, so much less complicated.

But another part of her knew that if he did keep his distance now, she'd be disappointed. And that was a problem, because she didn't want to have feelings about him, or about the sex, or about any of it. She simply wanted to chalk up their time together as a pleasant diversion that didn't require anything further from either one of them.

But, God, the man had made her body *sing*. Really great sex tended to confuse a person about what they did and didn't want.

The thing about assembling pieces of trash into a yurt was that after the plans were drawn, it was largely a physical exercise rather than a mental one. That meant she had plenty of time to think while she worked. And what she was thinking about was Liam. And that wasn't a desirable state of affairs at all.

She was just wrapping up for the day, cleaning up her materials and assessing the work she'd completed, when she heard a knock on the doorframe of the big barn.

Aria looked up to see Gen peering into the barn. She was wearing her black gallery dress, and her curly red hair was up in a loose bun.

"Hey there," Gen greeted Aria, making her way into the barn. She'd finally exchanged her pointy heels for more sensible flats now that giving birth was imminent.

"Hey." Aria was tired and dirty from a day of work, and she pushed her dark hair away from her forehead, letting out a sigh.

"I just thought I'd check in on my way home," Gen said. It was just after five p.m., and the daylight was fading, creating long shadows inside the barn. "I wanted to see how the yurt is coming along."

"Oh. It's good. Slow, but good."

Gen craned her neck to look up at the roof. "Did Liam get the skylight fixed?"

"He did."

There must have been something in the way she said those two words—*he did*—that pinged Gen's radar. She looked at Aria with more interest, her eyebrows rising as she focused on her.

"And …?" Gen asked.

"And what?"

"I don't know. It just seemed like there might be an *and*."

Aria let out a sigh, and her shoulders fell. "There is, but I'm not sure I want to talk about it."

"Uh oh." Gen peered at her with concern. "Did something happen? Something bad?"

"No, no. Not bad. Not bad at all. Just … private."

Gen looked thoughtful. "All right. I respect that."

"You do?"

"Of course. Especially since I can just get it out of Liam."

"Gen—"

"I'm kidding," Gen said. "Mostly." And then she gave Aria a little *toodle-oo* sort of wave and walked out of the barn.

Aria watched her go, one hand propped on her hip.

The story was going to be all over the ranch by morning. Not that it was a very long story. Of course, stories that centered around sex didn't have to be long to catch people's interest.

"Damn it," she said to the empty barn.

As it happened, Gen didn't have to get it out of Liam. She got it out of Ryan.

The three of them were gathered on the back porch at the main house, Liam and Ryan with bottles of beer in their hands and Gen sipping from a glass of sparkling water, when Gen started poking around.

"So. How are things going with you and Aria?" Gen asked Liam, waggling her eyebrows much the way Ryan had earlier.

"There's no *me and Aria*." Liam scowled and looked at his beer bottle so he wouldn't have to look Gen in the eye and lie to her.

"Really? I got the idea there was." She was leaning against the porch railing with her glass in her hand.

"Well, I don't know where you got that idea," Liam said. "Because it's not true."

"Oh, bullshit," Ryan said mildly.

"Ry ..." Liam started to protest.

"Just can it with the 'Ry' business," Ryan said. "I'm not going to let you stand here and lie to my wife."

"Ooh," Gen said. "So there is something."

"Well ... maybe," Liam allowed. "But I'm not telling you what, because it's none of your damned business."

Gen just smiled. "That's fair," she said. "But I have to give you some sisterly advice."

"You really don't," he said.

"I do, because I love you."

That stopped Liam, because he knew it was true, and even he couldn't give a ration of shit to a woman who was standing there saying she loved him.

"All right. Then say what you have to say. But I hope this is going to be quick."

"It is," she said. "Just … be careful."

That was it? That was all she had to say? "Well, hell." He took a swig of his beer, grateful that there wasn't more.

He should have known it wouldn't be that simple.

"There's something there. With Aria, I mean," Gen said.

Now he was the one pushing for information. "Something like what?"

Gen considered the question. "I don't know. Not really. But … I talked to her a lot before I offered her the residency. I talked to other people about her. I read articles about her, did my research, saw her resume, all of that."

"And?" Now Ryan was interested, too.

"And, after all of that, I don't know much more about her than I did when I started." Gen shrugged.

"*Hmph.*" Liam let out a sound that was remarkably similar to the one his mother often made. "You saying you don't approve?"

"I'm saying I don't know if I do or not," Gen said. "Because I don't really know her. And it's not for lack of trying."

"Well … maybe she's just private," Ryan said.

"Maybe. But I don't think so. I think there's something there." And without saying what that something might be, she took her glass and went back into the house, leaving Liam and Ryan alone on the porch.

"What the hell do you suppose she was talking about?" Liam asked Ryan after she was gone. "What kind of *something?*"

"You got me," Ryan said.

"Well ... she's your wife, you ought to understand her better than I do."

Ryan smirked. "If that's what you think, you're in for a big surprise if you ever get married."

Chapter Nine

Liam wasn't sure where he stood with Aria. The idea of sex with no strings or obligations wasn't completely unappealing. Still, he didn't want to be that guy who slept with a woman and then ignored her afterward, pretending she'd somehow become invisible, or that their encounter had never happened.

That was what he told himself as he headed toward the old barn-turned-studio the next day—that he was just going over there to avoid being an insensitive asshole. He wasn't doing it to see if he could make something happen between them again.

Still, if that was how things turned out, that wouldn't be the worst thing in the world, would it?

He had a lot of work to do on the ranch, and he couldn't really afford the time to pop in on Aria. On the other hand, what were his parents going to do if he was MIA for a while, fire him?

When he poked his head into the barn, he could see that she'd made quite a bit of progress on the yurt. She'd started to assemble the support structure, and a rough skeleton was beginning to form.

"You're really making progress," he observed, stepping into the barn.

She seemed flustered for a moment when she saw him.

Then she recovered herself and shrugged. "Yeah, I guess I am."

She turned back to what she was doing, resuming her work without engaging with him further. He was sure that was designed to send a message. Some variant of *fuck off,* most likely.

Liam considered his options. He could chat her up as though they were friends; he could make another pass at her; he could be blunt and ask her what her intentions were, as though the two of them were living in some kind of Victorian novel; or he could turn around and walk out.

He chose the first option, the friendly one.

"Just thought I'd come by and say hello, see how you're doing," he offered.

"I'm doing fine. Thank you for asking." Her delivery was cool and impersonal.

"Uh ... everything okay with the skylight?" he asked.

She glanced at him briefly before returning to her work. "It's hard to tell, since it hasn't rained. Mostly, it's just sitting up there."

He wasn't getting anywhere. Time to switch from Option One to Option Three: the blunt approach.

"What the hell's going on?" he asked.

She sighed and put down the piece of trash she'd been working on, turning to face him. "What are you talking about?"

"I'm talking about how you're pissed off at me, and I don't know why."

"I'm not."

He kept his voice neutral. "Well, that's bullshit, and I guess we both know it."

"I didn't ... I'm not ..." She threw her hands into the air, flustered. "I'm busy, that's all."

He was quiet for a moment as he considered how to respond to that. Finally, he nodded. "Well, all right. I guess I'll get going, then." He felt a little hurt, but his manly pride prevented him from acknowledging it. He turned and started to walk out of the barn.

"Liam?"

He stopped. "Yeah?"

"I'm sorry." And she did look sorry. She looked like a woman who was wrestling with unfathomable issues that Liam couldn't begin to guess or understand.

"Well, all right. You're just having a bad day, I guess. That happens to all of us."

"It does."

She didn't offer anything more, so he decided to get out of there and cut his losses. "Listen … you know where to find me," he told her. "And, feel free to do that. Find me, I mean. Any time."

The offer seemed to make her even more uncomfortable than before, and maybe a little sad. "All right," she said.

He left the barn before he could screw things up even further, without realizing what he'd done to screw up in the first place.

Aria *was* having a bad day, but it wasn't because she was angry with Liam. Quite the opposite.

She was having a bad day because she really, really wanted to see him again.

God, she'd been so rude to him, and she hadn't meant to be. He hadn't done anything to deserve it. But if she hadn't been rude—if she'd been polite or even friendly to him—he wouldn't have left. And if he hadn't left, she imagined she'd be naked, sweaty, and out of breath by now, with Liam lying heavily on top of her.

A large part of her regretted the fact that she wasn't in exactly that situation, and that made it even more important that she set her boundaries and stick to them.

She wasn't going to date Liam Delaney.

She wasn't going to sleep with him again.

And she certainly wasn't going to fall for him.

Falling for people led to loving them, and loving people had never led her anywhere she wanted to be.

Liam had other things to worry about, like the fact that Breanna wanted to drag him over to the house she wanted to buy.

What did he know about real estate? He'd never bought a house, had never even looked into doing such a thing. He'd lived at the ranch since the day he was born and had slept in the same room all that time. As a Delaney—with all of the wealth that implied—he could have chosen any house in Cambria, or anywhere else, for that matter. But the ranch had everything he needed, and he'd never seriously considered leaving.

Colin knew about real estate. Hell, even Ryan knew more than Liam did—at least he'd had a house built, so that was something. Liam knew as much about buying a house as he did about performing heart surgery.

"Come on. Please?" Breanna begged him after breakfast the next morning. "Just take a look and tell me what you think. That's all I'm asking."

The boys didn't have to leave for school yet, and they were roughhousing with Liam—something he managed to do while still keeping up his end of the conversation. "But why me?" He hefted Michael and tossed him onto the living room sofa as the boy laughed. "What the hell do I know?"

"You know about houses," Breanna insisted. "You've spent more than thirty years living in one."

"I've never bought one," he grumbled. Lucas launched himself at Liam, who picked him up with one arm and carried him like a sack of laundry. "I've never thought about buying one. Hell, I don't even watch those TV shows you like—the ones with the Realtors and the designers and all that."

Breanna had been a fan of HGTV for some time, a fact Liam blamed for his sister's insistence that she wanted a place of her own. If it hadn't been for all that talk about bonus rooms and open floor plans, she wouldn't be planning to leave, and he wouldn't be wishing he could punch one of those glossed-up TV remodeling experts right in the damned face.

"Take Dad," Liam said. "Take Ryan, why don't you?"

"Dad's already seen it, and Ryan's busy," she said. "And I'm asking you." She turned to her sons, who, at eleven and thirteen, were almost too big to play with their uncle, and shooed them upstairs to get dressed for school. Then she went to Liam, hooked her arm in his, and lay her head on his shoulder. "Please?" She batted her dark eyelashes at him.

"Aw, hell," Liam said.

"For God's sake, boy, go see your sister's house," Sandra grumbled at him as she passed through the room on her way from the kitchen to the stairs.

The truth was, he was pleased that Breanna had asked him, that she wanted his opinion. But he was afraid he wouldn't be up to the task—that he would give her bad advice, resulting in her committing to a real estate deal she would regret for years to come. Worse, he worried that he would inadvertently talk her into the purchase. He knew he'd miss his sister and nephews if they moved across town.

Still, his sister was asking him for a favor, and he couldn't exactly refuse her.

"Well, all right," he said. "I guess I can take a look this weekend."

"I kind of hoped we could do it today," she said. "The Realtor says there are other people looking at it, and I don't want to let it get away."

She did the eyelash-batting thing again.

"Aw, hell," he said.

The place was a dilapidated, rambling old farmhouse on Moonstone Beach Drive. The road ran along the Cambria coast, hugging a rugged, rocky beach crowned by a wooden boardwalk. It had mostly been given over to hotels and restaurants that catered to the tourists who flocked here every summer, but a few private homes sat snugged up next to establishments with words like *fireside* and *shores* and *sea otter* in their names.

At first glance, the house looked like a rundown mess. At second glance, it wasn't much different. But Breanna was bubbling over with enthusiasm as she and Liam, accompanied by a perky Realtor named Molly, made their way up the front walk.

"This house dates back to the nineteen twenties," Molly told them, her heels clicking on the brick walkway.

"Looks like it hasn't changed much since then," Liam muttered.

"Oh, but Liam, think about how wonderful it'll be with a little work!" Breanna told him, gushing.

"The location alone makes it worth the price," Molly put in.

That was probably true from a strictly financial standpoint, but even so, the price was substantial. For that, Breanna would get overgrown weeds, peeling paint, and a front porch that was sagging alarmingly. Things were likely even worse inside.

On the other hand, the lot was surprisingly big for a place at the beach. There was a roomy yard for the boys, and the property included the main house, a big, ramshackle barn, and a little guesthouse.

"Shall we look at the inside?" Molly suggested. Her voice was annoyingly upbeat, as though Liam and Breanna had just won a selection of valuable prizes.

"I guess," Liam allowed.

The interior of the house was pretty much what Liam had expected. Scarred wood floors, peeling wallpaper, and a musty smell that suggested the place hadn't been occupied in a while.

One of the kitchen cabinets was hanging on the wall precariously from one corner, and there was a dead mouse on the floor, its face locked in a permanent grimace.

"What do you think?" Breanna bounced on her toes in excitement.

"I think I tend to agree with Mickey over there." He gestured toward the mouse.

"Oh, come on," Brenna said. "I know it needs a lot of work, but have some imagination! It has five bedrooms and a parlor, and Liam, just imagine the boys growing up here, across the street from the beach! They could learn to surf, and—"

"They could do that now," Liam observed. "We only live a five-minute drive from the damned beach."

Her shoulders sagged, and her face fell. "Do you really hate it?"

Seeing her suddenly turn sad aroused his brotherly instincts, and he told himself to stop being an ass.

"Ah ... no. I guess it's got some potential, if someone wanted to put the work into it."

"It does! It really does!"

Molly, looking a little bit smug at this turn of events, gestured toward the stairway. "Shall we take a look around?"

Liam thought Breanna could do a lot better, given her almost unlimited financial resources. But he had to concede that, given those financial resources, she could really do something with the place.

"Why has it sat empty for so long?" Liam asked Molly when they were done with their tour of the property.

"It's changed hands a number of times," Molly told them. "Mostly among buyers who intended to use it as an investment. One had planned to tear it down and build a hotel here."

"Tear it down!" Breanna said in horror.

"Another one had planned to flip it, but ran out of money and let it go into foreclosure. The price has come down twice over the past year." Molly delivered the information as though she expected Breanna to squeal in delight. Which she might have done, if Liam hadn't cut her off.

"Bree, if you want a place at the beach, we can find you something on Park Hill, or maybe Marine Terrace. Someplace that's livable for you and the boys. Someplace that doesn't need so much *work*."

"But I *want* to do the work," Breanna told him.

It didn't seem like the kind of conversation they should be having in front of the Realtor, so Liam excused himself, took Breanna by the arm, and led her across the weedy, overgrown yard to the weathered old fence that lined the property.

"I'm just not sure you know what you're getting into here," he said.

"Neither am I," Breanna admitted. Her big, dark eyes were shining. "But I *need* this, Liam. I haven't had anything of my own since Brian died."

Liam blinked at her in surprise. "What do you mean? You have the boys."

"Yes, and they're my whole world. Which is great. But … sometimes I wish my world included other things, too. Things that are just mine." She put her hand on his arm and squeezed.

"Well … I don't see why you need my approval."

"I don't. But it sure would be nice to have it."

And all at once he realized how rare it was for anyone to seek his guidance on anything. When people wanted advice, they asked Colin. They asked Sandra. They asked Ryan, especially if the question had anything to do with ranch management or livestock. But it never occurred to anyone to ask Liam. The fact that she was asking now made him feel touched in a way he wouldn't admit to her, even under threat of torture.

"Well, I guess I can see how you could turn this place into something." He rubbed the back of his neck, his face scrunched up in a way that broadcast his misgivings.

"I could, Liam. I know I could."

"Well …" He still felt like he had a brotherly duty to talk her out of it, so he clung to one last argument. "What are you going to do with this much space? It's only you and the boys."

"I don't know," she said. She was practically vibrating with excitement. "But I'll think of something."

Chapter Ten

"What did you let her buy that ramshackle old place for?" Orin's face was pinched in dismay, his skin even ruddier than usual.

"Well, I don't guess I let her do anything," Liam protested. "She's a grown woman."

"Yeah, but that old place?" Orin ran a hand over his head. "Why, it's been sitting there falling apart for as long as I can remember. I was kind of hoping you'd talk her out of it."

"He tried," Breanna said. Orin and Liam had been talking in the living room, and they hadn't heard her come in. Liam felt a little abashed at having been caught discussing her. "I didn't want to be talked out of it."

"Well ..." It was what Orin always said when he didn't know what to say but didn't want to concede defeat.

"Anyway, it's too late," Breanna went on. "I put in an offer this afternoon."

"Those boys shouldn't be taken away from their family," Orin said, in one last effort to argue his point.

"That part really is unfortunate," Breanna said, deadpan. "It's a fifteen-minute drive from here to there. They're unlikely to ever see you again."

"Well ..." Orin said again.

Sandra came in from the kitchen, having apparently eaves-dropped on the whole conversation. "Now, Orin, I don't want you discouraging our girl. I think it's fine that she's buying her own place."

"Thank you, Mom," Breanna said.

"Well, I just think it's time, that's all. A woman needs a place that's just hers, a place where she doesn't have to compete with her mama to be the queen bee." She winked at Breanna and let out a rough chuckle.

"Like I'd even try to compete in this house," Breanna said.

"Not if you know what's good for you, girl," Sandra said. She puttered around the room straightening things, plumping sofa pillows and picking up empty drinking glasses from the side tables to take them back into the kitchen.

"It's going to need work," Liam put in. "A lot of work."

"I know, but that's the exciting part," Breanna said. "I can do whatever I want with it—flooring, kitchen countertops, bath-room fixtures—I can really make it mine. I like the floor plan, so if the place is structurally sound—"

"If?" Orin wanted to know.

"I'll be getting an inspection, Dad, and if something's really wrong, I can back out. But I have a good feeling about this."

"Well …" Orin rubbed the back of his neck. "I guess the location's going to be okay."

"If you like an ocean view and having your feet in the sand thirty seconds after you leave your front door, I guess it'll do," Sandra said, rolling her eyes at her husband.

"God. This is so exciting." Breanna did that bouncing-on-her-toes thing again. "I'm going to need a renovation guy."

"I can help out some," Liam said. "But, yeah, I guess you're gonna need someone who knows what he's doing."

"You ask your brother. He'll get you some names." Everyone in the room knew Sandra meant Colin, even though she hadn't said his name. Colin had supervised so many property developments up and down the coast that he knew a stunning array of people in the business.

"Well, I hope you're not making a mistake," Orin said, looking pained.

"I'm not. And if I am, it's my mistake," Breanna said. She kissed her father on the cheek and went upstairs to check on the boys.

"I still think you should have talked her out of it," Orin said to Liam.

Sandra grunted. "You just don't want the little birds to leave the nest," she told Orin. "But when they don't leave the damned nest, it's usually because they don't know how to fly."

The comment had been a casual one, but it still hit Liam hard. When Breanna was gone, Liam would be the only one of his siblings living at home. True, he'd been off in Montana for a few years, but now he was right back in the room he'd slept in when he was a boy.

He'd always thought he'd moved back into the house to be close to his work on the ranch. But was there more to it? Had he never learned to fly?

Maybe Breanna wasn't the only one who needed to think about making a change. Maybe Liam needed to jump out of the damned nest too, to see whether his wings would catch the air, or if he would fall flat on his ass.

Aria had never had the option of staying in the nest, as she'd never had much of a nest to begin with.

She'd had no choice but to fly. Though sometimes, rough weather made it a little hard to stay in the air.

Maybe that was why she was building the yurt—a nest of

items discarded the way she'd been discarded so long ago, and so many times since then.

She tried not to think of these things too often, and she kept right on not thinking about them as she worked to assemble the basic frame of the yurt. The various pieces of plastic flatware, water bottles, soda cans, discarded chopsticks from Chinese takeout restaurants, broken sand toys, and other random items were finally taking shape into something identifiable.

She was building the yurt in such a way that it could be disassembled for transport and then reassembled wherever she ended up showing the piece. After some consideration, she'd decided to create the floor as three pieces, and the shell of the thing as two parts that could be clipped together at its destination.

Creating two halves of the main yurt structure was more of a challenge than making it as one whole, but if she'd done it as one piece, moving the thing would be too much of a hassle.

And the yurt wasn't going to do her much good from a career standpoint if it stood here in the Delaney barn forever.

She was thinking all of this on a rainy Saturday partly because the work needed to be done, and partly to keep her from thinking about Liam.

She'd shooed him away the last time he'd come to see her, more than a week ago. At the time, that had felt like a necessary thing to do. But now, with the rain pattering on the roof and the gray light of the morning coming in through the open barn doors, she couldn't help feeling lonely and thinking how nice it would be to have someone here with her—particularly someone who might hold her and kiss her and make her, if just for a moment, feel whole.

It would feel nice—but that was the problem. It would feel *too* nice. So nice, maybe, that he would get to her, get under her skin in a way that would make it hard to extricate herself.

Still.

What harm would there be in a little pleasure? What harm could possibly come of continuing their casual fling with the understanding that it would never be more than that?

She thought about the rain and wondered if she might use that as an excuse to bring him here. It would help if the skylight were still leaking—which it wasn't.

She looked up at the skylight, speckled with rain. Then she looked down at the barn's dirt floor, which was completely dry.

It didn't have to be.

Aria retrieved a water bottle from her worktable, considered it, and then opened it and poured the contents onto the dirt beneath the skylight. Then she picked up her cell phone and dialed Liam.

When he answered, she said, "Liam. Hi. It's Aria. I'm sorry to bother you, but … I'm in the barn, and there's some water on the floor under the skylight. I wondered if you could come and take a look."

It wasn't a lie, after all.

Liam made his way to the old barn with his male pride wounded. How the hell had he screwed up a simple job like fixing the skylight? A man didn't have much in life if he didn't have his sense of competence at basic tasks.

Add to that the double insult that Aria had rejected him the last time he'd seen her, and his mood was all storm clouds and thunder as he walked into the barn and got out of the rain.

"What the hell? I thought I fixed the goddamned thing," he said, not so much to Aria as to the room itself, as he peered down at the puddle underneath the offending skylight.

"Mmm. I thought you did, too," Aria said. She'd been standing at her worktable doing some damned thing, but when he came in, she stopped doing whatever it was and turned to face him.

She was wearing those tight jeans again—the ones that hugged her curves so closely it made him dizzy—and some kind of loose sweater with a low neckline that gave him a dazzling view of her cleavage. Her hair was up in a messy bun, and the slight chill in the air made her cheeks pink in a way that made him want to kiss her.

Not that he was going to—not until she asked him to.

He craned his neck to look up at the skylight.

"Well, that's weird."

"What is?" she asked.

"It's still raining, but there's no leak right now." He'd expected to find water dripping from the roof of the barn, but there wasn't any—just the standing puddle of water where the leak should have been.

"Huh," she said. "I didn't see any actual leak. There's just water on the floor."

A hint of a grin tugged at her lips, as though she knew something he didn't. Which she probably did. The vast depth and breadth of the things Liam didn't seem to know these days was staggering.

"Well …" He rubbed the back of his neck. "I can't get up there again now, with the rain. But I can take a look again as soon as it clears up and the roof dries out a little."

"I'd appreciate that."

Standing here looking at Aria, Liam felt his insides grow warm and soft in a way that wasn't entirely unpleasant.

"I guess I ought to apologize," he told her, for lack of anything else to say. "I should have fixed it right the first time."

"Hmm." She walked over to him, stood well inside his usual bubble of personal space, and looked up at him with her big, amazing eyes. "It's nice to see you."

Was she coming on to him? It sure seemed like it.

At that moment, there was a kind of electric storm in Liam's brain that short-circuited any rational thought. If he'd been thinking clearly, he might have remembered the way she'd turned him away before. He might have considered the possibility they wanted different things out of anything that might happen between them. He might have thought to worry about what it meant when a woman wanted you, then didn't want you, then wanted you again.

But as it was, he wasn't thinking about any of those things. Instead, he was just focused on her nearness, and the smoothness of her skin, and the way she smelled like lavender and fresh rain.

He did, however, remember one snippet of thought he'd been having before she'd come so close to him.

"I'm not going to kiss you," he said, his voice rough.

"You're not?" She looked at him with eyebrows raised.

"No. Not unless you tell me you want it."

They were both quiet for a moment, standing so close they could feel each other's body heat in the coolness of the barn.

"I want you to kiss me," she said.

After that, his rational brain shut off entirely, replaced by a caveman brain that only knew the sensations of hunger and need.

He grabbed handfuls of her hair and took her mouth with a ferocity even he hadn't seen coming.

A groan came from deep within her throat as she responded to him, pressing her body against his and wrapping her arms around him.

His reaction to her was so strong and so immediate that there was no question of going to the guesthouse, or to his house, or to anywhere other than where they were at this moment. The delay simply would not have been tolerable.

He pushed her backward until her back slammed into the barn wall. Just for a second, he was conscious of what was happening, and of the fact that his sudden burst of aggression might be too much. Pressed up against her, he stopped and looked at her in question, the air between them hot and charged. When she grabbed his face and pulled him to her for a kiss, he had the answer he needed.

He thrust his work-roughened hands under her sweater, ran them up her body, and then took hold of her breasts over the fabric of her bra.

"Liam." It was a whisper, a prayer.

His name on her lips made him want her even more. He brought his hands down to her ass and lifted her so she could wrap her legs around him, her back pressed up against the rough wood of the barn wall.

The big worktable was a couple of feet away, and he reached out with one arm to sweep away the various bits and pieces—glue pots and trash and sketch pads that went crashing to the floor in the seconds before Liam lay her on the table, his body on top of hers.

It didn't occur to her to protest his manhandling of her work. In fact, it was ridiculously hot. She tore at his wet jacket and then his shirt. She couldn't get down to his bare skin fast enough.

After what seemed like a moment and also like forever, he was naked from the waist up, her sweater was pushed up to her neck, and he was raking her jeans down her body. She wasn't aware of the rain on the barn roof, or the open door where anyone could come in, or the morning chill. She was only aware of what her body felt, and what Liam was doing to her.

She reached for his jeans the best she could, lying on her back with him halfway on top of her, and that was the last bit of permission he needed. He unbuckled his belt, unsnapped and unzipped, and then fumbled for the condom he'd tucked into his back pocket before he'd come out here—a rash bit of optimism that was now paying off better than he could have hoped.

He ripped open the package with his teeth, rolled on the condom, and then thrust into her so hard and fast that it made her gasp.

The rough tabletop scratched at her back as she clutched at him, holding on to him, her fingernails digging into his biceps. She wrapped her legs around his body and he grabbed onto the sides of the table with his hands, his face buried in the hollow between her shoulder and her neck.

The raw power of him took her breath away.

She felt the orgasm coming, first from a distance and then closer, closer, until it slammed into her like a bolt of lightning. She cried out and clutched at him, and later she thought that she might even have blacked out for a moment. Her overwhelming, noisy pleasure pushed him over the edge, and his body stiffened and shuddered over hers.

When it was over, they both struggled to recover. It was a big table, so there was room for Liam to lie down next to her, breathing hard, the two of them gathering themselves with fragments of beach trash under their backs.

"That's not why I came out here," Liam said after a while, his voice raspy.

"Well, it's why I brought you out here," Aria admitted.

"It's ... what? What do you mean?"

She grinned, her eyes closed in remembered bliss. "There's no leak. You said it yourself. It's still raining, but there's no water coming in through that skylight."

"Wait. But the water ..."

"I poured a bottle of Evian on the floor."

For a moment, he didn't know what to say. The idea of her scheming like that, coming up with a fake leak to get him out here, was both surprising and flattering. He couldn't say whether a woman had ever used false pretenses to get him into bed—or in this case, onto a table—before.

"Well, you're just full of damned surprises," he said, not at all displeased with the situation.

After a while, they both became aware of the fact that they were half-dressed with the barn door wide open to the world, creating a potentially embarrassing situation for themselves if anyone should come by.

Aria was the first one to get up. As she rose, Liam tried to pull her into his arms, but she playfully smacked him away. "We're in public—sort of—and I've got no pants on," she pointed out.

"You look good with no pants on," he told her.

"I'm not sure your sister-in-law is going to think that."

"What's Gen got to do with anything?" Liam asked.

"Nothing, except that she comes around sometimes to check in and see how I'm doing."

Liam rose up on one elbow to watch her pull her jeans on, grinning. "Well, if she comes in now, she'll think you're doing just fine."

"Or she'll think I'm slacking off on the work I came here to do."

Liam noticed Aria gradually turning distant, as though he'd done or said something to offend her, though he didn't know what it might be. Unless his advances had been less welcome than he'd thought.

He got up off the table, fastened his jeans, and picked up

his shirt off the floor.

"Hey. Aria?" He pulled on the shirt and started to button up against the cool air.

She was pretty much put back together now, and she'd begun picking up the stuff he'd swept off of the table and onto the floor.

"Are you … I mean, is everything okay?" he said.

She stopped, a pot of glue in one hand and an empty soda can in the other. "Fine. Why?"

"Well, you just … a minute ago, you seemed pretty damned happy, and now I'm starting to wonder if maybe I overstepped."

She looked at him blankly. "Liam. What are you talking about?"

Frustrated, he ran a hand through his hair. "I'm talking about the fact that I was kind of rough with you, and I'm wondering … Jesus, what I mean is …"

She sighed and closed her eyes for a moment. "Liam, I wanted that. I lured you out here. You can relax. You're guilt-free."

Somehow, her reassurance on that point wasn't as comforting as it should have been.

"Then what's wrong?"

She began putting items from the floor back onto the table, not looking at him. "I need to get back to work, that's all."

He stood there, confused and hurt. He wondered if this was what high school girls felt like after their date screwed them in the back seat of a car and then never called again.

Not knowing what else to do, he went over to where she was and started picking art supplies and random bits of trash off of the floor.

"You don't have to help," she told him.

"That's all right. I did it, I should help clean it up."

She fixed that pale gray gaze on him. "I said you don't have to help."

Whatever this was, he didn't know how to fix it or what he'd done to cause it.

"Well, all right, then." He picked up his jacket off the floor, shrugged into it, and walked out into the rain.

Chapter Eleven

When Liam was gone, Aria picked up a few more things off the floor and placed them back onto the table. Then she stopped what she was doing, threw the items she was holding onto the table with enough force that they bounced, and said, "Damn it. Goddamn it."

She raked her hands through her hair and stood there, going over what had just happened.

Why had she acted like that? Why had she been so rude to him? She'd made him think that she was somehow upset or traumatized by what had happened—that he had somehow taken advantage of her.

Well, she *was* upset and maybe even traumatized by what had happened, but not in the way he thought.

The upset? That was because she hadn't wanted him to leave. The trauma? Well, that happened a long time before she'd even met Liam Delaney, and now he was the one who was suffering for it.

Damn it.

Aria had things she couldn't tell him, things she had no desire to tell anyone, ever. Those things made it impossible for her to sustain a meaningful relationship, not because she *couldn't,* but because she was never going to let anyone have the kind of power over her that Liam would have if she decided to let him in.

She wanted the fun and excitement and physical closeness that sex represented. She wanted that release, that joy. But she did *not* want anyone claiming a piece of her, because once that happened, she might come to depend on it.

And people didn't stay. That was one thing you could count on: people never stayed.

She'd learned over time that it was better to be the one who made that decision to cut things off. It was better to be the one in control of the goodbye. That way it would never take her by surprise, never leave her shocked and wounded in a way she might not recover from.

So far, imposing that distance between herself and the men who had come into her life had kept her safe.

But this time it was harder. This time, pushing him out felt wrong. It felt counterintuitive. Showing him the door had hurt— it had maybe hurt her more than it had him.

It occurred to her that if she was going to have trouble keeping her distance from Liam Delaney, then maybe it was best if she didn't have anything to do with him at all.

He was too dangerous.

But even as she was thinking it, her body was still vibrating with the fire Liam had ignited in her. Had she ever felt anything so … so *intense*? So powerful? So world-shakingly profound?

She was beginning to sound to herself like one of those silly, stereotypical women who let a guy under her skirt and then thought it was love.

This was not love, and it wasn't going to become love.

Not if she had any say in the matter.

Liam left the barn feeling pissed off and out of sorts.

Which didn't make any sense, since he'd just gotten laid in

the middle of the workday. Whenever that happened, you could generally consider it a good day. Except he didn't feel good at all—not at the moment.

Maybe that was why he decided to pick a fight with Ryan.

Ryan had called on his cell phone to say that he'd gotten his truck stuck in the mud out in the southwest pasture, and he wanted Liam to come out with the four-wheel drive and tow it out of there.

When Liam showed up with his F-150, he was already in a mood that had nothing to do with Ryan—though Ryan took the brunt of it anyway.

"Why the fuck did you take your goddamned truck out into the pasture in the rain?" Liam demanded. He'd started in before he was even fully out of the truck.

"Well, hello to you, too, Liam," Ryan said mildly. His boots were ankle-high in mud, and he looked like the cocker spaniel they'd had as kids after it fell into the creek.

Liam looked at Ryan's truck, which was bogged down halfway up its tires in sticky mud.

"Of all the stupid, boneheaded, dumbass ..."

"I brought the truck out because there's a break in the fence and I didn't feel much like hauling fence posts and barbed wire on the back of a horse," Ryan said, keeping his tone neutral. "If it's any of your business, which I don't figure it is."

"You made it my business when you called me out here to rescue your ass," Liam said.

"Well, I'm going to knock you on yours if you don't stop taking whatever's bothering you out on me." Ryan rarely got mad, and he didn't appear to be mad now. He was simply stating a fact.

Having his bad behavior laid out for him in such straightforward terms caused Liam to deflate a little. "Aw, hell," he said.

Ryan clapped Liam once on the back. "Let's get the truck out of the mud, and then we can talk about whatever's going on with you."

"Like hell," Liam grumbled. "I'll get your truck out of the goddamned mud, but I'm not talking about my damned feelings."

"Well, that's a relief, because I didn't really want to hear about them," Ryan said. "Now, are you going to put on the tow strap, or do I have to do everything?"

Liam had said he didn't want to talk about his feelings. But after he'd dragged the truck out of the mud and had helped Ryan to repair the break in the fence, he found himself doing just that.

They'd gone into the stables to get out of the rain, both of them soaked and muddy, and Liam started in before he even realized he was going to do it.

"I saw Aria today," he said. He sat down on an overturned bucket and wiped water off his face with his hands.

"Well, color me surprised that your mood has something to do with a woman," Ryan said.

"Ah, fuck off if you're gonna—"

"Sorry," Ryan said. "Go on."

The stable was dry and relatively warm, and the smells of horse, sweet hay, and wet animal hair surrounded them. Having grown up with the smells, Liam found them comforting.

"She and I kind of ... you know ..."

"You hooked up again," Ryan provided.

"Yeah."

"And, what? It was unsatisfactory?"

"Unsatisfactory?" Liam looked at him incredulously. "Hell, it practically blew the top of my damned head off."

Ryan pulled up a bucket, turned it upside down, and sat

down next to Liam. "Well, that's good news then, right?"

"You'd think so. Except, when it was over, she couldn't get me out of there fast enough. I don't know what the hell went wrong."

Ryan's eyebrows rose. "Was it maybe ... Shit, I don't know how to ask this.... Was it maybe not as consensual as you thought it was?"

Liam's expression turned dark. "What kind of Neanderthal asshole do you think I am?"

"I don't," Ryan said. "But sometimes signals get crossed. People think they're on the same page, but they're not."

Of course, Liam had wondered the same thing himself. Getting mad at Ryan was just a matter of habit.

"I asked her about that," he said, scowling. "She pointed out that the whole thing had been her idea. Which it was."

"Huh. Maybe you're just lousy in the sack," Ryan suggested.

"Bite me. Asshole."

Ryan gave Liam a half grin and got up off his bucket. "Well, maybe she regretted it, for whatever reason. Or maybe she's upset about something that has nothing to do with you. Either way, you could find out. Maybe have a conversation with her."

"I tried. She wouldn't talk. She just wanted me to leave."

"Women are an eternal mystery," Ryan observed.

"Yeah, but the thing is ... I just want to know that she's okay."

Ryan considered that for a minute. "Well ... Gen talks to her. You want me to have her check in?"

"Ah, hell." Liam rubbed at the stubble on his chin. Sending Gen to do what he should be doing on his own seemed ... unmanly. And yet, it might work. "Yeah. Would you? I just ... I want to know what I did. If I did anything. I don't want to be that asshole who hurts a woman and doesn't even realize it happened."

Liam got up and headed for the stable door.

"Liam?"

He turned back to look at his brother.

"You're not that asshole," Ryan said.

"Ah … shut up," Liam said, embarrassed. He went out into the rain to finish his day of work.

Chapter Twelve

By the time Gen showed up to check on Aria, the old barn was empty except for the sound of rain on the roof and the partially constructed yurt inside, like the abandoned shell of some giant, long-deceased tortoise.

Gen found Aria in the guesthouse. She opened the door to Gen's knock wearing sweatpants and an old gray sweater, a glass of wine in her hand. Her face was free of makeup, and her hair was pulled back into a ponytail, loose strands framing her face.

"Oh. Gen." Aria knew the greeting sounded less than enthusiastic—which it was.

"Hi. I just … you know. Wanted to drop by to say hello."

It was clear that Gen was uncomfortable about being here, and it took Aria less than a minute to figure out why.

"You might as well come in," she told Gen, stepping back to allow her to enter. "You're not going to get the dirt on what's going on with me standing out there in the rain."

Gen feigned surprise. "What? I'm not—"

"Please."

Gen's shoulders fell. "Okay, maybe I am." She came into the little house, which was warm from the fire in the fireplace. She shrugged out of her coat and hung it on a rack near the door. Then she put one hand to her lower back in a posture common to hugely pregnant women everywhere.

"Listen, I just wanted—"

"Liam sent you," Aria said, cutting her off.

"Well ... Ryan, actually."

"So, Liam told Ryan and Ryan told you? Is there anyone on the property who doesn't know that Liam and I had sex in the barn this afternoon?"

Gen's eyes widened. "Well, I didn't know until just now."

Aria could tell from her expression that it was true. She smacked her face with her hand. "Oh, God."

"So, you and Liam in the barn, huh?" Gen said, impressed. "One time Ryan and I—"

"Genevieve," Aria said, stopping her.

"Sorry."

The conversation had been confusing so far, and Aria felt a little disoriented. "So, if you didn't know, then why ... ?"

"Ryan said I should come and check on you, but he didn't say why. He only told me that Liam said you'd seemed upset about something." Gen hadn't exactly been invited to sit down, but she did anyway, settling in on the sofa in front of the fireplace.

"Oh. Well, that was ... gentlemanly," Aria said. Liam had probably told his brother exactly what had happened, but Ryan had kept his mouth shut about the details. It spoke well of him.

"Yes. That's my husband," Gen said fondly. She eyed the wineglass in Aria's hand. "God, I wish I could have some of that. Any time now." She laid a hand on her midsection as if to remind herself of the reason she was depriving herself.

"I've got some Perrier," Aria said.

"Great. I'll take it."

Aria went into the kitchen to put the sparkling water into a glass with some ice. Then she came back, gave Gen the glass, and perched her butt on the arm of the sofa.

"It was nice of you to come and check on me," she told Gen. "But unnecessary. I'm fine."

"Are you?" Gen cocked her head to the side and peered at Aria. "Because you seem a little"—she searched for a word—"out of sorts."

Aria *was* out of sorts, and it did have to do with Liam. And it would be nice to talk to someone. On the other hand, Gen was Liam's sister-in-law, so if there were sides to be taken, she'd probably come down on his. Plus, Aria didn't necessarily want Gen prying into things better left alone.

Still, she was here, and Aria was here, and Aria was on her second glass of wine …

"I never should have gotten things started with him," Aria said miserably.

"Well, I know Liam can be a bit of a challenge ..." Gen began.

"It's not that."

"Then what?" Gen looked at her with interest.

"It's just ... God! We've had two ... encounters, I guess you could say ... and afterward, he's sweet! And he wants to stay and talk, and he wants us to hold each other, and I guess that's fine for some people. I mean, I know it is. But I don't do that sort of thing!"

Gen rubbed at her face as though she were just waking up from a nap. "Wait a minute. You're telling me the problem is that Liam is too nice to you?"

"Yes! Sort of! Why can't he just ... you know. Be great in bed and then go?"

Gen's eyebrows shot skyward. "*Was* he great in bed? Wait! No. Don't tell me. I don't want to know, because whatever the answer is, I'll never get it out of my head."

Aria slumped onto the sofa cushions miserably.

Gen shifted in her seat a little—with some difficulty—to face Aria. "I don't think I'm out of line saying this, but there are women who actually like it when a man is sweet after sex. They especially like it when he wants to stay around."

Of course Gen couldn't understand where she was coming from on this. Gen probably was emotionally healthy, capable of sustaining long-term relationships that were nurturing and mutually fulfilling. She was married to Ryan and having his baby, and that seemed like a good indication. How could Aria explain her own essential dysfunction to someone who'd never experienced it herself? She'd sound like an idiot. She'd sound crazy.

"Aria," Gen said, her voice soft and reassuring, "I know we don't know each other all that well. But what's going on?"

Aria got up from her seat and started to pace in front of the fireplace, the wineglass in her hand. She downed the contents, then put the glass on a side table.

"What's going on is that I don't want to get into a relationship. I don't want to get into a ... a big thing. I just want a little mutually satisfying fun, and then I want to be able to walk away."

"Well, Liam's a grown man," Gen said. "If that's what you want, tell him. He's capable of understanding that. And then he can make his own decisions about whether he wants the same thing."

"You don't get it," Aria said.

"Isn't that what I've been saying since I walked in the door?" Gen threw her hands up in exasperation. "I really don't get it. So explain it to me."

"The problem isn't Liam. It's me." She felt a little quivery inside, maybe from thinking about Liam, or maybe because what she'd just said was more honest information about herself than she was used to sharing.

"Go on," Gen prompted her.

"When he wanted to stay? I ... I wanted that, too. I didn't want him to go."

"Okay," Gen said.

"It's just ... the sex," Aria said miserably. "It was ... I mean, I never ... Well, I have, but ..."

Gen nodded knowingly. "It was *too* good."

Aria stopped, started to say something, and then thought better of it.

Gen went on, "The sex was so mind-blowingly good that it's like you've been sprinkled with fairy dust and unicorns, and now you're thinking about things like kids and Christmas mornings and twentieth wedding anniversaries. Believe me, I've been there."

Was that what was happening to her? Aria realized it was.

"Well ... what happened with you?"

"I ended up married and pregnant," Gen said, looking satisfied with herself. She rubbed her baby bump lovingly.

"Well ... that's not what's going to happen with me and Liam. I just ... If we're going to be together now and then for great sex, that's fine, but he can't be all sweet afterward, wanting to hang around and talk and ... and cuddle."

Gen wrinkled her nose. "Liam's a cuddler? I wouldn't have thought."

"Not with me, because I didn't let it get that far," Aria said.

"But why not?" Gen seemed genuinely curious, as though she were examining a scientific specimen under a microscope.

"Because ... I'm just not going there."

Gen rearranged herself carefully on the sofa, either because pregnancy made her uncomfortable or to buy herself some time to think about how to say what was on her mind.

"I looked into you," she said at last. "When you applied for the residency. It's part of the process. I talked to people about you, and ... I researched you."

Aria felt a thin chill of dread run through her.

"And?"

"And, what I found out is that nobody knows you. Not really. They know your art, and they know your education, but ... nobody I talked to claims to really know you."

Aria straightened her spine and gave Gen a look of steely defensiveness.

"At the risk of repeating myself: and?"

"And, I'm just wondering what's going on. Look, if you've got something in your past that's making it hard for you to ... I don't know ... to have a connection with Liam, you can talk to me about it. I can listen. I know it's none of my business, but ..."

"It really is none of your business."

Neither of them said anything for a moment, and the air was thick with tension and potential hurt feelings. At last, Gen got up from the sofa, straightened her dress, and picked up her purse.

"I'm sorry for prying. I'll just go."

Aria knew she should apologize. Gen was reaching out to her, and Aria had been rude—every bit as rude as she'd been to Liam earlier that day. She knew Gen was trying to help, and she knew that was what people did—they talked about the things that mattered to them, and they formed relationships with other people. She knew, intellectually, that it was normal and healthy. But she didn't know if she was capable of it.

"Thank you for coming by," Aria said, forcing a little warmth into her tone.

When they were both at the door of the cottage and Gen

was pulling on her coat, she paused and turned to Aria.

"I meant what I said before. If you want to talk, I'm available."

"It was kind of you to check on me," Aria said, "but you can tell your husband and Liam that I'm fine."

Gen looked her over with an appraising gaze. "I'll do that."

Once Gen was gone, Aria went back to feeling like shit.

This residency was important for her career. Gen had connections—important connections that she intended to use to get Aria's new piece shown in an influential gallery.

Landing the residency was a coup for Aria. And what was she doing with it? She was getting entangled in a romantic mess instead of focusing on her work, and she was insulting and alienating the person she was counting on to help her take her art to the next level and get her the attention she needed to promote it.

She needed to focus, that was all. She needed to stop sleeping with Liam, stop getting into personal conversations with Gen, and stop letting herself get distracted by things that could only end badly.

One thing she wasn't going to do was spill her guts to Gen, or to anyone else. So what if she didn't want her past on full display for anyone who wanted to examine it? So what if she valued her privacy? She didn't owe an explanation to Gen or to anyone. Her past was her own.

And if it was preventing her from going anywhere beyond the physical with Liam, then that was just how things were.

She rubbed her face with her hands. "Damn it."

Another glass of wine seemed like a really good idea right now. She went to the kitchen to pour one.

Chapter Thirteen

Liam had too much shit to deal with in his day-to-day life without adding woman problems to the list.

He had the ranch. He had his continuing grief over his uncle, which he felt every day, in ways big and small, both predictable and surprising. He had a leg that didn't work right and might never be at one hundred percent again. And he had the stinging sadness of knowing that his ex was even now picking out throw pillows and potted plants for his cousin Drew's house.

He had a full schedule of crap to cope with, even without Aria Howard added to the mix.

But for some reason, he wasn't so much thinking about those other things.

Right now, he was just thinking about her.

He told himself to get his head back in the game at work. They were in the middle of calving season, so he had to check all of the pregnant animals to see if any were ready to deliver and to make sure none of them was in distress. Since Liam's ex had been their veterinarian, they were currently without one—or at least a steady one they knew they could trust. A vet they'd never worked with before was coming out today to check on a bull that had been showing signs of a respiratory illness, and Liam wanted to be there to evaluate the guy, see if he knew his ass from a hole in the ground.

On top of that, two of the ranch hands had quit unexpectedly—one to be near his elderly parents who were in failing health, and the other to go to law school—and Liam had to pick up the slack for them until they could find some new guys to take their places.

The bottom line was, he was busy, and he didn't need any distractions.

Be that as it may, he was distracted as hell thinking about Aria—so much so that Ryan had to repeat himself when they were in the barn looking at the bull.

Ryan had been saying something about discharge and Liam hadn't heard him.

"I wasn't ... What did you say?" It was like coming up from underwater.

"I said, the bull doesn't have any nasal discharge that I can see. Where the hell's your head?" Ryan looked at him appraisingly.

Liam scrubbed his face with his hands. "Aw ... hell, I don't know. I'm just not on my game today, I guess."

"You think?"

Liam expected to see amusement on Ryan's face—expected for his brother to rib him about who was the superior cattleman. But instead, he saw concern, and that was somehow worse.

"You okay?" Ryan asked.

"Yeah. Of course."

"You know, I can handle things here if you want to ..."

Liam scowled. "I didn't hear some damn thing you said, and now you think I can't do my job? I could work you into the ground any day of the goddamned week." It wasn't true—Ryan was every bit as formidable on the ranch as Liam was—but it sounded good.

Ryan didn't seem convinced. "Well ... all right," he said. "I just thought—"

"That's your problem, right there. You need to stop thinking," Liam snapped at him.

That ended it for the moment; they both went back to doing what they'd been doing, and the subject of Liam's lack of focus wasn't brought up again. But privately, Liam told himself he needed to get his shit together.

It wasn't that his heart was broken because Aria hadn't pledged her eternal love for him after two sexual encounters. It wasn't that he thought she should be slavishly devoted to him because of his prowess in bed. And it wasn't that he'd fallen hopelessly in love with her, pinning onto her all of his hopes for emotional fulfillment and the healing of his romantic scars.

Liam might, occasionally, act like an idiot. But he wasn't a big enough idiot to believe any of that.

His unsettled feeling had more to do with instinct. Something was telling him that there was more to Aria's hot and cold routine than she was letting on. Of course she had depths he didn't understand; they barely knew each other, and he'd had no real opportunity to get beneath the surface. But some vague itch in the back of his brain told him that whatever was going on, it was more than the usual things that made a woman change her mind about a man. Something told him that if he knew Aria's secrets—really knew—he'd be both fascinated and rocked by them.

That left the question of whether he was willing to do what it might take to find out.

Part of him wondered why he cared. They were her secrets, not his, and she didn't owe him any kind of explanation. They'd screwed twice. So what? He'd had fun, and so had she, and neither one of them had any obligation to the other.

But, for whatever reason, he couldn't get her out of his head.

Being preoccupied by a woman wasn't the safest state of affairs when you were dealing with large animals on a daily basis. The last time he'd let a woman really get into his head, he'd ended up with a crushed leg, a trip to the emergency room, and a surgery that hadn't fully restored him.

On the other hand, if he was thinking about Aria, it meant he wasn't thinking about his ex.

There was a lot to be said for that.

Aria didn't open up to people. She didn't mind sharing a little bit about her sexual escapades with Gen, but when it came to what was going on in her heart, that was her own business and no one else's. The habit of keeping her inner thoughts to herself had been formed over many years of hard experience, years in which she'd learned that her feelings didn't matter to anyone but herself.

If you told people your feelings, they could—and would—use them against you.

Because that attitude had been so firmly in place for so long, she was more than a little surprised when she found herself exploring those feelings with a man—one other than Liam Delaney.

It started with the skylight—the one for the yurt, not the one in the barn.

Aria had the idea of creating a multicolored glass mosaic made from the discarded bottles she'd found on the beach. But she hadn't worked with glass much, and she needed some instruction to get the effect she was looking for.

Gen knew a local artist who worked with glass, and the guy

had agreed to show her some techniques she could use on her piece. He had a studio with a glass furnace, something she might need and had no access to on her own.

That was how she ended up in Daniel Reed's outbuilding south of Cambria, showing him her sketches for the skylight and talking to him about the yurt, the concept behind it, and the overall feeling she hoped people would experience when they saw it.

Daniel, a tall, dark-haired guy with a two-day growth of beard that gave him a rugged, man-of-the-earth look, squinted at her drawings.

"If you want a stained glass look, then you don't need to fire it," he told her. "You can just cut the pieces and fit them together inside a frame."

She nodded. "Right. And that could work. But what I really wanted was to create the effect that the bottles are melting together. Like they're each distinct bottles—you have to be able to see the labels—but they're kind of slowly fusing to become one."

The idea of the bottles fusing together had to do with her themes of evolution, rebirth, and the unity of humankind, but she didn't tell him that. The concepts behind works of art were sometimes tiresome even for other artists.

"Huh. Well, you can do that with a torch." He showed her a hand-held blowtorch he used for smaller pieces. "I can show you, and we can do a few test pieces. Then, when you're ready for the real deal, you can come out here and get it done."

She'd offered to pay him for his instruction and for the use of his space, but he'd waved her off. "Gen's a friend. And my wife is one of her best friends. You get the wife's-best-friend discount."

The remark, and the way he'd casually thrown it out there,

made her wonder what it would be like to have a best friend.

"That must be nice," she said, before she realized she was going to say anything.

"What must be nice?"

She felt herself blushing a little. "Oh ... you know. Just ... the best friend thing."

He raised his eyebrows at her. "What, you don't have a best friend?"

And then it popped out: the truth. "I've actually never had one."

He looked stunned by the revelation. "Even when you were a kid?"

"Especially when I was a kid."

Aria immediately felt embarrassed to have blurted out such a thing. "Listen, that's ... Just forget I said that. Okay? Let's talk about glass."

They were standing in Daniel's studio late in the afternoon, with golden light slanting in through the windows. Though the day was cold, the room was still hot from when he'd used the furnace earlier that morning. Shelves and tables lining the room were covered in colorful pieces of glass: bowls, vases, and some amorphous sculptures that put her in mind of flowers and insects and running water.

He regarded her for a moment, then nodded. "Sure, we can do that."

He started to show her a piece of his own that used techniques similar to what he'd been talking about. "See, this one—"

"The thing is ... I don't want to talk about my personal life."

"Okay."

"But this ... this thing happened ... and I'm a little thrown."

"Yeah? What's the thing?"

What was she doing? Why was she getting into this with him? She tried backing off. "There's no thing. Really. There was never a thing." She waved her hands to clear the specter of the *thing* from between them.

"Oh, there's a thing," he said. "The question is whether you want to talk about it."

"Well ... I don't."

He nodded. "Fine."

"It's just ..."

He leaned his butt against the edge of his worktable and crossed his arms over his chest, looking vaguely amused.

"This wouldn't be the first time I stood in as somebody's girlfriend for the purpose of a personal confession," he told her. "I'm here, I'm done with work for the day, and I'm game. I don't have a dog in this fight, so whatever it is, I figure I'm perfect if you want to bounce it off someone."

When he laid it out that way, it was hard to argue with his logic.

"Do you know Liam Delaney?"

"Sure. Everybody knows the Delaneys."

"Well, I ... he ..."

He prompted her: "Does this involve one or both of you naked?"

She ran her hands through her hair. "Never mind. This is stupid."

"Sorry. Sorry." He held up his hands in a gesture of surrender. "I don't mean to be offensive. It's just my way. Seriously, I'm listening."

"Actually ... yes. What you said. Yes, it did."

Daniel looked at her for a moment, then pushed off from where he'd been leaning against the table. "Let's get a beer."

"A beer?"

"If I were talking about this kind of thing with a guy, there would be beer."

That seemed true enough, so she followed him out of the studio, down a gravel path through an expanse of golden grass, and to his house, which appeared to have been renovated recently. It looked as though the second floor and part of the ground floor were new, though they'd been designed to blend in with what looked like a 1920s cabin.

Daniel led her through the back door and into the kitchen, where a tall, stunning blond woman was standing at the sink, rinsing a plate. Aria recognized the blonde from Jitters, a coffee-house on Main Street.

"This is Lacy, my wife," Daniel told Aria.

Lacy greeted her with a smile. "Aria Howard, right?" She dried her hands on a kitchen towel and extended one to Aria to shake.

"Right."

"Cappuccino, one sugar," Lacy said, pointing at her.

Aria couldn't help smiling—something about the woman's sunny disposition demanded it. "Usually," she said. "Though sometimes I'm a nonfat latte with a dusting of cinnamon."

"Right."

Lacy turned to Daniel. "I'm headed out; Connor's leaving early to go to his cousin's thing."

"Did you eat?" Daniel asked her.

"Not yet, but I'll grab something at Linn's on the way."

They kissed, and Lacy gave Daniel's shoulder a quick, af-fectionate rub before she grabbed her purse and left the house.

Watching the two of them made Aria feel a nagging ache in her chest. Something about their easy, casual exchange, the way they seemed at home in the world together, made her long for that kind of comfort with someone. Then she told herself she was being stupid.

Domestic comfort was nothing but an illusion—she knew that.

Aria wondered if Lacy would have a problem with her and Daniel here in the house alone, talking about Aria's encounters with Liam.

"So ... is this okay?" she asked him. "With Lacy, I mean? The two of us, here, talking about my sex life?"

He took two bottles of beer out of the refrigerator, brought one to her, and sat down at the kitchen table. She sat across from him.

"As long as I don't become a part of your sex life—which I don't plan to do—we're good." He twisted open the bottle and took a drink. "So, shoot. What's up?"

For just a moment, Aria reflected on the absurdity of her situation. She was in a virtual stranger's kitchen, about to tell him her man problems as though they were gabbing at a hair salon, their newly set tresses under the big plastic dryers.

Of course, Aria had never gabbed with anyone while sitting under a dryer, so she really was in no place to make the comparison.

"Liam and I ... got together ... a couple of times. While I was out in the barn at the ranch, working on my piece. The skylight was leaking, and he came out there ..."

"And he worked on more than your skylight." He wiggled his eyebrows at her. "So, what's the problem? He being an asshole again? He's been known to do that."

"No." She thought about the question. "I think if there's an asshole in this scenario, it's me."

Daniel leaned back in his chair and threw one arm over the back of it casually, settling in for her story. "Okay. So, what assholish thing did you do?"

"The thing is, we had fun," she told him. "And that's all it was supposed to be. Just one time, just ... you know. Fun."

"Two times," he corrected her.

"Right. Exactly. It was supposed to be one time, but then it was two times, and he seemed ... I don't know ... like maybe he had other ideas. Like he maybe wanted more than that. And that's not okay!"

"Wait. You're upset because a guy you slept with seems like he's not just in it for your body?" Daniel raised his eyebrows at her.

"Well ... it sounds dumb when you say it that way."

"And yet ..."

"I just ... I think we've had some mixed signals, that's all. I want one thing, and he wants something different." She slumped in her chair and took a long swallow of the beer. It was very good beer; some kind of local brew with a citrusy flavor.

"Okay," Daniel said. "You've had a communication problem about who wants what. Talk to the guy. Straighten it out."

"I can't do that," she said miserably.

"Because?"

"Because if I talk to him, I'm going to want to sleep with him again."

Daniel rubbed his forehead with his fingers. "Help me out here. If you want to, and he wants to ..."

"You don't get it," she told him. "I need to be able to walk away. And if it's hard to walk away now, how much harder is it going to be if I sleep with him again? Or again after that?"

Daniel was starting to look like he might be developing a headache.

"But you don't actually *have to* walk away," he said carefully, as though he were trying to explain algebra to a toddler. "You could always, you know, try things out. Date. Like people do."

"Like people do," she repeated.

"Well ... yeah."

"Other people might do it, but I don't."

"You don't what? Date?"

"Date. Have relationships. *Get to know people.*" She put finger quotes around the last phrase.

"But ... why not?"

It was one thing to talk about what she had or had not done with Liam Delaney. It was entirely another to start unburdening herself about the chaos of her formative years and the emotional scars that had resulted.

"I just ... don't."

He let out a short laugh. "That's it? You just don't?"

"That's it." She took a long drink of her beer.

Daniel looked at her appraisingly. "Huh."

They were getting too close to the heart of things, things she didn't want to discuss. So she got up and put her purse strap over her shoulder.

"Thank you for the beer. And for the help with my piece. And for the talk."

"You're welcome." He rose from his seat, took both of their bottles, and tossed them into the recycling bin. "Come back when you're ready to do a test piece for your skylight concept."

"I will."

She was headed toward the door when he stopped her.

"Aria?"

"Hmm?" She turned.

"If you like to be able to walk away from people, but you're having trouble walking away from him, there might be a reason." He shrugged. "Food for thought."

Chapter Fourteen

This thing with Aria was like a nagging itch that wouldn't go away, no matter how much Liam tried to scratch it.

The fact that she was interested in him one minute and pushing him away the next was something he could have brushed off. It could mean anything or nothing. Who knew the mind of a woman?

But combined with what Gen said—the thing about nobody knowing her, and about Gen's sense that something was going on there—he had the itch. Liam wanted to know what the deal was.

Of course, it wasn't just curiosity.

He hadn't been able to make himself feel an interest in any other woman since Megan had left him. Lord knew he'd tried. Then Aria had showed up, and suddenly Liam was feeling desires he'd thought were lost in him.

He appreciated the role she'd played in reawakening something he'd sorely missed. And now that those feelings of wanting someone were back, he sure as hell wanted to indulge them.

So, yeah, it was that.

But it was also intuition. Liam's gut told him that Gen was right: There was something going on with Aria, something that ran deep. And he wanted to know what it was.

If anyone asked, Liam's mother would tell them that Liam had been her stubborn child, the one who wouldn't give up a fight no matter how ill-conceived.

He was going to find out what made Aria Howard tick, one way or another.

He just had to figure out what that one way or another might be.

Liam didn't consider himself to be a scheming kind of guy—he was more the no-bullshit, straightforward type. But if straightforward wasn't going to get it done, well, he could scheme.

It was one such scheme that brought him to Gen's gallery on a weekday afternoon while he just happened to be in town picking up a gallon of milk for his mom.

The day was gray and cool, and foot traffic on Main Street was sparse—not like it would be in summer, when tourists would be three deep on the sidewalks and on the boardwalk at Moonstone Beach.

There was one person in the gallery with Gen, browsing a selection of small watercolors on a display near the door. Gen, all done up in her professional art dealer persona, looked pleased and surprised to see him. The surprise made sense, because he rarely came into the gallery. Art wasn't much his thing.

"Liam." She got up from her desk and waddled over to him as the customer—a tourist, judging from the Cambria sweatshirt she was wearing—wandered out the door.

"Hey, Gen. You going to be taking off work soon?" Her belly was so big that he wondered how she managed to haul it around day after day.

"I figure I'll work right up until the big day," she said. "This job isn't exactly coal mining."

"Well."

"Is there something wrong?" The little space between her eyes furrowed in concern. "There's something wrong, isn't there? I can see it in your face."

"No. Not wrong, exactly. Just ... I wanted to talk to you about something." He felt awkward as hell.

He told her what he wanted, and when he was done, he looked at Gen expectantly.

"You want me to invite Aria to your house for dinner? That's it?"

He squirmed a little, shifting from one foot to the other. "Uh ... yeah. That's it. And you and Ryan have to come, too. But, yeah. That's the plan."

"Well ... if you want her to come over for dinner, why don't you ask her yourself? Why do you want me to do it?"

He opted for the truth. "If I ask her, she'll say no."

"I see. So, you want me to get her to do something that she wouldn't want to do if she knew the truth about why she was doing it." She looked amused, and also a little bit judgy.

"Pretty much," Liam admitted. "Look. I just want to get to know her better, that's all. In neutral territory."

She raised one eyebrow. "How is your house, with your parents and brother and sister and the whole deal, neutral territory?"

She had a point there.

"Well, okay. Not neutral, exactly, but ..." He struggled with his explanation, and she let him off the hook.

"You want to get to know her in a context where you both have your clothes on."

He rubbed the stubble on his chin and gave her a half grin. "That's more or less the idea. But if I ask her out on a date, she won't go."

"You could at least try ..."

"She won't go. You know her as well as anybody does. You know she won't."

Gen sighed. "You're not wrong."

"I know I'm not. So, will you do it?"

"Liam ..."

"I don't ask you for favors very often," he pointed out.

"That's true, you don't."

"And you want me to spoil that kid of yours when he gets here ..."

Her eyes widened. "You'd try to hold your nephew's happiness over me to get what you want?"

"Whatever works."

"All right. I'll ask her. Now, get out of here so I can work."

"Thanks, Gen. I mean it."

"You're welcome."

When he was halfway out the door, she stopped him. "Liam?"

He paused in the doorway and looked back at her.

"Just ... be careful, that's all. I don't want you to get hurt again."

The way she said it—the genuine love in her voice—made him feel a swell of emotion in his throat. He stuffed it back down in an effort to maintain his manly veneer.

"Hell. However it works out, I can take it."

As he walked out to his truck, he had to admit to himself that he might be lying. He might not be able to take it at all. But he was sure as hell going to find out.

Aria still hadn't met the rest of the Delaneys, so the dinner invitation was intriguing. She was living on the property of one of the wealthiest and most influential families on the West Coast.

Why shouldn't she indulge her curiosity?

The question of whether Liam had put Gen up to making the invitation occurred to her, but then she dismissed it. After the way Aria had treated him, it seemed unlikely that he'd be up for having her over to his house for dinner. And if he was behind it, that didn't seem like such a bad thing. It would give her the opportunity to show him she could be friendly while still setting appropriate boundaries.

And there *would* be boundaries. There had to be.

She made the walk to the main house late in the afternoon the following Saturday. The sun was already sinking in the sky, the colors of dusk painting the landscape. The air was chilly, so she had a warm sweater wrapped around her.

The house was a few hundred yards up a dirt road from the guesthouse, and she enjoyed the crunch of the road under her boots as she walked, the sound of birds in the Monterey pines, the rustle of small animals in the grass at the road's edge.

The Delaney place was a big white farmhouse with a wraparound porch that suggested summer evenings spent outside enjoying the cool ocean breeze. The house looked old but wellloved. Warm, golden light spilled out through the windows, and the multicolored Christmas lights hanging from the eaves made Aria realize with a start that it was already December.

For a moment, she just stood there looking at the house. She could imagine the Christmas mornings, the raucous family get-togethers, the chaos of kids getting ready for school.

Standing there on the path leading to the house, she felt a longing so deep it was like a fever that wouldn't break.

The normal things were what usually did it; those were the things that nearly brought her to her knees.

It wasn't hard to see where Liam got his demeanor.

Sandra Delaney greeted Aria with the same scowl that was frequently on the face of the woman's son. Sandra was brusque, ill-tempered, and crabby.

Aria loved her immediately.

"Well, you must be that artist that's been out there in our barn," Sandra said when she opened the front door for Aria. "I guess you'd better come in." She said it as though there had been some doubt whether Aria would be admitted, and she was letting her in with some reluctance.

Inside, the house was buzzing with happy disorder. Sandra, a small woman with graying hair pulled back into a ponytail, was bustling around with an apron around her middle and bunny slippers on her feet; an older man, probably in his sixties, had his feet propped up on a coffee table and was watching football on TV; two boys, either in their preteen or early teen years, were arguing over whose turn it was to use the Xbox; a woman in her thirties with thick, dark hair was setting a big wooden farm table with plates and silverware; and Ryan and Gen were messing around with the big Christmas tree in the corner, adjusting a string of lights.

"Aria. I'm so glad you could make it." Gen looked up from the tree and greeted her warmly. The smell of the tree combined with the aroma of roast chicken—the smells of a loving home— made Aria's eyes feel hot, and she blinked several times to steady herself.

Aria had brought a bottle of wine, and Gen took it from her and led the introductions. The older man in front of the TV was Orin, Gen's father-in-law. The woman setting the table was Breanna, one of the Delaney siblings. And the two boys were Breanna's sons, Michael and Lucas.

Only one person was notably absent: Liam.

Aria wanted to ask about Liam without seeming like she

was asking about him. She said, "Are we expecting anyone else?"

Gen looked at her innocently. "Anyone else? Like who?"

Flustered, Aria found herself babbling. "I didn't mean … I'm not …"

"Liam's on his way," Gen said, amused. "I'm not sure what's keeping him."

Liam was already late for a dinner he himself had arranged, and he knew he had to hurry up and get there. But he had one quick thing to take care of first.

That one quick thing involved him getting up on the roof of the old barn at near dark, and he sincerely hoped that he wouldn't fall twenty feet and mess up an arm to go with his poorly functioning leg.

Even worse, he might fall on his head—though some people claimed he must have done that already, long ago.

He knew what he was doing was silly and immature. And yet, here he was.

The thing was, rain was in the forecast over the next few days, and with the skylight over Aria's studio space fixed, there'd be little or no reason for him to come out here and see her.

But if the skylight were a little less fixed … well, then a man would have to do his part to help out a woman who was just trying to create her art without a steady flow of rainwater dripping onto it.

He went up onto the roof with a flashlight and a few tools. All he had to do was displace a few roof tiles and scrape away some of the sealant, and bingo.

If his brothers knew he was doing this, he'd never hear the end of it. But if Aria could use the skylight as a ruse, so could he.

Sometimes a guy had to be creative when it came to women.

Chapter Fifteen

Dinner consisted of roast chicken, mashed potatoes, green beans, freshly baked rolls, green salad, and apple pie for dessert. Ryan, a vegetarian, had skipped the chicken and had taken a double helping of everything else.

Sandra, at the head of the table, peppered everyone with her good-natured nagging.

"Now, Genevieve, I expect you to eat more than that, girl. How do you expect to grow a new person if you're not taking in enough calories to keep a damned flea alive?" She grunted at Gen and spooned more mashed potatoes onto her daughter-in-law's plate.

Instead of arguing, Gen simply thanked Sandra for the potatoes. Gradually, Aria realized that people didn't argue with Sandra much because there was no point in it. Any argument with Sandra Delaney was lost before it started.

"Orin, pass Aria some more of that chicken," Sandra ordered her husband.

"Oh, I shouldn't," Aria protested.

"Well, why the hell not?" Sandra wanted to know.

A little flummoxed, Aria hesitated. "I … really need to watch my weight."

"*Pfft*. You're fine," Sandra insisted.

"By God, that's the truth," said Liam, who'd finally arrived and was now sitting across the table from Aria. He grinned at her and winked, and she knew she'd been right when she'd told Daniel she might not be able to resist Liam. There was just something about the man.

Damn him. Why did he have to be so ridiculously appealing? Life went so much more smoothly when the man in her life—when there was one—was pleasant but unremarkable, someone she could spend time with or not, depending on her whims.

Liam Delaney was another kind of man entirely, with his cocky grin, the fine lines that fanned out from the corners of his eyes when he smiled, his lean, strong body, the way every molecule of him radiated easy masculinity. Every moment she spent with him, she could feel her own control of the situation slowly leaking away.

Why couldn't he take it easy on her and be a little less compelling, for God's sake?

Part of his magnetism was the fact that she could sense something beneath the surface, some deep well of feelings and meaning waiting to be discovered. Her instinct told her he was more richly layered than most people realized.

It was so tempting to just dive in and start excavating, peeling back the layers to see what lay at the deep heart of him.

But if she indulged that urge to really get to know him, it might mean that he, in turn, would really get to know her.

And that wasn't an option.

Aria tried to focus less on Liam and more on her meal.

She launched into a little small talk, asking the Delaneys about their family history (on the land since 1865, dedicated to cattle ranching for most of that time); life on the ranch (busy, messy, and sometimes dangerous); and Breanna's plans to buy the house on Moonstone Beach.

Then, the talk turned to her and her art.

"Mom says you're making a tent. That's really cool. Are you going to camp in it?" Michael, Breanna's oldest son, asked her. The boy, who looked to be about twelve or thirteen, had his mother's dark hair and deep brown eyes that reminded her of the deer she spotted from time to time outside the guesthouse.

"It's a yurt, which is kind of like a tent," she told him. "And I am going to camp in it, in a way." She explained her plan to install the yurt inside a gallery space and then live in it for a period of time yet to be determined.

"You're going to camp indoors?" Lucas, Michael's younger brother, asked in wonder. "What for? When people camp, it's usually so they can be around lakes and trees and stuff. And go fishing. Uncle Liam takes me fishing sometimes. And sometimes I go with Uncle Ryan."

Gen had explained to Aria that the boys' father, a Marine, had died in combat in the Middle East. The idea of their uncles stepping in to take them fishing—and to help fill the hole their dad's death had made in their lives—made Aria feel a sudden, unexpected love for the family.

Breanna ruffled Lucas's hair affectionately. "Maybe you and I can go fishing sometime soon," she told him.

Aria had just begun to think that the talk of fishing would save her from having to explain the concept behind her yurt, when Orin, the Delaney patriarch, picked up the thread of the conversation.

"I'd kind of like to know why someone would go camping indoors, too," he said. "Makes no sense to me, when a person's already got a perfectly good roof over their head."

"Well ..." Aria tried to think of how to explain without lapsing into the incomprehensible art-speak that people in her circles so frequently used. "The yurt is made of garbage. Things people have discarded on the beach, mostly. By building something out of it, and then living inside of it, I'm trying to show how the things we use every day—the things we choose to throw away—affect our world. Many times, people become so involved with the things they buy—most of which they're eventually going to throw out—that they shut out nature. The things become their entire world."

She considered the explanation she'd just given. It was incomplete, but it more or less touched on the major points she wanted to make.

"*Hmph.*" Orin looked down at his potatoes. "The last guy out there in the guesthouse was a painter. "You paint something, you hang it on the wall. It makes sense."

"If you think that last guy's paintings made sense ..." Ryan began.

"Orin, your opinion of art and two dollars is worth just about enough to buy you a cup of coffee," Sandra grumbled, a forkful of chicken paused halfway to her mouth. "Why, I think the yurt is a fine idea."

"You do?" Gen asked.

Sandra let out a grunt. "Most people are all about things. You buy this, you buy that. You feel unhappy about something, you buy something else. Then later on you realize you're not any happier than you were before you bought the damned thing. People act like if they've got enough damned stuff, they can block out everything they don't like about their jobs, or their families, or whatever's going on in the news. But it's all still out there, by God, no matter how many big-screen TVs you have."

"Yes." Aria looked across the table at Sandra. "That's exactly it." Sandra wasn't one of those people who tried to fill their world with things. She was immensely wealthy, but her home was simple and comfortable, the kind of home that someone making fifty thousand dollars a year would find familiar and accessible. The Delaneys were about the land. Of course they could understand a statement about the dangers of fouling it.

After a little more talk about art, Sandra asked the question Aria had been dreading.

"So, where're your people from?" Sandra threw the question out there casually, as though it didn't mean anything. Which, for most people, it probably didn't.

"I grew up in the Bay Area," Aria said. It wasn't an answer; she hoped no one would notice that.

But of course, someone did.

"What's your family like?" Ryan asked. "Are your parents artists, too? I figure that kind of thing's genetic, at least some of the time."

Aria looked at her plate to avoid making eye contact with anyone. "No. They aren't artists," she said.

She hoped to God the conversation would end there, but Orin kept it going. "What do they do? And what do they think of the whole yurt thing?"

It wasn't as though Aria had never had to deal with this kind of questioning before. She knew she should just come up with a lie, something benign and ordinary, something about her father being a pharmacist and her mother an elementary school teacher, something so bland that it would immediately prompt a change in topic. But she could never bring herself to lie, so instead, she inevitably floundered around offering evasive answers, feeling an oppressive pressure building in her chest.

"The dinner is delicious," she told Sandra. "If I could just use your restroom?"

As she was walking out of the room, she heard the Delaneys talking about her.

"What did I say?" Orin asked plaintively.

"Nothing. It's not you," Gen reassured him.

"Well, what is it, then?" Ryan asked. "She looked upset."

"Just ... everybody drop it, okay?" Liam said.

"Drop what? What did I say?" Orin asked again.

"The woman doesn't want to talk about her damned family," Sandra said, in a tone of voice that said the matter was closed. "Why, there are times I don't know why I'd want to claim any of you people. Lucas, stop playing with your napkin and eat your dinner."

Fortunately, by the time Aria returned to the table, the talk had changed to Breanna and her house. Aria listened gratefully as Breanna talked about how her offer had been accepted, and what she was going to do next.

"The place is barely inhabitable right now, which is why it's so great that I don't need to move in right away," Breanna said, her face alight with excitement. "I've got a two-week escrow, and after that, what I really need is a contractor."

"Two weeks?" Aria said. "Isn't that fast?"

"Yes, but we can do it because it's a cash deal," Breanna told her.

"I don't know what the big hurry is," Liam said, sounding a little irked. "The house is about ready to fall down. You ought to take the full thirty days, or even longer, and really check it out. You don't know what you're going to find if you really get to looking."

"I'm going to have it inspected, Liam," Breanna said. "I'm not an idiot."

"Yeah, well." Liam pushed his food around on his plate with his fork.

They talked a little bit more about real estate, and contractors, and Breanna's plans for remodeling the house. Once the tension of trying to avoid talking about her family blew over, Aria found that she was genuinely enjoying the Delaneys' easy banter. Aria had never owned a house—she'd always had apartments—but she joined in the conversation about open vs. closed floor plans, the benefits of en suite bathrooms, the importance of having a guest bedroom, and the various ways in which the house would have to be adapted for use by a couple of young and boisterous boys.

When the meal was over, Aria offered to help clean up, and Sandra shooed her away. She chatted with the family for a bit in the living room, then excused herself, saying she wanted to make it an early night.

The guesthouse was only a short walk away, but it was dark, and the rain had started pattering onto the roof. So when Liam offered to drive Aria back to the guesthouse in his truck, she accepted.

"I really like your family."

The truck was bumping over the dirt road leading to the guesthouse, the rain drumming on the roof and windshield, the wipers making a soothing *swoosh-swoosh* sound.

"Yeah. I kind of like 'em, too. Most of the time," Liam said.

"So, what was going on with you and Breanna?" she asked. "Why don't you want her to buy a house?"

"Ah … it's nothing." He shrugged. "I just think she's rushing things, that's all. One minute she's happy living on the ranch, and the next she's buying a place that's so rundown it's about to fall in on itself. I just don't get it."

"Maybe she's not as happy as you think she is," Aria suggested.

Liam shot her a look before focusing on the road again.

"Well, hell. Why wouldn't she be happy? What's she got to be unhappy about?"

She'd hit a nerve, clearly. She could either back off or poke at it and see what happened. She decided to poke.

"Sometimes a woman needs a home of her own, Liam."

"Is that what you want? A home of your own?"

They'd arrived at the guesthouse, so he parked the truck and turned off the engine. She suddenly felt very aware of the intimacy of being here with him in the dark truck, both of them dry and protected from the storm.

"We're not talking about me. We're talking about Breanna."

"Yeah, I noticed that. The part where we're not talking about you, I mean." His voice was a low rumble that made her flash back to the moments she'd spent with him, moments when she'd lost her sense in the feel of his body.

He waited for her to take the bait, and when she didn't, he sighed and rubbed his face with his hand.

"I just don't want her to go, I guess."

"You and she are close?"

He considered that. "You know, I'm not sure I realized we were until she started talking about leaving. Then, once she started making plans ..." He left the thought out there, unfinished.

"She'd probably appreciate it if you'd be supportive. Stop giving her such a hard time about it."

"Maybe. But if I didn't give her a regular ration of shit, she'd wonder who the hell kidnapped her brother and replaced him with a lookalike." He gave her that grin, the one that made her all soft and stupid.

After a moment, he tried again: "If you've got brothers, you probably get that—"

"Liam. Don't." She cut him off before he could go any

further.

"Don't what?"

"Just … don't." She gathered up her purse and went for the door handle. "Thanks for the ride."

"Aria. Wait." Liam put a hand on her arm, and she paused. "What?"

Liam didn't know how to answer her. What was it he wanted to say? How could he get her to stay here with him, or better yet, to invite him in?

"I'm sorry," he said. That always seemed to work well when women were pissed at him. "I shouldn't have pushed the thing with your family. You obviously don't want to talk about it, and—"

"You're right. I don't." It was dark in the cab of the truck, but the full moon was making the cloudy sky all silvery and pale, so he could see her face, see the challenge in her eyes. Still, she wasn't leaving, so that was something.

"So, we won't talk about that."

"Good."

They were quiet for a moment, watching each other, the tension thick between them.

"Instead, why don't we talk about why you're shutting me out?" he said.

She closed her eyes. "Liam …"

"We've had a good time together. At least, I know I was having a good time. But you … changed. One minute you were interested, and the next, you couldn't wait to get rid of me."

"That's not—"

"Just wait. Let me finish. Now, I'm not some guy who's going to try to pressure you into something you don't want. I mean … shit, I'm not that guy. I just want to know what I did."

"You didn't do anything." Her voice was softer now.

"I didn't?"

"No."

"Then what the hell's going on?"

She didn't say anything for a while, and he thought maybe he had a chance. Maybe she would answer him, tell him something real that would explain her sudden change of attitude.

Instead, she opened the truck door. "Goodnight, Liam. Thank you again for the ride."

Chapter Sixteen

Liam was far from the first man to become puzzled by the mystery of women. He found it comforting to know he was no more or less clueless than the next guy.

Reassuring as that thought was, it didn't help him with the situation at hand.

What was going on with Aria? What was the big secret about her family? And why did she keep pushing him away when she obviously was attracted to him?

Maybe he was tired of being alone after his breakup with Megan. Maybe his male ego needed answers. Or maybe he just didn't have enough to keep him busy.

Whatever it was, he was determined to solve the puzzle of Aria Howard.

The more she put him off, the more his substantial stubborn streak kicked in and he decided that he was going to figure her out or die trying.

He hoped it would be the former rather than the latter.

He thought about all of that the next morning while he went about his work at the ranch and waited for Aria to call him.

She was going to call sooner or later—if only because he'd sabotaged her skylight and it was raining like the heavens had unleashed the wrath of God.

He was out in the southeast pasture, riding a big black gelding and checking on the stock while trying not to notice the rain pounding down on him.

The cattle didn't always care about coming in from the rain, but today it was coming down hard, so Liam and some of the hands were putting dry bedding under a big, open-sided shelter they used when the weather got bad. They had too many animals to put them in the barn during a downpour, but the shelter, with its high, arching canopy, could hold quite a few of them.

They were just getting everything set up with fresh hay and a full water trough when Liam's cell phone rang. He'd closed it up in a Ziploc bag to keep it safe from the elements, since he was so wet he looked like he'd fallen into a lake.

He stood under the shelter, took the phone out of the bag, and answered it.

"Yeah?"

"Liam."

Just the sound of her voice could make parts of him stand at attention.

"Hey there," he said, a grin tugging at his lips. "You keeping dry?"

"Well … that's what I called about. The skylight's leaking again."

His eyebrows shot up, as though this were actually news to him. "You're kidding."

"I'm afraid not. I hate to bother you with this again, but—"

"It's no bother." At least that part was true. "I'm just finishing up here. I'll be out there in a bit to take a look." He ended the call feeling pleased with himself.

Who said Colin was the smart one?

When Liam got to the old barn, he saw that he'd done a

better job of sabotaging the skylight than he'd realized.

Where there had been a slow drip before, now there was a steady stream.

"Oh. Crap." As he looked up at the place where the water was coming in through the roof, his surprise was genuine. The effect was more dramatic than he'd thought it would be.

"Yeah," Aria agreed.

Liam, feeling a little bit guilty, asked, "It didn't get your ... your yurt ... wet, did it?"

"A little. Luckily, it wasn't directly in the line of fire."

"Well, that's good." He gazed up, his hands on his hips.

"You're soaked," she pointed out, as though he might not have noticed on his own.

"Yeah. That's a thing about ranching. The work doesn't stop just because it rains."

"I guess it doesn't." She reached out and wiped a drop of water off of his face with her finger. He felt it all the way down to his feet, and for a second, he didn't realize that he wasn't breathing.

"I'll have to wait until the rain stops to get up there and look at the skylight," he said, his voice a little hoarse.

"I know. That's ... I know."

She was standing closer to him than people having a casual conversation about a skylight usually did. Even that distance seemed too far. He took a small step closer to her, until he could almost feel her body heat.

"I guess you need to get back to work," he said, his voice just above a whisper.

"You too."

"Yeah." But he didn't leave, and he didn't move away.

She swallowed hard, and he saw her throat move with it.

"It's pretty cold and wet out there," he observed.

"It is."

He reached out and touched a lock of her hair that had come loose from the pins that had been holding it.

"It would help warm me up a little if I could maybe kiss you," he said. "Just once."

"Liam …" She started to protest.

He wasn't going to push it. He wanted her to want him; that was the point. And if she didn't, well, he guessed there was nothing for it.

"All right," he said. "I'll be back when it's dry."

He'd started to walk toward the door when she caught his arm. He turned to her, and then she was holding his face in her hands and kissing him.

He sank into the kiss, opening his mouth to her, caressing her with his tongue. His whole body seemed warm and liquid.

Then she pulled back and let go of him.

"Just once, you said."

He grinned at her. "So I did."

He walked out of the barn feeling happier than before, barely noticing the rain.

The kiss settled Liam down in a way he hadn't expected. Now that he knew Aria still wanted him, there was no need to hurry. He could take his time to find out what was going on with her, what had her so off balance.

He had no doubt that he would find out eventually, somehow. The fact that she didn't want him to discover whatever it was she was hiding was barely a factor in his imaginings.

It wasn't that he wanted to force her into any kind of relationship—it wasn't that he wanted to push her somewhere she didn't want to go.

But Liam had suffered a certain amount of damage in his

life: over his uncle's death, his heartbreaks, the physical injuries he was still struggling to overcome. He figured that one damaged person probably had a special knack for spotting another one.

And he'd spotted Aria, all right, as though she were lit up in neon.

If he figured out whatever it was that was troubling her and he still couldn't help—and if she still didn't want to be with him—well, that was fine. He could be a man about it and walk away.

But sometimes when you got a little air onto a wound, it started to heal. And if he could make that happen for her, it seemed like a worthwhile thing to do, whether the whole thing ended with the two of them together or not.

The question was, how to get her to open up to him. Or, failing that, how to find out the truth some other way.

Liam pondered all of that as he went back out into the rain to finish his workday.

The question distracted him to the point where Ryan had to call him out on it twice, once when he completely missed something the man was saying to him, and once when he didn't look where he was going and found himself up to his knees in a mud puddle.

"What's going on with you?" Ryan asked as they were wrapping things up for the day, grooming their horses in the big stable, the smell of wet animal permeating the air.

"Not a damn thing," Liam said, with little hope that Ryan would accept the answer.

"Well, that's bullshit," Ryan said amiably. "Are you okay?"

"Yeah. I really am," Liam said, meaning it.

Ryan considered his brother. "You know, it seems like you are, for a change. But there's something on your mind."

Liam glanced Ryan's way as he combed the gelding's coat.

"Well, I figure it's my mind, so I don't owe you an explanation for whatever's on it."

"Sure," Ryan said.

The first thing Liam tried was talking to Gen, but that didn't go anywhere. Gen told him the same thing she'd already told him—that Aria had been vague about her background when applying for the residency. When he pressed her for more information, like the specifics of what Aria had put in her application, Gen had balked.

Liam had expected as much, so he wasn't daunted. Next, he did what anyone would do in a situation like this: He consulted Google.

After Liam showered and ate dinner, he went up to his room, closed the door, and, with a beer in his hand, settled down in front of his laptop to search for whatever there was to know about Aria Howard.

He entered what he knew about her: her name, her profession, and her connection with the Bay Area, where she said she'd grown up, and Portland, where she lived now. He began wading through the entries on his screen.

At first, things seemed promising. There were a lot of hits, mostly about her work. He learned that she was well-regarded in the West Coast art scene, and that she'd had her work displayed in various high-end galleries and a few museums.

He read a little bit about the art itself, which was experimental and avant garde, combining visual art with performance. She'd once done an installation in which she had set up a table and chairs in the middle of a contemporary art museum and had sat across from one visitor at a time, silently looking at them. Liam would have thought that was a pretty pointless excuse for art, except for the articles he read about the visitors' reactions.

People had felt emotionally moved by the experience. They'd talked to her about their lives, though Aria herself didn't speak. Some had stayed for extended periods of time. Some had cried.

"What the hell?" Liam muttered as he read a review of the installation, which was decidedly positive. He tried to imagine what it was about sitting across a table from a stranger that might make a person cry, and as he thought about it, he decided it wasn't as odd as it seemed.

Aria had listened to people without talking, had looked at them without breaking that contact until the other person was ready to leave. How often did you really get that in life? So many times when you tried to talk to someone, they were so busy thinking of what they were going to say next that nobody really heard each other. And as for people taking the time to really *look* at each other? Well, hell, that was even more fraught with awkwardness and self-consciousness.

He wanted to pretend he thought the whole thing was stupid, but he could kind of see what she was getting at. He wondered what it would be like to sit across a table from Aria and really be seen by her, to really be listened to by her.

The interesting thing, though, was that she'd stayed silent even then. It was no coincidence that her performance art had involved her seeing into other people instead of them seeing into her.

He read some more articles on art-related websites, and a few archived newspaper pieces about her and her career. He found a couple of pictures of her, either performing or attending the gallery openings and lectures of others in the field.

Interesting thing, though: the earliest mention of her was from about five years before, when Aria was around twenty-three. That was odd. Just as a test, he Googled himself and found mentions that went back decades, ranging from his appearances at local charity events to articles in various financial magazines to his exploits on his high school football team. He guessed it was possible that a person's early life might not turn up much on a search engine, but his own name was all over the place—and he'd never made any kind of effort to put himself in the spotlight. Aria, on the other hand, was a performer. She intentionally put herself out there. So why wasn't there more of her online?

He found a few interviews, and reading them, he found pretty much what he expected. It was all about her art, with nothing about her personal life or family background.

"Well, shit," he said. His room was dark except for the desk light that illuminated his screen. He leaned back in his chair and took a deep drink of his beer.

Was it possible that Howard wasn't the name she'd grown up with? He didn't think she was ever married—if she was, she'd sure as hell never mentioned it—but it was possible. Or maybe Aria Howard was a stage name, like actors sometimes used.

"All right," he said to himself, thinking it over. "All right."

He searched online until he found a website that offered background checks for the bargain rate of $26.95. He fished his wallet out of his back pocket, found a credit card, and entered the information.

Now, he just had to wait.

Chapter Seventeen

The rain stopped the next day, and after waiting a respectable amount of time to let the barn roof dry in the sun, Liam went out to Aria's studio space with his ladder and his toolbox to fix what he'd intentionally broken.

It was a little after ten a.m. when Liam knocked on the frame of the open barn door and peered into the cavernous space.

"Anybody home?" he called out.

She emerged from the shadows with an apron tied around her waist, a pair of latex gloves on, and her hair up in a ponytail away from her face. "Hey. I was just doing some work on the khana."

"The what?" He squinted at her.

"The khana. It's the lattice frame that the walls are made out of. I was just finishing it."

He came into the barn to where she'd been working, and saw what she meant.

He'd seen her making the equivalent of long two-by-fours out of trash, and now they'd been used to build a kind of lattice framework for the walls of the yurt. Plastic water bottles and used grocery bags, beer bottles and the odd individual item—a toothbrush here, a Barbie doll there—made up what basically looked like an octagonal, six-foot-high fence.

Before, he'd looked at the project as some kind of unexplainable oddity—some crazy thing beyond his understanding—but now, seeing the thing begin to take shape, he started to become interested.

"Huh. But … how are you going to move it once it's done? It's going to be pretty big."

They talked for a while about how the yurt would be disassembled and then reassembled on site.

He found himself absorbed in the project, partly because construction was something he could understand, and also because it reminded him of the model airplanes and cars he used to build when he was a kid. The problem of a project, the questions of how to accomplish a specific goal, had felt soothing to him, occupying his brain in a way that pushed out all of the day-to-day concerns and anxieties that otherwise would have plagued him.

He could see that this was much the same thing for her. If she really was troubled about something—and he'd have bet his family's entire net worth that she was—then throwing herself into building a yurt, or whatever else she might be working on at any given time, would be a welcome release.

But he hadn't come here to talk about a yurt. He hadn't come here to fix a skylight, either. He'd come here to talk to her, so he figured he'd better focus on that before she caught on and kicked him out—which could happen at any moment.

"It was nice having you to the house for dinner," he said, figuring that was a safe gambit to begin a conversation. "My mom liked you."

"I liked her, too," Aria said.

"I know it gets a little crazy, with so many people and the kids and everything …"

"No," she said. "It was nice."

Now that Liam was here with her in the private, quiet space of the barn, she expected him to make a move on her. And she probably wouldn't have resisted him if he had. Instead, he simply talked to her—about her work, and his family, and his day on the ranch.

It was comfortable, without the usual tension she felt when she was around him.

She was starting to regret the fact that they were standing in an old barn instead of sitting somewhere quiet with beverages and maybe a fireplace to keep them cozy and protected from the afternoon chill, when he clapped his hands once to mark the end of something—or the beginning of something.

"Well, I guess I'd better get to that skylight," he said.

"Yeah, okay. Thank you. It's weird that it started leaking again."

He was walking away from her, and she was observing how cute his butt was in a pair of faded jeans, when he turned a little and said over his shoulder, "Not so weird."

"Huh? Why not?"

He gave her that grin that made her knees weak. "Because I got up on the roof and screwed with it to make it leak."

She was so stunned by the revelation that she stared at him, stammering. "But ... but why?"

"To give me an excuse to come out here and talk to you." Then he winked at her—God, that wink—picked up his ladder and his tools, and went to work.

Later that night, when Aria was settled in the guesthouse, wearing her pajamas and drinking a glass of wine, she spent some time thinking about whether it was cute or creepy that

Liam had sabotaged the skylight so he could spend time with her.

Yes, she'd spilled a bottle of water to make him think there was a leak. But he'd gone a step further and had actually created one.

When she considered what her gut said about it, she settled firmly on cute.

She'd never had anybody sabotage a skylight for her before. It was an interesting first.

She was thinking about how adorable it was, and about how adorable *he* was, and about how much she'd liked his family, and about how pleasant it had been just listening to him talk today, when she realized what was happening.

It was like she'd gone wading in knee-high water, and now the water was gradually rising and she was drifting out further and further, until eventually she would be in over her head without a raft or even a life jacket.

Damn it.

She wanted Liam—God, did she want him—but she didn't want the eventual pain and heartbreak that would come from allowing herself to really have him.

Aria raked her hands through her hair, sat back on the sofa, and decided to lose herself in a mindless TV show, or maybe a book.

Anything but thoughts of Liam Delaney.

It didn't take long for Liam to get the results of the background check he'd ordered on Aria.

He opened his e-mail, and there it was: a message with the subject line, YOUR BACKGROUND CHECK IS READY. He took a breath, steadied himself to push back the feeling that he was meddling in something that wasn't his to meddle in, and clicked on the link.

He had wondered if the $26.95 would turn out to be a waste—if he'd end up with nothing but the prior address of some other Aria Howard. But the report was surprisingly thorough. He learned a lot for his money.

He found Aria's address in Portland, which he was sure Gen already had. Before that, she'd lived on 35th Street in the Outer Sunset district of San Francisco, and before that, in an apartment complex in Oakland. She'd had two parking tickets: one for rolling through a four-way stop, and one for driving fifteen miles per hour above the speed limit.

She'd worked at an art supply store, a restaurant, and a convenience store, and she'd attended an extension course through UC Berkeley a few years before.

But there wasn't any information earlier than that—and he quickly saw why.

Aria Howard had legally changed her name five years before. Her real name—or, at least, the name that had been hers before then—was Lindsay Clifford.

He took a moment to digest that. What had made her change her name? Was it simply a professional decision? Had she changed it because she thought Aria Howard sounded better for a woman in the performing arts?

He had some hope that Googling the name Lindsay Clifford might produce something useful. It wasn't the most unusual name he'd ever heard, but it was better than something like Jane Brown—a name that would certainly send him down dozens of false avenues before he found the one he was looking for, if he ever did.

But Lindsay Clifford had some potential. How many of them could there be?

There were a lot, it turned out, but by adding some of the

other information he knew, such as her connection to the Bay Area and to art, the pool was narrowed down quite a bit.

Liam sat back against the headboard of his bed, his computer on his lap. He felt a little weird about what he was doing, but, hell, it wasn't like he had some dark motive. She'd sparked his curiosity, that was all. She'd made him want to *know*.

He started sorting through the hits for *Lindsay Clifford artist Oakland*. There wasn't much—she'd been young when she'd changed her name, and he figured public records relating to anything that happened while she was a minor probably had a certain amount of privacy protection.

He did find something that caught his eye, though.

It was a PDF of a newspaper article, dated fourteen years earlier. The article was about an art contest held by the Westerley Camp, one of those residential programs for troubled teenagers that operated under the theory that long hikes and Spartan accommodations could convince a kid to stop smoking pot and telling his mom and dad to fuck off.

The article included a photo of the winner: a chubby fourteen-year-old girl with dark hair and angry eyes. He zoomed in on the girl's face and found himself looking at a young Aria Howard.

Chapter Eighteen

Liam considered what he knew about Aria: She didn't talk about her family or her background. She'd had a difficult childhood—difficult enough to have attended a camp for troubled teens. And she'd changed her name as a young adult, not as a result of marriage, but apparently in an attempt to forge a new identity separate from the person she'd always been.

He could look into it further, maybe call Colin and get the name of a private investigator. Colin had to know at least one—he must have employed them from time to time back when he was practicing law for a large firm.

But that was too intrusive. Liam wondered whether he'd crossed a line by doing what he'd already done. Going further with it seemed like it would be counterproductive. When she found out about it—which she would, because he would eventually tell her—she'd be less likely to trust him than ever.

He shut his laptop, sat back, and closed his eyes to think about it.

Maybe what he already knew was enough. Maybe now that he had some idea what she was hiding from, it would allow him to at least start a conversation and see if he could encourage her to open up.

It seemed worth a try.

Why did he even care this much about Aria's history? If she wanted to keep secrets, then who was he to stop her from doing it? Who was he to say that starting over and burying the past was wrong?

But wanting to know was like an itch that was going to nag at him until he managed to scratch it.

How could he get her to talk to him?

When you wanted to get to know a woman, the usual thing to do was to ask her out. But judging by the way she'd been acting toward him, she would say no. He and Aria had taken things out of order—they'd had sex before they'd done the usual process of gradually getting used to each other—so the standard procedures didn't apply.

Aria had placed Liam neatly into a cubbyhole marked CASUAL SEX, when he wanted to be in the one marked POSSIBLE RELATIONSHIP. How could he get from one cubbyhole to the other?

Liam's brother Colin knew more about dating—and, in fact, more about most things—than Liam did. He knew that if he called Colin for advice, he'd never hear the end of it. His brother would hold it over his head that Liam had acknowledged his superiority, which would mean that the family's upcoming Christmas dinner was likely to result in Liam wanting to pour a punchbowl full of eggnog over the man's head.

Still, he decided that might be worth the risk.

Liam called Colin the following day during a break from work, when it would have been late afternoon in Montana. Even though Colin was a part-time rancher now—he spent the rest of his time managing the family's finances—he still sounded like he was wearing a thousand-dollar suit. Which he might have been.

"You're calling me for help. With a woman." Colin stated

the facts in front of him as though he were trying to make sure he wasn't hallucinating. "I don't think this has ever happened before."

"Yeah, yeah," Liam said. "Are you going to give me a ration of shit about it, or can we just get to it?"

"How about first I give you a ration of shit about it, and then we get to it?" Colin suggested.

"Ah, hell. I knew this was a mistake. I'm hanging up," Liam said.

"No, no. Wait. I'll help. Just ... give me a minute to adjust."

Liam filled him in on the basics. He didn't tell Colin any of the private things he'd discovered about Aria's past—only that she'd been alternating hot and cold toward him and that she didn't seem to want to talk about herself. Given the fact that they'd jumped past the preliminaries and had gone straight to bed, how could he back things up now and spend some time getting to know her as a person, the way he should have done in the first place?

"You don't want to be used for your body. That's sweet. Really," Colin said, falling into the pattern of brotherly teasing they'd perfected while growing up.

"Well, hell, I like being used for my body on occasion," Liam said. "But she's got me ... curious."

"Curious," Colin repeated.

"Well ... yeah."

"Have you thought about asking her out? You know, on a date? Where everybody's dressed?"

"Yes, I have, smartass. But she's gonna say no."

He'd expected Colin to argue with him on that point, but he didn't. Instead, he was quiet for a moment while he considered the question.

"Well ... you could take an interest in her art."

Liam protested, "It's a yurt. Made out of trash."

"It sounds like she's still got a lot of work to do on it, right?"

"Yeah," Liam admitted.

"Ask her if she needs some help."

"Help?" He said it as though the word itself were an unfamiliar concept to him.

"Sure. Go over there and see if she needs anything. See if you can ... hell, I don't know. Find more trash for her. Or glue something."

Liam was skeptical. "It's art. What the hell do I know about art?"

"It's a trash yurt," Colin pointed out. "She's not painting the Sistine Chapel. And anyway, even Michelangelo had assistants."

"He did?" Liam asked.

"I have no idea," Colin admitted. "But it sounds right. He must have."

"Huh," Liam said.

A day or two later, Aria was out in the barn working on the exterior of her yurt.

She didn't often question her own choices when it came to her art. Generally, once she decided on a particular project, she just went with it, throwing herself into the work until it was finished.

But when she considered how much work this damned yurt was going to be, she had to wonder if she'd lost her mind.

The basic frame was done, but there was still the roof with its glass panel and its multiple layers, the inner and outer wall coverings, and the floor ... not to mention that there had to be some kind of door.

She was beginning to think that she'd still be gluing pieces of trash while presidential administrations rose and fell, climate changed, fashion trends came and went, and several more versions of the iPhone were introduced.

There was something soothing about the process of building the structure, the hours of systematic work that allowed her mind to wander wherever it would. And yet her back hurt, her shoulders were stiff, and she thought she might be starting to develop carpal tunnel syndrome from the repetitive process of brushing glue onto things.

She was just standing to stretch, pressing her hands to the small of her back, when she realized she wasn't alone.

"Back trouble?" Liam was standing in the doorway of the barn, sunlight streaming in around his silhouette. Now that the rain had passed, the weather had turned crisp and clear.

She straightened up self-consciously. "Not trouble, exactly. I'm just a little stiff."

It was a perfect opportunity to make some kind of pass. She halfway expected him to offer her a massage. Instead, he said something she didn't expect.

"Need some help?"

"I ... you mean with the yurt?" She thought she must have misunderstood his offer.

"Sure. I've got a little time, I could"—he gestured vaguely toward her construction area—"just do whatever needs doing."

When she didn't say anything for a moment, he backpedaled a little.

"I mean, I know it's your art. You've gotta be particular about how it's done, so ... if I shouldn't have offered ..."

"No! It's not that. It's a nice offer."

"Even Michelangelo had assistants," Liam said. "I mean, I guess he must have."

"He did," she agreed. "All right, thanks. Come over here, and I'll show you what needs to be done."

The sudden introduction of help was a godsend. She showed Liam how to glue pieces of refuse together to create the outer covering of the yurt, and he got to work. This part of the project was going to be a long and painstaking one, perhaps taking up the bulk of the time Aria would spend on the piece. Having someone to help her with it would cut the time investment considerably.

"Reminds me of putting together model cars when I was a kid," Liam told her as he chose pieces, applied glue, and then stuck the pieces to plastic trash bags to create the outer skin of the yurt. "Or maybe those paper-mache projects they have you do in school."

He talked about his brothers and the things they'd all built—the tree house when Liam was eight; the science experiments; the endless Popsicle stick structures and clubhouses made of cardboard boxes; the bike Ryan had put together from parts.

"Your brother built his own bike?" she said. "Aren't you guys ... you know ..." It seemed indelicate to say it.

"Rich?" Liam filled in the blank for her.

"Well ... yes."

"We are. But my parents never believed in spoiling us. I remember having to work like hell for my two dollar a week allowance when I was in third grade. Still, Ryan could have bought a bike. He built one himself because he wanted to."

"And how old was he then?"

Liam considered it. "About ten."

"That's a big project for a kid that age," Aria said.

"Yeah, well." He was quiet for a moment. Then he said,

"My uncle Redmond helped him with it."

There was something there—something in the way he'd said his uncle's name.

"Did your uncle do things with you, too?"

"He ..." Liam cleared his throat. "Yeah. He did."

Aria knew she'd hit a particularly sensitive spot, and she knew that if she pressed him on it, he'd likely change the subject. It's what she would do. Instead, she simply kept working quietly beside him.

"My uncle died a few years ago," he said finally.

"Yeah. I remember reading about that," she told him. Redmond Delaney's death had been news because of his vast wealth. It had hit the financial magazines and websites, not that Aria made a habit of reading those. She remembered the headlines, though—including those saying Redmond had left most of his fortune to a son nobody had known about.

"What was he like?" she asked.

"Redmond?" Liam shrugged. "He was just ... Redmond." He let out a low laugh, as though in response to a private joke. "He was quiet. Strong. Kind. Tough as hell. Simple. At least, we thought he was."

She proceeded carefully. "I seem to remember something about the will. How some things came out that were ... unexpected."

He glanced at her as he continued to work on the yurt. "Unexpected. Yeah, I guess you could say that." He applied a thin layer of glue to a crumpled cigarette box and affixed it to a kind of sheet Aria had made out of plastic bags. "He slept in his childhood bedroom from the time he was born until the day he died. Except for a few years when he was off in Montana." He shook his head. "Never had a wife. Never had a girlfriend that we knew about. I mean ... did we think it was odd? Yeah, sometimes. I guess. But … if he'd been gay, he might not have been the kind of guy who felt comfortable saying it. We figured it was his own private business. Turned out he never had anyone because he was in love with a married woman he met out in Montana. So in love with her that he was never interested in anyone else." He considered that for a moment. "Can you imagine being in that kind of love? The kind where you'd rather be alone for the rest of your life than settle for anyone else?"

"No. I can't," she said honestly. Sometimes she thought that any kind of love—even the kind that flamed out quickly and came to earth in a painful, devastating crash—was beyond her grasp.

"Well. It must have been something," he said.

They worked side by side for a while longer, and she thought he'd said everything he intended to. Then, just when she'd thought he had closed down on her, he started to talk again.

"Finding out I had a cousin I never knew about—that was a hell of a thing. Hated his fuckin' guts when I met him. You want to know what's the most crazy-ass thing about it? I didn't start to like him until he stole my girlfriend." He shook his head as though he still couldn't believe that particular development.

"He … what? How did that play out?" Aria asked.

"Ah …" He shrugged. "She's better off with him. I mean, sincerely. They're more right for each other than she and I ever were. I was kind of a mess. I had some things to work out."

"And did you?" she said. "Work them out, I mean?"

He glanced at her. "Mostly. But it's fair to say I'm still a work in progress."

"Aren't we all?" she muttered.

Liam stayed for about an hour before he had to get back to

his own work wrangling cattle, or whatever it was he did on the ranch.

When he was gone, the barn seemed more empty than it had before he'd arrived. Before today, she would have said that having a visitor in her studio while she was working on a piece would be intrusive and distracting. But she'd found it surprisingly soothing to listen to his voice while she worked. And he'd helped her make significant progress.

She found herself missing him almost immediately, and missing him made her wonder if and when he might come back. And that made her scowl in dismay.

Damn it.

If he thought he could worm his way into her heart and mind ... then he was right. It was working. And she couldn't let him do it. There was too much at stake. She just couldn't go there.

It would have been so much easier if he'd just come here to get her into bed again. She would either say yes or no, and either way, they could move on without any confusion or complications.

Instead, he'd come here and talked to her as though they were friends, as though they had a relationship that went beyond the physical. He'd told her true things and had made her get to know him a little. Which was going to make it that much harder to walk away.

She tried to get back to work, but she was too distracted, her mind too focused on Liam and the way his voice had sounded, the way he'd looked ...

She gave up with a sigh and plopped down onto a folding chair at her worktable. Then she pulled out her cell phone, and in an impulsive move, called Daniel Reed.

"Reed," he said.

"Hi, Daniel. It's Aria."

"Oh. Hey. If you're ready to get started on that skylight, I can—"

"It's not the skylight. It's Liam."

"Ah. Just ... wait a minute."

"For what?"

"For me to get in girl-talk mode." She heard him rustling around on the other end of the line—scrubbing at his face, maybe, or finding a comfortable seat—and then he said, "Okay. Shoot."

"He ... he tricked me into a goddamned date!" She hadn't even realized that was what he'd done until she'd said it out loud. "He knew that if he asked me out, I'd say no, so he came to the studio and started talking and being all ... all *Liam* ... and that's really not fair! How am I supposed to keep control of this situation if he's going to *trick* me like that?"

"That bastard," Daniel said, mock-serious.

"You're not helping."

"Sorry. I guess I'm a little confused about why it's such a bad thing that you're starting to like him. I mean, beyond the obvious thing about your taste ..."

"Daniel."

"Sorry. Again. But I'm serious. If you like him, and he likes you ..."

She'd already chosen Daniel as the person she wanted to open up to about all of this, so she decided to tell him just one true thing, one bit of why a real relationship with Liam Delaney—or with anyone—would be a cataclysm.

"If we start to get to know each other—really know each other—then he's going to find out some ... things ... about me that I'd rather not have anyone know. Because if he knows them, then things that are in the past won't be in the past anymore. They'll be here, now, and ... I just can't deal with that. Not now, and not ever."

From Daniel's silence, she guessed that he was taking a moment to adjust to this new information.

"The past is never really the past, Aria. Not when it's affecting your present."

"Very philosophical," she said dryly.

"I mean it. Whatever the thing is that you don't want people to know, it won't go away just because people don't know it."

She felt the sting of tears in her eyes, and wiped at them with her fingers.

"Did you kill somebody?" he asked after a while.

"What? No!"

"Then I think there's a chance he can handle whatever it is," Daniel said.

"It's not about what *he* can handle. It's about what *I* can."

"All right. Then, can you handle pushing away a guy you might have something good with if you could just get past your baggage and let it happen?"

She pressed her lips into a hard line and didn't answer him.

"It's something to think about," he said.

Chapter Nineteen

Liam hadn't meant to say all that stuff about Redmond. In fact, he found that the less he thought about Redmond, the easier life was. But he'd started talking, and it had just come out.

The fact was, he was still raw with grief, and the more he could push it down and think about other things, the easier it was to get through every day, doing his job and living his life.

During the first year or so after Redmond had died, Liam had sometimes sneaked into his uncle's room just to sit, to feel the essence of the man in the space where he'd lived for so long.

But Sandra had finally packed up Redmond's room, giving some of his things to Drew and putting the rest into boxes that were now stored in the garage.

After that, Liam had sometimes gone to visit with Redmond's horse, Abby, when he'd wanted to feel close to the man. But Abby, who'd been growing old, had passed on about a year before. Now, the only place he could go was the cemetery.

He hadn't been up to the cemetery in a while, but talking to Aria about Redmond had stirred something up in him again. He waited until he had to go into town on an errand—that way, he wouldn't have to explain himself—and drove up to the graveyard at the top of Bridge Street, with its headstones and stone benches amid groves of trees, quiet except for the rustle of the breeze through the leaves.

Liam was pretty sure he was the only one in the family who still came up here. It wasn't that the others didn't care, or didn't miss Redmond. But they'd moved on. If they knew how he still felt, how the loss of his uncle still tore at him, then the others would wonder why he hadn't gotten past the grief as easily as they had. After all, Redmond was his uncle. It wasn't like losing a father.

Except for Liam, it was exactly like losing a father.

Liam had Orin, of course, and Orin had been a solid and reliable father, as steady as the earth itself. But Liam had always suspected that he was his father's third favorite son. Orin never would have said as much, but Liam could feel it. Ryan was the kind, principled, salt-of-the-earth one. Colin was the smart one.

And Liam was the other one.

Hell, if Liam were to talk to a therapist about it—which he'd never done and would never do—he would probably find out that he'd adopted the role of the family's hot-tempered lunkhead because it was the only part that hadn't already been cast. And maybe it had seemed like the only way to get his father's attention.

But it hadn't worked—not really. Orin had been busy with the ranch and with his other children, and Liam had felt angry and left out.

Redmond must have spotted that, because he'd stepped in where Orin had left off. Redmond had spent time with Liam one on one when Orin either hadn't had the time or the interest. There had been camping trips, fishing. Redmond had been the one who'd taught Liam to ride.

Redmond had been the one who'd showed up when Liam was in high school and had needed a ride home from a party because he was too drunk to drive and didn't want his parents to know.

Redmond was the one who'd talked to the other kid's parents when Liam had gotten into yet another fight.

Redmond had been the one who had shown up to all of Liam's football games. Orin had come to a lot of them, too. But Redmond had come to every one.

Liam settled in on a small granite bench next to Redmond's grave. The weather was cool, with a light wind ruffling his hair. He pulled his jacket around him.

This cemetery wasn't like others, with their strict rules about what could and could not be displayed on the graves. Here, families created informal shrines for their loved ones, with framed photos, mementos, handwritten letters, and other symbols of love and loss adorning the grave sites.

Liam thought that if it helped people feel better, it was probably good. But that wasn't his style, so he didn't bring anything when he came here. He wasn't religious, and he wasn't under the illusion that Redmond could somehow see the flowers or the letters from the great beyond.

Redmond was just gone.

A set of wind chimes hanging from a nearby tree tinkled in the breeze, and Liam found the sound unbearably eerie and sad. He found himself getting teary-eyed, as he always did, and he wiped his face with his hands.

"Damn it, Redmond."

It wasn't okay that he'd died, and it wasn't okay that Liam was left behind feeling stuck with his grief, feeling so incapable of moving forward with his life.

When Drew McCray had shown up, having been named in the will, Liam had been seething with anger and jealousy. Mostly because *he* had felt like Redmond's son, and the thought of someone else stepping forward to claim that status had been too much to take on top of the pain of loss.

As it had turned out, Liam and Drew had a certain amount in common. Both of them had been cut down by grief—Liam over a man he'd been close to, Drew over the father he'd never known and never would know. Both of them had reacted with anger. Both of them had shut down, unable to move on.

But lately, Drew had moved on, all right—with Liam's ex. Hell, good for him. If that was what it took to break out of the cycle of anger and self-defeating behavior, then so be it.

At least one of them had gotten out.

Sometimes, Liam felt like he was ready to move on, too. Meeting Aria had made him think maybe he was ready to go forward—if not with her, then with someone.

He needed to stop being the angry Delaney and find a way to just be himself.

He sat there on the bench, alone in the cemetery except for the occasional squirrel scampering up a tree, and wondered what Redmond would do. But then he rejected that thought.

Redmond had failed to acknowledge his only son because he hadn't wanted to rock anybody's boat. Probably not the best role model to look to for guidance on self-improvement.

"Okay," Liam said, wiping away the last of his tears and standing up from the bench. "Okay."

He walked out of the cemetery, gravel crunching under his feet, to go back to the ranch and just get on with it.

Chapter Twenty

Christmas was only a few weeks away, and Aria had no one to shop for. Usually, that kind of thing didn't bother her, but this year, in the wake of her dinner at the festively decorated Delaney house, she wished she could enjoy some of the trappings of the holiday the way other people did.

She couldn't just randomly buy gifts for any of the adults surrounding her—Gen or Liam, or maybe Daniel—without making them feel obligated to reciprocate, and that was an awkwardness she just didn't want to deal with.

But kids? That was another story. You could always buy Christmas gifts for kids, and nobody thought it was weird, or felt obligated, or wondered about your motives.

She'd been out walking on Main Street late on a Wednesday morning, enjoying the cool ocean air and the relative dearth of tourists, when she'd come across a toy store and had gotten the idea.

If she bought something for Breanna's kids, Lucas and Michael, it might lift her spirits nicely, and she wouldn't have to tell anyone that it was her only chance to participate in a holiday ritual other people took for granted. She could just say it was a thank you for the family's hospitality.

She went into the store, exchanged polite greetings with the shopkeeper, and began browsing through the board games and kites and skateboards. She was just looking at a Lego set when she heard a voice behind her.

"I'm surprised to see you here."

The voice alone was enough to send an electric tingle of warmth down her spine.

She turned, and there he was, that sexy grin on his face, that long, tall body looking out of place amid the brightly colored toys.

"Liam." She put down the Lego set and turned to him.

"Who are you shopping for?" he asked, nodding toward the box she'd just replaced on the shelf.

"Michael and Lucas. Kids and Christmas, you know … I just thought it would be fun." She felt a little self-conscious, as though her explanation were transparent and he'd be able to see how pathetically lonely she was.

"Same here," he said. "Plus, I wanted to pick up something for Ryan and Gen's baby."

"You're Christmas shopping for a baby who hasn't been born yet?" That was unexpectedly sweet, coming from a guy like Liam. She found herself charmed—even though she didn't particularly want to be charmed.

"Yeah, well." He looked at his feet, and that was charming, too, damn it—she could see the child he'd once been, shy and self-conscious and all boy.

"Since you're here, you can give me some insight. What do your nephews like?"

They talked about that for a while. Michael liked arts and crafts, building, projects, that kind of thing. Lucas liked super-heroes, particularly Spider-Man and the Hulk.

He told her that he didn't know what you were supposed to buy for a not-yet newborn, he just knew that he wanted to get something to show his enthusiasm for being an uncle again.

With Aria's help, he settled on a newborn-approved stuffed rabbit with legs that made a crinkling sound and ears that doubled as teethers.

Aria found an art set for Michael and a couple of action figures for Lucas, and they both paid for their purchases before emerging onto Main Street with their shopping bags in hand.

"Lunch?" he said.

Aria was surprised by the one word, seemingly coming out of nowhere. "I ... what?"

"It's almost noon," he said. "I'm starving. You want to get some lunch?"

She'd vowed that she was not going to date him. Would lunch be a date, or would it just be lunch? A date would be planned in advance, wouldn't it? Did the fact that this was so impromptu exempt it from potential date status?

Aria was so flummoxed by the simple equation of whether lunch equaled a date that she didn't even realize she hadn't answered him yet. She tried to come out with something—anything—and found herself stammering.

"I wasn't ... I didn't ..."

"Come on." He didn't wait for her to answer. Instead, he started walking down Main Street with long, easy strides.

The arrogance of him literally walking away without her left her speechless. What the hell was she supposed to do now? Chase after him like a puppy? Or just let him go?

Damn it, she thought, not for the first time in relation to Liam Delaney.

She was hungry, and she was lonely, and he looked so damned good as he walked away. She grabbed her bags and hurried after him.

•••

Aria had been so certain that Liam was trying to lure her into a date that it was utterly unexpected when he walked straight past several nice-looking restaurants and led her to a taco truck at the corner of Main Street and Burton Drive.

"This isn't a restaurant," she said, realizing as she said it that she sounded stupid.

"You don't like tacos?" he asked, his eyebrows raised.

"That's not ... I mean, sure. I like tacos."

Apparently, *I like tacos* was all the input he needed from her. He placed an order and paid, and after a short wait, he was handed a very aromatic sack and two takeout cups of whatever he'd ordered for them to drink.

"All right, come on," he told her, and started walking down Main Street.

"Is that the way you do things?" she said, hurrying after him. "It's just, 'Come on, woman,' and then you go and wait to see who follows you?"

"I never called you *woman*," he said, not unreasonably.

"You were probably thinking it."

"Do you want your tacos or not?" He stood there looking at her with that half grin, his eyebrows raised in question.

The bag smelled good, and her stomach rumbled in response.

"Yes, I want my tacos."

"Well, all right, then." He walked down Main Street a little farther with Aria chasing after him, then he turned on Bridge Street.

He didn't slow down until they'd reached a small park with a stretch of grass dotted with trees, a tiny wooden building that a plaque said was a Chinese temple, and an Asian-inspired fountain that trickled water onto smooth rocks below.

He led her to a bench in the shade, and she sat beside him.

"This is lovely." She looked around in surprise, having neither seen nor heard of this park before in her explorations of the town.

"Yeah. The creek's right over there, behind the trees." He motioned with one hand. "You can hear it, this time of year. Water's fairly high after the rains."

She listened, and he was right: She could hear that, and so much else. The breeze rustling the branches of the trees. Some kind of small bird calling to its brethren. The gentle sounds of the fountain. And the occasional car passing by on Burton Drive—locals going about their day, or maybe tourists on the way to somewhere else.

"I got you a Coke," he said, holding out one of the cups. "I figured everybody likes Coke."

"You wouldn't have had to guess if you'd asked," she grumbled. "But, yes, I like Coke. Hand it over."

"If I'd asked, it would have given you time to change your mind," he said, as casually as if he'd been asking her to pass him a napkin. "Chicken or beef?"

"And why a taco truck?" she asked.

"Same deal. If I'd taken you into a restaurant, the whole time we were waiting for a table or looking at the menus, you'd have been planning to go to the ladies' room and sneak out the back door." He looked around the park. "There's no back door here. Now, do you want chicken or beef?"

She stared at him for a moment, surprised at how accurate his assessment was. "Chicken."

"Good choice, though I'm partial to beef, myself." He dug a taco out of the paper bag and handed it to her.

She unwrapped the taco, looked at it, and belatedly said, "I wouldn't have freaked out if we'd gone to a restaurant." It was bullshit, and she knew it.

"Really? You wouldn't have figured that was too much like a date, when you've already told me you don't date? You wouldn't be in your car on your way back to the ranch right now?"

"Well …"

"Eat your taco."

She wanted to be irritated at how smug he was, but he was right. And the taco looked damned good. She took a bite and savored the flavors of tender chicken, chiles and spices.

"Wow. This is really good."

"Isn't it? That truck's been in the same spot for years. I go a couple times a week, at least."

They ate in companionable silence in the cool, crisp air.

"So, you going home for Christmas, Aria?"

He said it so casually that it had to be idle conversation—it couldn't have been him prying into her private life. And yet, the question sounded like an accusation, or an interrogation.

"The residency is three months," she said, avoiding what he was really after—some tidbit about her family or friends, some juicy bit of information about who she was when she wasn't here.

"*Hmm.*" He took a bite of his taco, chewed thoughtfully, and swallowed. "I don't imagine Gen's got you chained to the guesthouse, though."

Smartass.

"No. I'm not going anywhere for Christmas," she said.

"Well, good. Then you can come to our place for Christmas dinner." He sounded entirely too pleased with himself.

"That's very nice, but—"

"Hell, it's not me being nice. It's self-preservation. If my mom finds out you're all alone in that guesthouse because I didn't have the manners to invite you, she'll have my ass."

Aria wanted to protest, but she figured it was probably true.

"Your mother's quite a woman," she said.

He nodded seriously. "Yes. She is."

If he'd asked about hers, it would have plunged the conversation into an abyss of avoidance and awkwardness that would have killed the friendly mood. But he didn't. Instead, he told her a story about Sandra.

"My mother grew up on the ranch," he said.

"But she's not a Delaney by birth, is she?"

"No. She's not. What happened is, her dad was a ranch hand—got a job working for my grandfather when my mother was only about five, six years old. Her mom had taken off—God knows where—and her dad had to bring her along when he came to work. Now, my grandmother was a sucker for kids, especially little girls, since she didn't have any of her own. So she kept an eye on my mom during the day, taught her how to bake pies and tend a garden, that kind of thing. Then, as my mom got older, she started to notice my dad."

Aria wiped some salsa from her mouth with a paper napkin. "What did your grandparents think of that?"

He let out a low, short laugh. "Not much one way or the other, since my father was a lot older, and he thought she was just some annoying little kid who followed him around everywhere."

"I guess he didn't stay annoyed for long," Aria remarked.

"Well, that's the thing about my mother. When she sets her mind to something, she by God makes it happen. Every time." He unwrapped another taco. "She says I'm the most like her, out of all her kids."

Was that a warning? A challenge? She shot him a glance before reaching into the bag for another taco.

She'd thought he would make a move on her the last time

she saw him, when they were together in the barn. He hadn't. She thought the same thing now: surely he would make some kind of play to get her back to the guesthouse—or back onto the table in the barn.

Part of her really wanted that.

But again, he defied her expectations. When they were done with their tacos, he crumpled up the bag, threw it into a trash can, and walked her back to her car, which was parked on a side street up from the toy shop where they'd run into each other.

"I guess I'll see you back at the ranch," he said. His tone was annoyingly casual, as though there were nothing going on here except two acquaintances bumping into one another for a chat about the weather.

"Um … okay. I guess so."

The thing was, she hadn't wanted this to be a date, and she hadn't wanted him to kiss her. But now that she'd gotten her wish on both counts, she felt acutely disappointed.

She got into her car and started the ignition, thinking simultaneously about the excellent tacos and about sex.

Those two things didn't usually go together in her mind, but for Liam, she could make an exception.

Liam drove back to the ranch wondering if he'd played it wrong. Should he have kissed her? Should he have made some kind of move?

He'd wanted to—so much that he'd barely been able to think about anything else. But she was so skittish that he figured he had to proceed carefully, bringing her so gently into a relationship that she wouldn't even know she was in one until she was already there.

If he'd moved too quickly with her at the start—jumping right to sex, and thus putting himself in the *casual hookup* category—he couldn't make the same mistake again.

But, shit, it had been hard to hold back, hard to be friendly and chatty, keeping his distance like the two of them were just old friends.

He couldn't fuck this one up. He had to play it smart.

And wanting to be smart made him think about his mother and the story he'd told Aria. Maybe it wouldn't be such a bad thing to talk to Sandra about this thing he had going on.

If Sandra always got what she wanted—and she did—then maybe she could teach her son a bit about how she did it.

Chapter Twenty-One

If Liam had to make a list of things his mother enjoyed, listening to other people's complaints about their love lives probably would have ranked somewhere near the bottom, between foreign documentaries and toenail fungus.

That was why she was giving him this particular look, the one that said she was barely putting up with him but was doing it, nonetheless, out of a sense of motherly duty.

"What the hell do I know about dating?" she grumbled as she stood in her bedroom folding a basket of laundry that was fresh from the dryer. "I've only ever dated one man in my life, and even that wasn't what you'd call romantic. My God, the man didn't even know how to propose. 'Guess we might as well get married,' that's what he said. *Hmph.* I'm not exactly the damned voice of experience."

Liam was standing with his hands in his jeans pockets, feeling sheepish. As much as he hated doing laundry, he figured he'd feel less awkward if he had something to do with his hands, so he grabbed a few random shirts and socks off the top of the basket and started folding them.

"Not like that." Sandra slapped at his hand as he made a mess of folding a T-shirt. "Like this." She demonstrated, producing a shirt folded so neatly it could have been on a shelf at

Macy's.

He folded another shirt and held it up for his mother's approval.

"Better." She nodded. "Now, if you're going to be standing there, I guess you'd better get on with it and tell me whatever the hell's on your mind."

He picked a pair of socks out of the basket and rolled them into a tidy bundle. For a moment, he didn't say anything.

"I want to get to know Aria better." He'd considered a few strategies for broaching the subject, and had decided on the direct approach.

"Well, what's stopping you, boy? Don't tell me you want somebody to Cyrano the thing for you, hiding in the damned bushes and feeding you lines of poetry?" She chuckled at her own humor.

"No."

"Then what's the problem?"

"Well … she is. I mean, she's not a *problem*. That's not how I meant to say it. It's just … she's kind of private. We'll be having a conversation, and I'll ask some innocent question, and she just shuts down."

She let out one of her Sandra grunts. "I saw some of that when she was over for dinner. She's got some secrets, that one. Not sure they're any of your business, either."

"They might not be." He folded a pair of his dad's underwear, trying not to think too much about that as he was doing it. "But I don't want to cross-examine her. I just want to get her to go out with me."

"I don't suppose you've tried asking."

"She'd say no." She was about to ask him how he knew that, but he cut her off. "I just know, all right?"

She grumbled a little and snapped a shirt in the air to broadcast her disagreement. "Only a damned fool would sit around wondering why a woman won't go out with him when he's never asked her on a date. But if you're sure you're a psychic, well ...'"

He ignored the fact that she'd just called him a damned fool. He'd actually been one more than a few times when she hadn't noticed, so it all evened out.

"The thing is, if she knows I'm trying to get something started with her, she's going to shut me down. So I have to kind of ... you know ... get in there sideways."

"You want to date the woman without her knowing that's what you're doing," Sandra summarized.

"Well ... pretty much."

"What the hell are you asking me for?" she asked irritably. "Do I look like a damned relationship counselor?"

"No, but you get what you want about ninety percent of the time, so I figure you must know something I don't."

She shot him a look that was part annoyance, part amusement. "Well, boy, I know a hell of a lot that you don't. So at least you're right about that."

They folded in silence for a few minutes while she thought about his question.

With a lacy bra in her hands—Liam tried not to think about whether it was hers or Breanna's—Sandra glanced at him. "She doesn't seem to get out of that guesthouse much."

"I guess."

"Woman's been here for weeks—the middle of all this natural beauty—and she just works most of the time." She shook her head and *ts*ked. "Seems to me she could benefit from a tour from somebody who knows what's what around here."

The space between his eyebrows furrowed as he considered that. "If I offer to show her around, that's pretty transparent. I mean, I—"

"That's why you're not going to do it, boy. Gen is. It's all part of the service, with the whole artist thing."

"She is?"

"That's right." Sandra nodded decisively. "Then, when the two of 'em are already out there, looking at an elephant seal or some such, Gen's going to have an emergency at the gallery. Luckily, you'll be available to take over and save the damned day."

"Huh." Liam was impressed by his mother's ability to devise a scheme on the fly. "That's really sneaky."

Sandra grunted. "How the hell do you think I got your father to marry me? If I'd left it to him, he'd still be single and you kids wouldn't exist. Though sometimes that scenario sounds pretty relaxing, to tell the truth."

"I'll talk to Gen," he said.

"No, you'd better let me do it," Sandra said.

"Why?"

"Because she can say no to you. But the girl's smart enough not to cross her mother-in-law." She considered what she'd just said, then nodded crisply.

All in all, Liam considered himself fortunate that Sandra was on his side.

When Gen called Aria to offer her a tour of the area—everything from Hearst Castle to the elephant seal habitat to the cookie bakery in Cayucos—she knew something was up. Why a tour? And why now, when Aria had already been here for weeks?

She knew there was a scheme of some kind at work, but she misread what it was. She thought it was Gen feeling sorry for her because she rarely got out of the guesthouse and the barn. She thought it was an attempt to force her into getting out and socializing—something she was more or less open to.

Her error became clear when Liam invited himself along on the outing at the last minute—and Gen suddenly had an "emergency" that caused her to abandon the whole thing barely one hour into it.

If she'd had any doubt that the situation had been orchestrated, it was banished when she realized Liam had insisted on bringing his own vehicle.

Of course he would, wouldn't he? Otherwise, he and Aria would have been stranded down in Cayucos at the fish and chips place by the pier, which was one of the first places they'd stopped.

It was around one in the afternoon, and Gen had just finished her Caesar salad when she made a big production of feeling some Braxton Hicks contractions, saying she needed to visit her obstetrician to get checked out.

Aria knew it was a scheme rather than the real thing because Liam just let her go. If Gen had really been concerned about her pregnancy, Liam would have called off the outing and taken her to the doctor himself.

"Oh, jeez. I'm so sorry. God. If I'd had any idea this was going to happen ..." Gen said as she gathered her purse and prepared to dash off like a rabbit fleeing a coyote.

"Uh huh," Aria responded, her eyes narrowed.

"You're mad," Gen said. "I don't blame you. Really. But I don't want to take any chances." Gen was cradling her belly with one arm.

"Sure," Aria said, a french fry in her hand.

When Gen was gone, Aria glared at Liam. "Well, that was convenient."

"What was?"

"Her having to leave, all suddenly like that. With you here. Leaving me alone with you. When you just happened to have your truck handy to drive us home."

Liam raised his eyebrows. "I have no idea what you're talking about."

They finished their fish and chips and had another round of beer, then they walked out on the pier with the ocean wind tousling their hair and prompting them to pull their jackets tight around themselves.

"You're telling me you didn't arrange this?" she said as they headed back up the pier toward town.

"You think I'd do something like that?" He put his hand to his heart, wounded.

"Yes. I do."

"Well … you're right. I might have set you up." As they walked, he put his hand on her back in a way that was protective and comforting. She knew she should shake him off, but instead, she wanted to lean into his touch, close her eyes, and lose herself in him.

"Why didn't you just ask me out instead of scheming like this?"

"Because you'd have said no," he said simply.

"You don't know that."

"Sure."

"Okay, I might have," she admitted. "But, Liam, it's not you. It's just that I don't—"

"You don't date," he supplied.

"That's right."

"But why?" He stopped halfway down the pier and turned to her. A couple of kids with a dog ran past them, and Aria could smell the aroma of some ill-fated fish that had been caught and gutted.

"It's not something I particularly want to talk about."

"Yeah. I get that." He ran a hand through his hair and looked down at her, frustration lining his features. "You've made that clear. But you know what? It's bullshit."

She opened her mouth to reply—some retort about his arrogance, maybe, or about his lack of respect for her personal autonomy—but he cut her off.

"You have to let people in, Aria. I get that you've got things in your past that you don't want to talk about. But you know what? We all have shit in our pasts. I've got mine, you've got yours. You work it out by forming relationships with people. By relying on people. You can't just go on shutting down the conversation whenever it gets too close to what's real."

"I don't do that."

"The hell you don't. You're the most closed-off, secretive—"

"What if I am?" Anger pulsed in her chest, and she glared at him. "Who are you to tell me that's wrong? It's gotten me this far. It's helped me to survive, which is more than I ever thought I'd manage to do."

She'd said too much, and she knew it. They stood in the middle of the pier in the thin winter sunlight, gulls cawing overhead. She couldn't take back what she'd just told him; there was nothing to do but own it. She glared at him, her chin tilted up in defiance.

"What the hell happened to you?" he said after a while.

She'd wanted to stay angry—anger was the required response here—but she was mortified to feel fresh tears stinging her eyes.

"I can't do this," she said.

"Do what?"

"I can't have this conversation. I can't ... I can't relive it just to prove that I'm sensitive, and ... and open ... and whatever it is you need me to be. I can't do it, Liam."

Angry that she'd given in to her emotions, she wiped tears from her cheeks with a fist. She turned and started to walk away from him, and he reached out and caught her hand.

"I don't need you to be anything," he said, his voice soft now. "I just want you to be happy, and you're not. I'm not the most perceptive guy in the world, but even I can see that."

"I don't know how to be happy." It was the most true thing she'd ever said to him.

"I could help you figure it out." He reached out and touched her face, ran a gentle thumb over her cheek.

God, how she wanted to believe he could.

They came to a kind of compromise. She promised to let him be with her—just be with her without expectations on one beautiful, clear day—and he promised not to pry.

It was working well enough as they walked hand in hand on the beach.

Despite the cold, surfers in wetsuits rode waves toward the shore or plunged into the water, their boards flying into the air. Kids in jeans and sweatshirts dug in the sand with buckets and shovels, and a few parents sat by in beach chairs, reading or watching the waves.

They walked from the pier south past shops and expensive oceanfront houses. Aria occasionally bent down to pick up a shell, a smooth rock, or a piece of refuse she thought would work with her piece.

"So, how'd you get the idea for the yurt? The trash part of it, I mean." Liam asked.

"I was looking around my apartment one day, and I realized how many things in it are meant to be disposable. Food wrappers, junk mail, magazines and newspapers, napkins—all of that stuff. That seemed so odd—the huge, unmanageable amounts of trash—but also very familiar. If we were to eliminate everything in our homes that's destined to become trash, there would barely be anything left."

"So you decided to build a home out of trash," he said.

"Yes. Because we all already do that, every day." She was warming to her topic now, gesturing emphatically with her hands. "I'm not going to lecture people about pollution or global warming or any of that—even though it's important—because they wouldn't listen. They hear it all already, and they're closed off to it. But the hope is that a visual representation of the trash in our lives—the pervasiveness of it—will communicate the idea more clearly than words would."

Liam smiled, and she read it as condescension. She stopped walking and scowled at him.

"You think it's dumb," she said. It was not a question. "You think art is a waste of time unless it's, what, a painting of fruit and flowers you can hang on your wall. Well, it's more than that. It's—"

"I never said it was dumb."

"You were thinking it."

"No. I really wasn't. I was thinking it's nice to see you all fired up about it, that's all." He kept his tone mild, his pace easy as they made their way down the beach.

"Oh. I thought—"

"I know what you thought. You thought that a guy like me couldn't appreciate what you do. You thought, hey, all he knows how to do is shovel cow shit. Don't worry about it. You're not the first to come to that conclusion."

His tone was casual, no different than it had been when they'd talked about the weather or the quality of the fish and chips. But she'd touched a nerve.

"I'm sorry," she said. "I made an assumption. I shouldn't have."

"Yeah, well." He took her hand again, as though it simply belonged in his. "I don't know if you have brothers or sisters. And I'm not going to ask," he put in quickly, when she shot him a look. "But if you do, you might know how it is. One of my brothers is this nice guy who everybody loves, and the other one is a goddamned genius. And then there's me."

"What does that mean?" she asked tentatively.

"Well …" He shrugged. "My parents are great. They loved all of us. But I was never going to be as much of a good guy as Ryan—I'm just not built the way he is. And I was never going to be as smart as Colin. But I had to be something."

She could see it. He'd had to stake his claim in the family in some area that wasn't already dominated by someone else, so he'd become this: quick to anger with a tough exterior that said nothing could ever really hurt him. That's just what it was, though—an exterior. Beneath that, he was as much a mass of seething insecurity as anyone else.

She noticed his limp as they walked on the sand. It didn't slow him down much, but it was there, all the same.

"Your injury must have been hard on you."

He shrugged. "Yeah, and it wasn't just that. It was a lot of things. My uncle died, and I didn't take that too well. And then my girlfriend … Did I tell you that she dumped me right after I broke the leg? I mean, *right* after. I was still in the hospital."

She blinked at him in surprise. "That's awful."

"Yeah. It was. Hell, it wasn't all her fault, though. Probably not even mostly." He ran his free hand through his hair. "I didn't mean to go off like this. Things are pretty much okay now. I'm surviving."

"And you wouldn't let anyone know if you weren't. Would

you?" She stopped walking and faced him.

"I guess you'd know something about that," he said.

"I guess I would." It was the closest she'd come to admitting to him that there were things troubling her, things she couldn't or wouldn't talk about.

"Well, it's good to know we've got something in common." He gave her a slow half grin. "People have built relationships on less. Especially when you add good sex into the mix."

That word—*relationship*—could have made her shut down and back off, and it still might. She couldn't guarantee it wouldn't. But right now, with him looking at her the way he was, she just wanted to kiss him.

"The sex wasn't good." She went up on tiptoes and pressed a soft kiss to his lips. "The sex was *incredible*."

His hands moved to her hips and rested there, and his eyes slid closed at the touch of her mouth to his.

"Well, then, I definitely think we should include that in the tour." His voice was a low, sexy murmur.

"Whatever you say. You're the guide."

The scheme he'd worked out with Gen had worked better than expected, he thought as he snuggled in with Aria in the guesthouse bed. They'd come back here and had proven that their previous encounters hadn't been flukes. Two great sexual experiences might be put down to luck or circumstance. But three? That pretty much sealed it: they really were good at this.

They were spooning, with his long, lean body pressed against her back, his hand caressing her arm. He stretched his leg out on top of hers, and she let her hand run down its length.

She paused when she got to the scar from his surgery, then let her fingers continue their lazy trip toward his foot.

"How did it happen?" she said.

He told her about it: How he'd been thrown from his horse, and the horse had reared and come down on top of him. How he'd heard the bones break. How he'd thought, for a moment, that if the big Arabian came down on him a second time, it might kill him. And finally, how he'd thought for just an instant that he would welcome that.

She turned in his arms to face him. "Liam …"

"I wasn't suicidal," he told her. "Nothing as dramatic as that. It's just … I'd been having a hard time since my uncle died. And I knew Megan had a thing for my cousin. I knew it. I was on borrowed time. And the thing about dying—well, it wasn't even a thought, really. It was just a flash, for one second. This one, clear instant of knowing how much easier it would be."

He'd never told anyone that, and had never thought he would. It had just come out. It wasn't just that he'd never articulated it to anyone. He'd never even acknowledged it to himself until he told Aria about it.

She brushed a lock of hair from his forehead with her fingers and let her thumb trail down along his temple.

"I didn't have a childhood like yours," she whispered to him. "I don't know if I have any brothers or sisters. My mother …" She trailed off and didn't continue.

"It's okay." He pulled her in tight. "You don't have to."

It was something, and it was a start. If she didn't tell it all today, that was all right. He could wait until she was ready. He could wait as long as he needed to.

Liam had been having such a good time with Aria that he hadn't checked his phone for most of the day. Around mid-afternoon, he'd seen that he had a call from Ryan, but he figured that could wait. He'd silenced the phone and shoved it back into his pocket, forgetting about it.

Now that he was back in his truck and ready to head home, he pulled the phone out of his pocket to find out what he'd missed.

There were two more calls from Ryan and one from his mother, along with a couple of texts urging him to call.

With worry beginning to stir in his gut, he started up the truck and headed back toward the ranch, calling Ryan through his Bluetooth on the way.

When it went straight to voice mail, he called his mother's cell phone. She picked up on the first ring.

"Mom."

"Well, it's about time you called, boy. All hell's been breaking loose around here, and you about missed the whole damned thing."

The buoyant tone of her voice made him sag in relief. Whatever had happened, it wasn't bad. She sounded as close to giddy as he'd ever heard her.

"Okay. So what whole damned thing did I miss?"

"You missed your new nephew coming into the world, boy. Genevieve had her baby."

Chapter Twenty-Two

Aria was losing her grip on the situation with Liam, and now that he'd left and she was alone, no longer immersed in the hormonal bliss of recent sex, she was cursing herself for her stupidity.

They hadn't just had sex. They'd *made love*, and then they'd talked in each other's arms, and that was exactly what she *hadn't* wanted. That was exactly the kind of thing that led to heartache and misery.

"God, I'm an idiot." She berated herself for her weakness, for her lack of resolve, as she poured a glass of wine at the counter in the little kitchen. She knew better than this. She did. And yet, she'd not only had let it happen, she'd thrown herself into it with inexcusable abandon.

Just because he was ridiculously sexy with the whole badboy cowboy thing, just because he was kind, and sweet, and unexpectedly complex, it didn't mean she had to give in to him, and it certainly didn't mean she was in love.

Love. How had it happened that she was even thinking that word? When, exactly, had she lost her goddamned mind?

"This is not okay," she told herself. "This is definitely not okay."

She plopped down onto the sofa with her wine, her anxiety

mounting. She knew what happened when you started to feel an attachment to someone. And it wasn't anything good.

After a few minutes, she decided that she wasn't going to be able to relax—she had to get out of the house and do something with her pent-up energy. She thought about going to her studio to get some more work done, but instead, she got her coat, grabbed her purse and keys, poured her glass of wine into the sink, and got into her car.

She needed people, noise, distraction. She drove down the dirt road to Highway 1 and headed south toward town.

When Aria had visited Ted's before, it had seemed festive and friendly. But then, she'd been accompanied by Gen, as well as Liam and his brother. Now, coming into the bar alone, it seemed seedy, as though the scent that permeated the place wasn't spilled beer, but failure and despair.

Still, a little failure and despair didn't seem so bad right now. She entered tentatively, found a seat at the bar, and settled into it, her purse strap slung across her body to protect her bag from drunks, pickpockets, or both.

"You're Liam's friend, right?" Ted, the owner, was looking at her expectantly from the other side of the bar.

How could she answer that? Was she Liam's friend? Was she more? Right now, she didn't want to be his anything.

"I … yes. I was in here with him and his brother and sister-in-law."

"Surprised Liam's not here with you," Ted went on. "He loves a good beer, can't imagine him passing up the chance." He chuckled.

"Um … Ted? Could I maybe get a shot of tequila?"

She knew it didn't look good—a single woman here alone, drinking tequila. But at the moment she didn't really give a damn.

When she had the drink in front of her, she ignored the lime and salt that Ted had placed on the bar for her and slammed back the shot, wincing as it burned its way down her throat.

"Get you some water with that?" Ted asked, looking at her with a little concern.

"Yes, please. And a refill." She gestured toward the shot glass.

Ted tilted his head to look at her. "Ma'am? You doing okay?"

"I will be, once I get the refill." She shoved the glass toward him.

As soon as Ted had finished pouring, she slammed that one, too. The warmth of it spread through her, and the world was already beginning to get a little soft around the edges.

She might have been feeling a little self-destructive, but that didn't mean she was entirely stupid. She stopped after the second shot and switched to the water. Aerosmith was playing on the sound system, accompanied by the murmur of bar patrons talking and laughing. It was the middle of the week, so the place wasn't full. A few guys in their twenties sat at a table in the middle of the room, a couple more were at the other end of the bar, and three guys were gathered around one of the pool tables. She was the only woman in the room.

The lights were dim, and the music was loud. She thought she smelled the faint aroma of pot, as though someone had sneaked a toke in the men's room.

Later, she would tell herself that she hadn't come here looking for trouble. She'd simply come to be among people, to get out of the confines of the Delaney guesthouse. But she knew that wasn't true.

She'd come here to do something so stupid it would burn her budding relationship with Liam to the ground, saving her from all of the danger and risk love would bring.

That was why, when one of the twentysomethings from the table in the middle of the room came over and asked if he could sit next to her, she said yes.

She could have blamed it on the tequila, but that would have been a lie. She wanted disaster and ruin. She wanted to do something to push Liam Delaney out of her life for good.

They did the little things people do. They exchanged names, small talk, the questions of what she was doing here alone, and what she was drinking, and whether she wanted another one. He was younger than she was, and he hadn't shaved that day. He smelled like beer and sweat.

When he asked her to dance, she slid off the barstool and followed him into the middle of the room, and they swayed to "Crying" by Roy Orbison with the guy's hands on her ass.

He started kissing her halfway through the song. Hands grabbing her, sour breath, his tongue in her mouth, making her want to gag.

All she could think of was Liam.

The guy cupped her breast in his hand, and she heard some of his friends whooping and cheering.

And she couldn't—she just couldn't.

She pushed him away and headed back toward the bar. But he grabbed her hand and wouldn't let go.

"Where you going?" he said, his voice slurred with alcohol. "I'm not done dancing."

"But I am. I'm done." She tried to yank her hand away from him but he grabbed her harder, hurting her wrist.

"Come back. I wasn't doing anything." He still wouldn't let go. He was tugging at her, pulling.

"Back off. Back the fuck off. Let go of me." Her voice was shrill, and her heart was pounding with adrenaline.

"Hey. Hey, hey, hey." Ted was out from behind the bar now, a baseball bat in his hand. "Let go of her. Chuck? You let go of her before I smack your goddamned head over the left field fence. You got me?" He waved the bat menacingly.

"Yeah." Chuck let go of her and raised both hands in the air in a gesture of surrender and innocence. "I didn't mean nothing."

"I don't need this shit here. I'm trying to run a goddamned business."

"Yeah. Okay. Yeah."

Chuck tried to head back toward his friends at the table, but Ted raised the bat again. "No way. Go home."

"But—"

"You're done here. Go home." Ted held the bat just above his shoulder like he was getting ready for a fastball.

There was some back-and-forth between Chuck and his friends regarding whether they would leave with him. They didn't. He left alone, glaring at Aria through narrowed eyes as though it were all her fault.

Which, it seemed to her, it was.

A sudden wave of self-loathing swept over her, and she started to cry.

"Are you okay?" Ted put a hand on her arm, but she shook it off and rushed to the back of the bar and into the ladies' room.

Liam was at the hospital in Templeton crammed into Gen's room with various other family members and well-wishers when he got the call.

He was watching Sandra hold the baby, whose pinched skin

and perplexed facial expression made him resemble Yoda, when the phone in his back pocket buzzed.

He didn't recognize the number, but he hoped it was Aria. He stepped out into the hallway to take the call.

"Liam?"

"Yeah?"

"It's Ted. I'm at the bar, and I've got a … a situation."

Liam sat up. "What kind of situation?"

Ted filled him in. Liam hadn't even hung up before he had grabbed his coat and was headed out the door and toward his truck.

When Liam got there, Ted came out from behind the bar to meet him before he was more than ten feet into the room.

"She came out of the bathroom about ten minutes ago," Ted told him, gesturing toward a small corner table where Aria sat. "She wanted to leave, but I told her I couldn't let her go until she sobered up." He looked worried, and he was wringing a bar rag in his hands as he talked. "Sorry to bother you, man. She seems better now. But when I called you, she'd locked herself in the ladies' room, and I could hear her in there crying …"

"Okay. I've got this." Liam clapped Ted on the back. "Thanks for calling me."

"Well … I didn't know who else to call. She was in here with you that one time, so …"

"Yeah." Liam nodded. "It's okay. I'll handle it."

As he walked through the bar to the back, where Aria was sitting, he wasn't at all sure he really *could* handle it. He was beginning to think that where Aria was concerned, he was in over his head and sinking like he had rocks tied to his feet. But walking away wasn't an option—not now, not for him.

He got to the table and stood there awkwardly for a moment. Then he pulled out a chair and sat down across from her.

"Aria? You okay?"

Her face was red and blotchy from crying, and her mascara was smudged, making dark shadows under her eyes.

"Liam, go away."

"Well, not until I know you're all right."

"Why are you even here?"

"Ted called me."

"What? Why did he ... I didn't ... but ..."

She started to cry again, and he pulled her out of her chair and onto his lap, wrapping his arms around her.

"Take a breath," he told her, his voice gentle. "Just ... relax. Take a breath. You're okay. Everything's okay." He had no idea whether that was true, but it sounded good, and anyway, it was all he had. He rubbed her back gently with his hand.

Liam didn't know exactly what had happened, or why. Ted had told him some. He knew that Aria had come in alone, and that some guy had hassled her. He knew that Ted had chased the asshole off, and that Aria had retreated into the bathroom, upset, and at first had refused to come out.

But the circumstances that had led to all of that eluded him. Why was she here? Had she been meeting someone? He refused to consider the alternative: that she'd come in looking to get picked up. Even if that were true, he could worry about it later. Right now, she needed his help.

"Let's go," he said. "Let me take you home."

"But, my car—"

"You can't drive, not like this. I'll bring you back to get it tomorrow. Come on."

They walked out to where his truck was parked on Main Street, and he deposited her into the passenger seat with care, as though she were a piece of china or a baby bird.

She went quiet while he drove. Shame made her face hot, and she wiped at it with a wad of bar napkins she'd grabbed at Ted's.

Liam was mercifully silent, not asking her anything about what had happened or why. If he'd asked, she might have told him everything: how she'd come here looking to get in trouble—the kind of trouble that would make him never want to see her again.

And she'd failed even at that.

Ted probably thought she was upset because of that asshole Chuck. But that wasn't it. Chuck was an annoyance, but she'd never thought she was in any real danger.

No, she was inconsolable about what she'd almost done to Liam. He'd been cheated on before, and had been badly hurt by it. She'd known that was one way to burn the bridge between them—annihilate it so that it could never be rebuilt.

She'd wanted—no, needed—that separation from him because she knew she was losing herself to him.

In the end, she hadn't been able to go through with it. She hadn't been able to hurt him, even to save herself.

None of it made sense, really. She and Liam weren't in a relationship. They weren't dating. They weren't anything. They'd slept together a few times, but so what? Neither of them had any claim on the other.

And yet, her heart knew what her mind hadn't yet acknowledged.

Her heart knew that she and Liam belonged to each other.

She didn't want that, and yet there it was. You might not want gravity to exist, but your feet were held to the earth, nonetheless. It was incontrovertible.

Aria had always thought of herself as a strong person.

Despite everything she'd gone through, everything that had happened to her, she'd survived. She'd made a life for herself, protected herself. She'd gotten through. But now, knowing that she was helpless against her feelings for Liam, she was as frightened as she'd ever been.

Liam drove silently through the dark, quiet streets toward the ranch.

Liam wasn't sure what the hell had happened back at Ted's, but he knew one thing: Aria was either going to tell him, or she wasn't. He couldn't make her talk about it, any more than he could make her talk about whatever she was hiding from her past.

He drove silently, careful to keep up his casual guy act. He had to play this right, or he would lose any chance he had with her. He couldn't pressure her, as much as he wanted to. He couldn't nag or insist or freak the hell out, the way he wanted to. That would send her into her shell of silence, and she might never come out.

He wanted to shake her and demand to know what had happened, who had upset her, whether anyone had hurt her. And if someone had, he wanted to hunt them down and pound them into a screaming, bloody pulp. But that wouldn't get him anywhere. He had to act more mature than he felt.

He had to let her make the decision to come to him.

If she didn't, well, that would be one hell of a disappointment. But this thing wasn't going to work any other way. Liam wouldn't have considered himself to be particularly smart about human nature. But he did know that much.

He glanced at her out of the corner of his eye as he drove. She looked smaller than usual somehow. She looked like the strain of whatever had happened had taken a toll on the physical part of her as well as the emotional.

He couldn't just drive and do nothing, so he reached out his hand to her, and she took it. That gesture—that little bit of acceptance of his comfort—heartened him. He kept his eyes on the road, his posture in the driver's seat relaxed, but his heart had sped up, and he felt her touch like an electric current running through him.

He wasn't sure what was happening between them, but he knew it mattered. He knew something had changed, and there'd be no turning back from it.

Chapter Twenty-Three

When they got back to the guesthouse, neither of them spoke. Aria got out of the truck and went up the front step, and Liam followed her, thinking only to walk her to the door like a gentleman, to ask her if she was sure she was okay.

But once she had unlocked the door, she took him by the hand and led him inside. She didn't bother to turn on the lights. She closed the door behind them and brought him into her arms, the house dark except for the silvery moonlight filtering through the windows.

She kissed him, and the kiss wasn't like those they had shared before. Something had shifted; he could feel that in every cell of his body.

He knew he should walk away. He should ask after her welfare and then say goodnight, going back to his house and the safety of the life he'd lived before he met her. He'd been hurt before, but that would be nothing compared to what Aria could do to him. She had the power not just to hurt him, but to ruin him. He wasn't sure how he knew that, but he did. And he suspected that whatever had happened tonight at Ted's had a lot to do with her power over him and what she intended to do with it.

Walking away, as wise as it might be, didn't feel possible.

Holding her like this, in the quiet darkness, was all he wanted to do, no matter the risk. Inside her were tempests, raging storms he couldn't fathom. But this, having her in his arms, felt like safety. It felt like shelter.

She kissed him, and he sank into the feel of her mouth on his. The warmth of her, the way she yielded to him—he was lost.

She pulled back from him, took his hand, and led him into the bedroom. The only sounds were the rustling of clothing as they undressed, and the gentle movement of their breath.

When they were both nude, she came to him and wrapped her arms around him, and the soft warmth of her erased his fear, his uncertainty. He buried his face in her hair.

She took him to the bed and they lay down together. He started to touch her, to reach for her, and she gently moved his hands away as she began to kiss him—first his mouth, then his body. He let out a soft gasp as her tongue moved from his neck toward his chest, her lips grazing over him, making his skin tingle.

He wanted to reach out and grasp her in his arms, but he knew what this was: This was her giving to him in a way she hadn't before. This was a gift.

He kept his hands relaxed at his sides as she moved downward, running her lips and her hands down his body, over his skin. She dipped her tongue into his navel, and he trembled with the effort of lying still.

He was as hard and aching with need as he'd ever been, and when she took him into her mouth, he groaned with the pleasure of it. The ecstasy of this—of having a woman, this woman, worshipping his body in this way—transported him out of this room, out of this place, to somewhere infinitely kinder. Somewhere holy.

Liam gave himself over to her completely. This was something entirely different from what he'd had with Megan, or with anyone. This was everything.

This was Aria.

Later, when they were lying warm and sated under the covers of her bed, he told her about Gen and the baby.

"Oh, my God." She sat up and gaped at him, a sheet tucked over her breasts. "When she said she was having contractions, I thought it was a ruse to get us alone together."

"Yeah. So did I," Liam admitted. "When the new baby excitement wears off, Ryan's going to kick my ass for letting her go off alone."

"And she said Braxton Hicks! Doesn't that mean they weren't real contractions?"

He grinned. "Well, they must have been pretty damned real, because the baby came out."

"God." She lay back on the bed, marveling. "What's his name?"

"James Redmond Delaney. It's nice, don't you think?"

"It is." She snuggled up against him, and he pulled her into his arms.

They talked for a while about Gen and Ryan, and the baby, and family. And then, just as he expected her to pull back and go quiet, she told him the truth.

"My parents are dead, Liam. That's why I don't talk about my family. I don't have one." Her father had committed suicide when she was a baby. She'd never been told the details of that, but a bit of research in her teen years had revealed that he'd hanged himself from the rafters of the family's garage. After that, her mother had descended into a hell of depression and drug abuse. She'd gone to prison on drug charges when Aria was a toddler, and lacking any other relatives, Aria had gone into foster care.

"She got out of prison when I was six, and I went back to live with her for a little while," Aria told Liam as he held her and stroked her back. "Maybe six months later she died of a heroin overdose while I was at school. I wasn't the one who found her, so at least I was spared that."

"Who did?" he asked softly.

"Our neighbor. My mom was supposed to pick me up after school, but she didn't come. The neighbor, Mrs. Wilkens, had been listed as our emergency contact, so when the school couldn't reach my mom, they called her."

Liam felt the horror of the story like a gut punch, but he stayed still and quiet, afraid that if he reacted, she'd stop talking. And he didn't want her to stop talking, now that she'd finally started.

"When Mrs. Wilkens got the call that I was sitting there in the office at school, she came to our house and knocked on the door, looking for my mom. There was no answer, but the door was unlocked, so she peeked her head in. My mother was on the sofa, already gone. They didn't tell me what happened at first. A social worker came to the school to get me. And that was it. I never went home again."

With what she was telling him, he would have expected tears, great shuddering sobs that he would soothe with soft, whispered words. But her tone was flat, emotionless, and that worried him more than any display of grief would have.

"I spent the rest of my childhood in foster care," she said, and he braced himself for what was to come. Abuse? Neglect?

He was relieved that this part, at least, wasn't as bad as he'd feared.

"The foster parents I lived with were good people," she told him. "You hear horror stories, but ... they were just people, you know? Trying to do the best they could."

She told him how she moved through a succession of foster families, partly because of the temporary nature of foster care, and partly because her ferocious anger was more than some of them could handle, and she had to be reassigned.

When she aged out of foster care, she didn't have much of anything to fall back on—no home, no parents to offer her a safety net until she could provide for herself.

She did have one thing going for her, though: a high school counselor who recognized both her potential and the challenges she was facing in realizing it.

"She helped me find scholarships, financial aid." Aria's voice warmed a little. "She helped me get registered at the local community college and walked me through the process of applying for jobs and finding a place to live."

That time was so full of contradictions, she told him: Terror at being cut loose from any support system she might have had, and elation at finally being able to take charge of her own life. The stress of not knowing how she was going to be able to pay the rent on the tiny apartment she shared with two roommates, and the excitement of going to school not because she was being forced to, but because she wanted to.

"I looked into you a little bit," Liam said after a while, knowing that he had to come clean now, while they were talking freely, or risk having to explain later why he hadn't. "I know Aria Howard isn't your real name."

"It is." She pulled back from him a little so she could look at him. "I changed it legally. It's the real name of the person I am now. It's as real as anything else in my life. The person I was doesn't exist anymore."

That seemed like an important distinction to her—the question of her identity now, versus who she'd been then.

"I created this person, this version of myself," she said. "No one else did that. Just me."

He had so many questions. There was so much he wanted to know about how her past had affected her, how she felt about the life she had now, and—maybe most importantly—whether she was capable of loving him, when she'd known so little love over the course of her life. But he couldn't ask her any of that, not now. She had to choose to tell it on her own, in her own time. If she even knew the answers.

"You're lucky, Liam," she told him as they lay in the dark, wrapped around each other. "Your family, what you have here—you're so lucky."

She was right. Whatever issues he might have with his family—from feeling overshadowed by his brothers, to feeling crowded by his ever-present family members, to struggling to find his own identity within the larger group—he had never in his life lacked for love.

He wanted to say something to her, something that could help to heal her scars or soothe her decades-old hurts, but there were no such words. Instead, he said, "Thank you for telling me. I know it wasn't easy."

The rest of it—the story of whatever tonight had been, whatever demons had driven her to go to Ted's and do whatever it was she'd done there—could wait. She could tell him when she was ready to tell him. But he was fairly certain it had something to do with him, and with feelings that were more and stronger than she knew what to do with.

What mattered was that she was here now, with him, and whatever barriers had separated them were gone.

Whether they would stay gone, he didn't know. A person who'd been through what she had been through learned to protect themselves from a lot of things—including feelings.

It occurred to him as he lay there that he might be wholly unequipped to handle the complexities of Aria. Trying to have a relationship with her might be like trying to build a space shuttle when he'd barely passed auto shop in high school.

But he knew he had to try.

Megan had hurt him, and Aria had the power to hurt him so much more. But if that happened, so be it. He could risk it.

He was a hard man to break.

Chapter Twenty-Four

The next morning, Aria woke up in Liam's arms. That was something new. She'd gone to bed with men here and there over the years, but she'd never awakened with one still in her bed when the sun came up. It was a novel and not entirely unpleasant experience.

But that didn't mean it wasn't troubling.

God, she felt comfortable lying here in the warmth of his arms, but comfort was deceptive. Comfort could make you soft and unprepared—and weak.

Aria had never allowed herself to be weak, and she wasn't going to start now.

Okay, so she'd opened up to Liam last night. She'd told him things she had never intended to tell him. Now he knew, and there was no way to undo that. But that didn't mean he could see her as a victim who needed to be rescued. She wasn't that, and she wouldn't allow herself to become that.

Carefully, trying not to wake him, she eased herself out of his arms and got out of bed. She grabbed a robe from where it lay draped over a bedside chair and pulled it on. He started to stir, and she slipped into the bathroom and closed the door before he could wake up and see her.

She leaned against the door, tipped her head back, and

closed her eyes. She'd crossed a line last night, and she didn't think she could step back over it even if she wanted to.

But did she want to?

Standing there with the cold bathroom tile under her feet, she felt as though she had jumped out of an airplane without a parachute and was having second thoughts on the way down.

Aria heard Liam stirring, and she knew she couldn't hide in here forever. She used the facilities, washed her hands, took a deep breath, and walked out of the bathroom to find him standing next to the bed, pulling his jeans on.

"Hi," she said, feeling awkward as hell. *Hi* seemed like such an inadequate conversational gambit that she chastised herself for her failure to come up with something better. But, really, it was hopeless. Liam had found her crying in a bar after she'd thrown herself at a stranger, resulting in an emotional meltdown of regret. And then she'd slept with him in a way that had bared her soul as well as her body.

There was no clever, pithy, non-mortifying thing you could say the morning after that.

"Come here." He held his arms out to her, and she walked over and stepped into his embrace. It was exactly the right thing for him to do and say to break down her defenses even further. And it was exactly the wrong thing for him to do and say if she wanted to maintain the strength and self-sufficiency she'd worked so hard to build.

She sighed and relaxed into him.

Sometimes, when you'd already jumped from the plane, it was best just to enjoy the fall.

Liam didn't want to leave her, not now, not after the way she'd opened up to him the night before. But he was hours late for work on the ranch, and his mother wasn't likely to let him hear the end of it, especially with Ryan out for a few days.

"Listen, I've got to get going," he told her, gently disentangling her from his embrace. "I hate to, but …"

"No, of course," she said, a blush rising to her face. She turned away from him so he wouldn't see it. "I get it. You've got to work."

"I do. I'm usually out of the house at dawn, and my mother—"

"Right." The sun was streaming brightly through the windows. Aria hadn't checked the clock, but clearly, dawn had come and gone hours before.

"Can I see you later?" Liam picked up his T-shirt from the floor beside the bed and pulled it on. "I'd really like to."

He expected her to make an excuse—to tell him that she was busy, or that she was involved with someone in Portland to whom she'd be returning once the residency was over. She could tell him that last night had been fun, but that she wasn't in this for the long term. She could simply tell him she wasn't interested.

But she didn't do that. Maybe, like him, she'd begun to acknowledge that this thing between them was inevitable.

"All right," she said. "I'd like that."

He could feel his body relax. He'd been expecting the excuse, the brush-off. He'd been falling, too.

Liam rode out into the pasture that morning wondering how the hell he was supposed to play this. Not that he considered any of it a game.

Aria had made herself emotionally vulnerable to him for the first time, and he knew from the undefinable current running between them this morning that part of her regretted it. But he didn't want her to take a step back, not now. He had selfish reasons for that, but he also sensed that her past had been holding her back in ways big and small all her life. If she could talk about it, face it head on, and be open about it with someone—anyone, even if it wasn't him—that had to be a good thing. That had to be something that would lead to some kind of healing.

Somehow, he had to make her feel that what she'd done— telling him what she had—was a good thing, and he wasn't sure how to do that. She was oriented toward survival, and for good reason. Her fight-or-flight response was likely kicking in right about now.

The day was crisp and blue and beautiful, and Liam took a deep breath of the chilly ocean air, feeling the powerful animal under him and the breeze surrounding him. The tall grass whispered its unknowable secrets.

He found his father out in the northeast pasture, where he and a few of the ranch hands were getting ready to move the herd. The cattle regularly had to be rotated from one pasture to another in order to fertilize the soil and provide the animals with fresh grassland.

Orin, who was mostly retired but who was stepping in for Ryan, peered at Liam from under the brim of his hat. "Well, it took you long enough to get here."

Orin's tone was mild, but Liam knew his irritation was real. You didn't show up late for work on the ranch if you could help it. Liam was going to get a ration of shit at home about it later.

"Your mother says you didn't come home last night," Orin commented, his voice low enough that the hands couldn't hear him.

"Did I miss curfew?" Liam remarked dryly.

Orin made a scoffing noise. "You can give me whatever kind of attitude you want, son, but I don't think it's going to work as well with your mother."

It might have said something about Liam's life—and probably nothing good—that he still had to worry about his mother yelling at him. But he figured everybody had something. If it wasn't his mother, it would have been his boss, and he didn't have one of those, so that was something to be grateful for.

Nobody was going to care that he spent the night with a woman—by God, he was an adult, and he could do whatever he wanted with whomever he wanted—but showing up late for work? That was something a Delaney just didn't do.

Now that he'd done it, there was no help for it but to work his ass off making up for the lapse. So that's what he did for the rest of the day: When Orin took a break, Liam didn't. When they got the call from Sandra that lunch was ready, Liam worked through.

If he'd thought that was going to make a damned bit of difference, he was wrong.

"It's no wonder you're about to starve," Sandra remarked at dinner that night as she eyed Liam's plate, which he'd loaded up higher than usual with meatloaf, mashed potatoes, gravy, rolls, and green beans. "Couldn't be bothered to come in for lunch. *Hmph.* I don't spend all my time cooking for you people because it's good for my health."

He glanced up, his fork already loaded. He wondered if maybe he could sidestep this conversation if he avoided eye contact.

"I was busy." He focused his gaze on his food and not his mother.

"Well, I suppose you had a lot of catching up to do," Sandra said. "Got out into the pastures a good three hours late, I'm told. By God, if you worked at the damned grocery store and showed up three hours late, I guess you'd be looking for a new job."

"I guess it's a good thing I don't work at the grocery store, then," Liam remarked.

"Aw, let him be, Sandra," Orin said, looking uncomfortable at the idea of disagreeing with his wife. "Boy knows how to work, and I'd say he does enough of it."

Liam stopped eating and blinked at his father. Orin rarely spoke up when Sandra was reprimanding one of their progeny. The fact that he was doing it now—and on Liam's behalf—was surprising enough to make Liam forget how hungry he was.

He wasn't sure how to feel about it. On one hand, it was nice to have his father's support. On the other, hearing his father disagree with his mother was so unusual and so jarring that it made him feel unsettled and guilty for having brought it about.

"It's not gonna happen again," Liam said, shoving meatloaf into his mouth so he wouldn't have to say anything more.

"*Hmph,*" Sandra said again.

"The fact that Liam was late is less interesting than the *reason* he was late," Breanna remarked, looking at Liam significantly. Lucas and Michael, sitting on either side of her, were too young to hear about that reason, but neither of them seemed to be listening. They were both focused on their food, particularly their rolls, which each of them had slathered with a shocking amount of butter.

"Now, Breanna," Orin began, nodding toward the boys.

"So, did anybody see Gen and the baby today? How are they doing?" Liam asked, in an effort to change the subject.

"Is everything all right with Aria?" Breanna asked, as though he hadn't spoken. "I heard some ... things ... about what happened at Ted's last night."

Liam wanted to snap at Breanna to keep whatever she'd heard to herself, but she looked so genuinely concerned that he couldn't bring himself to do it.

"Things are good," he said instead, though he wasn't entirely certain that was true.

"Is Aria your girlfriend?" Michael asked, suddenly finding his roll less interesting.

Liam opened his mouth to respond, then realized he had no idea what the answer was. "Eat your meatloaf," he said.

"Well? *Is* she your girlfriend?" Breanna said.

"I guess what she is or isn't is none of your business," he said.

Sandra, who'd been silently listening to the exchange, said, "I hope you're bringing the girl here for Christmas dinner. She shouldn't be alone out there in that guesthouse on a holiday. Why, if you haven't already asked her, I'm going to wonder if I taught you any manners."

"I ... uh ... I did already ask her," Liam admitted.

"Well, fine, then." Sandra nodded, looking satisfied with herself.

"So, she *is* your girlfriend, then," Michael commented. "You don't invite a girl for Christmas unless she's your girlfriend."

"What do you know about it?" Liam asked mildly. "You're a kid."

"Well, I figure he's a kid who knows when a man has a damned girlfriend and won't admit it," Sandra snapped at him.

All in all, it was a puzzling and somewhat uncomfortable discussion. Liam figured he'd be better off if he just kept his mouth full of food. So he did that.

When Breanna started talking about the escrow on her house, which was scheduled to close in a few more days, he was relieved to have the focus off of him.

He should have thought of the house when she'd been grilling him about Aria. He could have changed the subject easily by asking something about floor tiles or paint color. Not that he gave a damn about floor tiles or paint color.

But the new direction of the conversation didn't make him feel any better, even if it wasn't about him. The idea of Breanna and the boys moving across town filled him with a deep sadness that almost made him lose his appetite.

The thought occurred to him that he might consider starting a family of his own, even buying a place of his own. Then maybe he wouldn't feel so invested in whatever his sister decided to do.

The thought surprised him with its sudden intrusion into his head.

Start a family? Where had that come from?

But he knew where it had come from. He knew very well. And if Aria knew he was starting to think this way, she'd pack her stuff and flee the Delaney Ranch so fast he'd see nothing but the dust in her wake.

He couldn't let that happen. He didn't know how he could prevent it, but he was a resourceful guy—he'd figure something out.

Chapter Twenty-Five

Liam's confidence about winning over Aria might have been shaky. But, as he stood outside the house that now belonged to Breanna, it occurred to him that it was rock steady compared with his feelings about whether it would ever be possible to fix up this dump.

"Bree. Are you sure about this?" Liam squinted at the house, rocking back and forth on his feet, his hands stuffed into his jeans pockets.

"Well, it would be too bad if I weren't," she said happily. "It's done."

"Yeah, but that doesn't mean you have to keep it. You could ... hell, I don't know. Just put it back on the market, I guess. The land alone's worth a lot."

She shot him a look that was part annoyance, part sisterly indulgence. "You said yourself that I was stupid to buy it. Why would anyone else want to?"

Liam shrugged. She'd made a good point. "Hell, I don't know. Someone stupider, I guess."

She slugged him in the arm in much the same way she had when she was eight and he'd torn the head off one of her Barbies.

"Ow." He rubbed at his arm. It didn't hurt much, but there

was the theater of the thing to consider.

"God, there is so much to do," she said.

Liam smirked. "You think?"

Breanna glanced at him uneasily, her brow furrowed. "Do you really think this was a mistake?"

He did, but looking at the worry on her face, he realized that his job right now wasn't to throw cold water on her enthusiasm. His job was to be a good brother and encourage her.

"Aw, hell." He rubbed the back of his neck. "No, I guess not. I can see there's a lot you can do with it. This place was probably really nice once."

"I know, right?" Breanna's bubbly joy was back, and that was a beautiful thing to see. Liam had been right to shut up about his misgivings. "Let's go inside!" she said, grabbing his arm and pulling him toward the house. "I can't wait to get started."

The inside looked even worse than Liam remembered, but that didn't stop Breanna from racing from room to room, fantasizing about what she would do with each one.

"These floors are the original oak! They need to be refinished, but they're going to be gorgeous. Do you think I should have this wall taken out to open up the kitchen? I want to have this wall redone to include lots and lots of windows for the ocean view. Look at the fireplace!"

It seemed as though she was talking to Liam, but he knew she wasn't—she was talking to herself. All he had to do was nod and occasionally utter an *uh-huh* or a *yep*.

"You know you're going to have to talk to Colin about this," he said when she'd finally stopped moving and had come to a halt next to him.

"Why?"

"Because he knows all the good contractors, and you're

going to need one."

"Ryan knows a contractor. The guy who worked on his house did a terrific job."

"Ryan knows a contractor because Colin found one for him," Liam pointed out. "Besides, Colin's coming home in a couple of days. What are you going to do, tell everybody not to mention the fact that you bought a damned house?"

"Do you think that would work?"

"Breanna ..."

"I'm kidding. Sort of." She paced the big, empty room and turned to face Liam from fifteen feet away. "I don't want a lecture, that's all."

"Well, he's going to give you one, so you might as well get used to the idea."

"I guess." She looked glum for a moment, and then suddenly perked up. "Hey! Come look at the boys' rooms!"

Liam and Breanna were so prepared for Colin to disapprove of Breanna's purchase that they were both astounded when he didn't.

He'd arrived in town with his wife, Julia, a few days later, and when Breanna had broken the news of her new house, he'd stayed stone-faced, betraying nothing of his initial reaction.

Now, standing in front of the house with a spreadsheet, the purchase contract, and the inspector's report in his hands, he finally pronounced his verdict.

"I think you got a deal," he said. Liam watched as Breanna squealed and jumped up and down. Julia grinned and rubbed Breanna's arm affectionately.

"Really? You really think so?" Breanna said.

"I do. This location is one of the best lots in town. And the inspector's report shows that the house is structurally sound. If you renovate, you can make a substantial profit."

Colin, forever in lawyer mode, flipped through the paper-work that Breanna had given him. While the rest of them were in jeans and sweatshirts or flannel shirts, Colin wore crisply pressed khakis and a sky blue button-down shirt. Living on the ranch in Montana might have relaxed him some, Liam reflected, but not enough to get the stick completely out of his ass.

Still, he was making Breanna happy, and that was some-thing.

"I thought ... Oh, it doesn't matter what I thought," Bre-anna said, giddy with happiness.

"You thought I was going to give you hell for buying a run-down house that's been occupied mainly by rats and spiders for the past twenty years," Colin said, deadpan.

"Well ... yes."

"I guess that's why you didn't ask me what I thought beforehand." Colin handled the family corporation's finances, and consulting him about money matters was usually a given—until Breanna had rebelled.

She looked embarrassed. "I didn't want you to try to talk me out of it. I love it, Colin. This house makes me happy. And I didn't want to be talked out of something that makes me happy."

"Fair enough," Colin said.

Breanna and Julia started talking about things like area rugs and kitchen upgrades, and they walked inside, leaving Colin and Liam standing on what would be the front yard but was now just a mass of wild grass, weeds, and poison oak.

Liam glanced at his brother. "You really think she got a good deal?"

Colin nodded thoughtfully. "Probably. But renovating this place is going to be one hell of a headache, even with a top contractor."

Liam sighed and clapped Colin companionably on the back. "Come on. Let's go in and take a look at the damage."

It was nice having Colin and Julia back home, even if it was only for a week. What was nicer still was the fact that Liam's cousin, Drew, had declined an invitation to come to the ranch for Christmas.

Liam had no hard feelings toward Drew—not really. But that didn't mean he wanted to have to watch him and Megan making kissy faces at the dinner table every night for as long as they decided to stay.

In truth, Drew had every right to be here, as he was part owner of the ranch, besides being family. If he had decided to come, Liam would have had to suck it up. It was just easier with Drew up there in British Columbia and Liam down here.

The guy had stolen Liam's girlfriend—which wasn't a helpful way to think of it, he supposed, since she was a woman and not a possession to be owned or taken—and he'd also stolen Liam's sense that he'd really known his uncle.

Truth be known, that was the worst thing. Liam had loved Megan, but they'd never been a good match. But what Liam had felt for his uncle Redmond? That was real. That was true. Until they'd all found out about Drew, throwing everything any of them had known about the man into question.

Liam thought about all of that as he sat on the sofa at the ranch house, watching Breanna, Lucas, and Michael putting decorations on the big, green Christmas tree set up in the corner of the room.

The boys were arguing about where a particular ornament—Darth Vader's head, with a festive red bow at the top—should be placed on the tree, and Breanna was mediating the argument, trying to find a suitable compromise that would satisfy both of the kids.

"I thought you were done decorating that tree weeks ago," Liam observed.

"So did I," Breanna said, shooting a reproving but affectionate look at her boys. "But then Lucas saw these Star Wars ornaments and just had to have them, and now here we are."

"Star Wars is stupid," Michael put in.

The kids bickered about that a little as Liam half listened to them. He enjoyed the noise of a full house, even if it came in the form of arguing. But the place didn't feel as full as it should have, not without Redmond. The man had been mostly silent as a rule, but still, without him, the house seemed quieter than normal, less full of life.

Thinking about Redmond made him think about the inevitability of death, which made him think about the necessity of living life to its fullest, which made him think about maybe having his own kids someday—which made him think about Aria.

"Have you seen Aria lately?" Breanna asked, as though she'd read his mind.

"Hmm?" He was roused out of his reverie by her question. "Uh ... yeah. I saw her for a bit this afternoon."

By "seeing her," he meant, of course, that he'd gone over to the guesthouse and made love with her. That was what they did, mostly—they had life-changing sex, then they both got dressed, said their goodbyes, and went about their daily routines. Since that night at Ted's, they'd fallen into that pattern, which was not at all unpleasant.

But Liam wanted more, and he knew he'd have to proceed carefully in order to get it. She'd taken a big step that night when she'd told him everything she had, but that didn't mean he could push her even further. He had to ease her along.

"So, what are you going to give her?" Breanna asked.

"Give her?" He blinked like a baby bird emerging from its egg into the sunlight.

"Yeah. For Christmas. Give her. The way people do."

"Well ... shit."

It wasn't that it had never occurred to him to give her a gift. It was just that the question of what to give her was so fraught with danger that he'd put the question out of his mind. Now that Breanna had brought it up, he realized that he didn't have much more time to delay. Christmas was in three days.

"You didn't get her anything," Breanna said flatly, her tone of voice broadcasting her harsh judgment of him.

"Well ... I wasn't quite sure what to get."

She looked at him with pity. "It's a good thing you have me."

"What, you're gonna help?"

"Of course I'm going to help. You think I'm going to let you show up on Christmas morning and give the woman in your life a toaster? Or the clock you got for opening a new account at the bank?"

"I didn't open a new account at the bank, smartass," Liam said.

"But if you had, you'd be giving her the clock. Don't deny it."

Breanna was looking at him with a combination of scorn and affection. It was the affection that made him squirm. The scorn, he was used to.

"I wouldn't give her the damned clock."

She scowled at him, letting him know she wasn't so sure that was true.

"Let me think about it," she said. "I'll kind of poke around and get back to you."

He wasn't entirely sure what poking around entailed, but he knew it sounded uncomfortable.

The poking didn't take much time. By the next morning, Breanna had decided what Liam should give Aria.

"I talked to Gen, and she says Aria likes Daniel Reed."

For a moment, Liam thought she was suggesting that Aria wanted the actual man—which would, obviously, be out of the question, at least from Liam's perspective. Then he realized with some relief that she was talking about his art.

"What, the glass?"

"No, a little Daniel Reed action figure. Yes, the glass, you idiot." Breanna had her hands on her hips in much the stance their mother used when she was scolding them about something.

"Okay. Okay." Liam nodded. "So, what, should I go to Gen's gallery to pick something out?" The Porter Gallery usually carried a selection of Daniel's glass pieces.

"No, Gen says you should go to his studio. She's got a few things, but she's sold most of the best stuff. There's a better selection at Daniel's place right now. She says he's been working on some new things that she hasn't seen yet, and you might want to take a look."

Liam's head bobbed. "I can do that."

It seemed like a good solution. Personal, but not so personal that it would freak Aria out. Expensive enough to say she meant something to him, but not so extravagant that it would make her think he was overstepping the bounds of their current relationship, or using his fortune to buy her affections.

Giving gifts to women was a minefield, and Liam would just be grateful if he could get to the other side with all of his body parts intact.

Chapter Twenty-Six

Liam went out to Daniel Reed's studio just after lunch. By the time Liam had called him to set up the visit, Daniel had already spoken to Gen and had set aside a few things to show him.

It was a cold, overcast day, and Liam pulled his jacket around him as he walked from his truck and down a dirt path lined with tall grass to the outbuilding that served as Daniel's studio.

Despite the chill, Reed's T-shirt was damp with sweat around his neck and armpits when he answered the door. Once Liam stepped inside, he knew why.

The man had no fewer than three furnaces going, and the inside of the studio had to have been more than ninety degrees despite the fact that the windows were open. Liam stripped off his jacket as soon as he stepped inside.

"I guess we should leave the door open, let in a little cool air," Daniel said. "I forget how hot it gets in here." He shrugged. "I'm used to it."

Reed was a tall, dark-haired guy women found especially attractive—at least, according to Gen. And it must have been true, because the guy had managed to marry the smoking hot Lacy Jordan, who'd been one of the most sought-after women in town until Daniel had taken her off the market. Liam talked to him from time to time, mainly because he was Ryan's friend, and because he worked with Gen. That was how it was in small towns—all interconnected.

"So, you and Aria Howard," Daniel said, leaning his rear against a worktable covered in various cast iron implements used for God knew what.

"Yeah, so? What about it?" Liam knew he was going to come off as a dick, but so much of the time, he couldn't seem to help himself. It was just his way.

Daniel shrugged. "Don't get your panties all twisted. I'm just making conversation."

Daniel was a good guy, mostly, so Liam wasn't sure at first why he felt like punching him in the face. Then, on reflection, he knew. It was because Aria had told him that she and Daniel were friends, and that they'd spent some time together working on her yurt.

Liam was jealous, especially since he was now, for the first time, noticing Reed's pecs, and his height, and the robustness of his hair, and all of the other things guys didn't notice about other guys until they sensed there was a need to compete.

He forced himself to relax and bring his shoulders down from where they'd been perched somewhere up around his ears.

"My panties are fine," Liam said. "I mean … shit. Yeah. Me and Aria Howard."

Daniel nodded, appraising Liam, his arms crossed over his chest. "Okay."

There was something in the *okay,* something fraught with meaning.

"Spit it out, Reed. You've got something to say, so say it." Might as well get it all out on the table so Liam would know whether he could get in that punch after all.

Daniel shrugged. "She's great, that's all. But she's going to be … a challenge. For you, I mean. I'm just wondering if you're up to it."

Liam's hackles rose, and he puffed up a bit, ready for a confrontation. Then, without warning, his defenses fell and his shoulders sagged. He rubbed his face with his hands.

"Well, hell. I hope so."

Apparently, that was the right answer, because Daniel seemed to relax a little. Then he smiled and smacked Liam on the back. "Come on, I'll show you what I've got finished. Lucky for you, she told me what she liked."

It turned out that what Aria liked was a six-foot-tall sculpture that Daniel had been making for the lobby of a boutique hotel in New York. The piece was done in shades of blue and green, and it had a kind of amorphous shape that dipped and swirled in various places. Liam thought that it looked familiar somehow, though he'd never seen anything exactly like it. Then he realized: It looked like water. It looked like an ocean wave that had been thrown skyward by a storm and had frozen in place.

"Wow."

Daniel appraised his own work with his hands on his hips. "I've been working with the idea of water—ocean water, specifically—since I did that big piece for Eden."

The job—a ceiling fixture for a Las Vegas hotel and casino—had been a turning point in Daniel's career. Liam had never seen it in person, but he'd seen pictures. This new piece was similarly inspired but had a feel and a shape all its own.

"Obviously, you can't give her this," Daniel said, gesturing toward the man-sized sculpture. "But I did some small studies of this concept that might work for you." He took Liam over to a big wooden cabinet, opened it, and carefully took out a piece about the size of a large apple. It didn't have the grandeur of the larger piece, but it had the same colors, the same sense of motion. The same … Liam searched for a word, and then found it. The word was *grace*.

"That's beautiful." Liam wasn't the kind of guy to particularly appreciate art, nor was he the kind of person to give compliments out of courtesy, especially to a guy he saw as a potential rival. But, screw it. The truth was the truth.

Daniel set the piece on a worktable and stood back, looking pleased. "Yeah, I think that ought to work."

"How much?"

Daniel told him, and Liam thought it sounded about right. He'd be spending enough for it to mean something, but not enough to scare her away.

Money changed hands, Daniel packaged the piece in a box with plenty of bubble wrap, and Liam figured his business here was done. He thanked Daniel and headed toward the door.

"Don't give up," Daniel said to Liam's back when he'd just about passed through the doorway.

Liam stopped and turned, his eyebrows raised in question.

Daniel looked uncomfortable, and he fidgeted a little, shifting his weight from one foot to the other. "I'm just saying … she really likes you. A lot. So … she's going to make it hard for you, but keep trying."

Aria was definitely *not* getting Liam a gift for Christmas. Gifts were for children and for people with whom you were in a relationship. Liam didn't fit either of those criteria, so why should she bother herself with choosing a gift?

The very fact that she was going to his house for Christmas dinner said *relationship* in giant neon letters. If she gave him a gift on top of that, the whole thing would be blown out of pro-portion, and before she knew it, she'd be washing his socks and nursing him to health the next time he caught a cold.

No. She would show up to visit the family—a family being hospitable to a guest on their property—and nothing more. She'd bring a nice hostess gift for Sandra, the things she'd bought for the boys, and a little something for Gen and Ryan's baby.

That would have to be enough.

She was already nervous as hell about the dinner. Adding gift-giving anxiety to the mix might just put her so far over the edge that she would be unable to function.

The whole Delaney family. At the same time. On a major holiday. Scrutinizing her for her potential as a mate for Liam.

When she thought about it, she alternated between chas-tising herself for agreeing to such a thing and reminding herself that if she didn't go to the Delaney house for the holiday, she would be alone.

And being alone sucked, especially at Christmas.

She was running all of that through her head the morning of Christmas Eve when Gen called.

They chatted about how she and the baby were doing and who was and was not getting any sleep, and then Gen got to the real point of her call.

"You're still coming, right?"

"You know, I'm not really sure that—"

"Don't do that." Gen's tone was stern. "Don't give me some excuse for why you can't come, because it won't work—it's going to be so transparent that we'll all be at the dinner table talking about you, and I know you don't want that."

Aria, alone in the guesthouse, was taken aback by that thought. "You'll all talk about me?"

"Of course. We've already exhausted every other topic of conversation."

"But—"

"Just come." Gen's voice was softer now, somewhere between a wheedle and a plea. "It'll be fun, and Sandra's a really good cook. What are you going to eat if you're in the guesthouse alone? A frozen Swanson's dinner?"

That was exactly what she had planned, but Aria didn't say that. She wondered for a moment why Gen was being so insistent, and then it came to her.

"Liam told you to call me."

Gen didn't answer, and that was, in itself, an answer.

"Oh, God, he did. I knew it."

"Aria—"

"Why didn't he call me himself if he's worried about it? Why—"

"Because he really wants you there, but he doesn't want to pressure you."

"But it's okay if you pressure me?"

"Apparently," Gen said wryly, as though she'd made that argument to Liam herself, unsuccessfully.

"Look, Gen …"

"Sandra's been cooking for days." Apparently, Gen thought the Sandra guilt approach would work better than the prospect of Aria potentially disappointing Liam. "She baked twelve kinds of cookies. Twelve."

"Well, I'm sure she didn't do that for me."

"She normally bakes two kinds, three max. But she asked Liam what your favorite kind was, and he didn't know, so she baked twelve kinds *just to cover all the bases.*"

Aria stood with the phone in her hand, speechless and wide-eyed. Then she realized she was being manipulated—and artfully, at that.

"She did not. You made that up."

"Well? Did it work?" Gen said.

Aria didn't want to admit that yes, it sort of had.

"I don't know why you think I've changed my mind," she told Gen. "I said I would be there, and I'll be there."

"Oh." Gen sounded surprised. "Good. Great. That's great."

Aria ended the call cursing her stupidity—not just for agreeing to come to the Delaney Christmas dinner, but also for getting involved with Liam in the first place. For letting him get to her. For letting her stupid, pathetic self fall in love.

As soon as that thought popped into her head, she knew it was true. She was in love with Liam.

God help her—and him.

Chapter Twenty-Seven

Christmas morning was cold and clear, with frost on the ground and the smell of the ocean in the air. Aria bundled up in a pair of fleece-lined jeans, boots, a sweatshirt, and a down jacket, then poured hot coffee into a Thermos and headed out to the barn, her shoes crunching on the dirt path.

Thinking about work was easier than thinking about her feelings for Liam—or facing his family with those feelings surging through her. So she threw herself into constructing the yurt.

The structure was really taking shape. The exterior was more than halfway covered with the detritus she'd recovered from the area's shorelines.

She'd thought she wouldn't be able to find much trash in Cambria, which looked to her like an unusually clean town, but when she expanded her search from the beaches to the bed of the creek that ran through the area and out to the ocean, she struck gold.

It turned out that the area's homeless favored the creek as a kind of home base, and an abandoned encampment had yielded fast food wrappers, Styrofoam cups, plastic shopping bags, syringes (she carefully washed these in bleach and removed the needles for her safety), beer and liquor bottles, stained mattresses (not much use to her for her current purposes), chip bags, and so much else that she likely wouldn't have to look anywhere else for the remainder of her project.

Once she was settled in the barn with adequate lighting and a space heater blowing warm air, she sorted through the boxes of crap she'd brought back from the creek and began the painstaking process of arranging it like pieces of a jigsaw puzzle on the exterior of the yurt.

Before the baby came, Gen had been talking to galleries about taking the piece—with Aria herself as an integral part of it—and she was beginning to see some interest. There were certain logistics involved in showing a performance piece of this nature and of this size, and that had eliminated a lot of places from the outset. But Gen had a good list of galleries that had the capacity to handle the piece and that also meshed with Aria's artistic vision. She was focusing mainly on the West Coast because of the difficulty of transporting the piece. It was going to have to travel by truck rather than by air, and while it wasn't out of the question to have it moved cross-country via roadway, it would be simpler and cheaper to stick to Los Angeles, San Francisco, or possibly Seattle.

A gallery in Santa Barbara was considering it, Gen had said, and that would certainly be easy enough to manage, given the proximity. But Aria wanted the piece in a gallery that would boost her visibility and reputation, and that meant a major city. The piece would be easier for Gen to pitch when it was finished, though, so Aria threw herself into it, gluing Big Mac containers and empty Cheeto bags, orange juice bottles, and Budweiser cans onto the structure.

She'd been working for hours—warm now both from exertion and from the space heater, her mind busy with plans for her career and her life—when she realized she wasn't alone in the barn.

The realization came so suddenly and took her so much by surprise that she gasped, standing up straight with a piece of trash in one hand and a bottle of glue in the other.

"Hey, hey. Sorry. I didn't mean to scare you." Liam was standing in the doorway of the barn, looking tall and manly and impossibly appealing. He was just standing there, neither advancing nor retreating.

"I didn't hear you," Aria said.

She was surprised she hadn't *sensed* him—lately, it felt like she was so attuned to him that she might know where he was or what he was doing even if he were in China, maybe, or the wilds of Alaska.

"Yeah, I didn't want to disturb you," he said. "You looked so busy. And … it was nice just to watch you."

The idea that he'd been standing there silently watching her might have been creepy, but instead, it was hot. And she didn't want him to be hot right now. Not that there was a damned thing either of them could do about it.

"Ah … I was just …" She gestured toward the yurt, feeling unexplainably flustered.

"Merry Christmas." He grinned, and she felt it seep through her like warm honey. "I brought you something," he said.

She didn't see the small, wrapped gift in his hand until he came over to her and held it out. She looked at it but didn't take it.

"It's just something I thought you'd … I was going to give it to you at the house, but …" His face was coloring slightly with embarrassment.

Of course Aria had known that he might give her a gift, but somehow the gesture was surprising all the same. He was standing there with such hope and nervous anticipation on his face that it nearly broke her heart.

"It's not much." He shrugged. "Just a little something. Here, take it."

Her failure to take the gift from him was becoming awkward for both of them, so she accepted the square, wrapped package and held it in both of her hands.

"Open it," he prompted her.

She untied the red ribbon, then carefully removed the paper—red and green with cheerful Santas—to reveal a plain cardboard box. She opened the box, pulled out an object covered in bubble wrap, and then began uncovering the contents.

When she saw what Liam had given her, Aria simply stared at it. The piece of glass in her hands caught the glow from the skylight over her head, and it shone in fiery, sparkling shades of green and blue.

"This is one of Daniel's," she said, still looking at the piece, at the way the sunlight flashed and played within it as she turned it in her hands.

"Yeah. Gen said you liked his stuff, so I went over there and asked him if he had anything he thought would be right. I hope it is. Right, I mean." He shifted uncomfortably from one foot to the other, his hands shoved into the pockets of his jeans.

He'd gotten it right—so right that it was hard to imagine the reason for his uncertainty. The piece was beautiful, dramatic in its shapes and colors, graceful in its undulating curves, as though it were made especially to fit in the palms of her hands.

"Liam." That was all she could seem to say.

"Do you like it?"

"It's beautiful."

When she'd seen Daniel's full-sized piece for which this smaller one was a prelude, she'd been awestruck, feeling that squeeze to the heart that only came from art that truly spoke to someone. It had reminded her of so many things: the sky, the ocean, calm summer days with a storm lurking over the horizon. It had reminded her of something she couldn't name, some feeling of safety and belonging that she'd never quite managed to grasp in her own life.

And now that feeling was here, in her hands.

She was starting to get emotional, and that wasn't okay—not with Liam here, watching intently for her reaction.

"I ... I really need to get back to work." She put the piece of glass on her worktable, grabbed a bucket full of various pieces of creek trash and a bottle of glue, and climbed into the yurt to work on the interior.

She knew she was acting like a kid who hid inside a blanket fort to avoid some unpleasantry like cleaning her room or eating peas. But this was an unpleasantry much more daunting than either of those things.

This was love.

"Aria?" Liam, standing just outside the entrance to the yurt, sounded confused.

She poked her head out. "Thank you for the gift, Liam. I ... thank you. I'll see you at dinner, okay?"

He rubbed the back of his neck, and she saw a range of emotions cross his face: dismay, irritation, resignation.

"All right. I'll come to the guesthouse about five, unless—"

"That's all right. I'll meet you at the house."

"But—"

"I have a lot of work. It's better if I just go over there on my own."

She could see that he was hurt, and she felt a tight squeeze inside her chest. He nodded, turned, and walked out of the barn without another word.

Aria sat back in the yurt, sighed, and covered her face with her hands. She let out a scream of frustration, muffled so he wouldn't hear. Then she picked up her materials and got back to work.

"She hated it."

Liam was in the kitchen at Ryan and Gen's house, where Gen was bouncing James on her shoulder, apparently trying to get him to burp. Ryan was at the sink putting dishes into the dishwasher, a job that apparently hadn't been done in a while. The kitchen looked like hurricane-force winds had recently passed through.

Liam leaned back against the counter, his hands in his pockets.

"What?" Gen said. "That's crazy. She didn't hate it."

"Well, she acted like she hated it." He scowled, pulled the hands out of his pockets, and stuffed them into his armpits.

"Did she *say* she hated it?"

"Well … no." In fact, it had seemed as though she liked the gift—right up until the moment she kicked him out of the barn and refused to let him pick her up for dinner.

"Then what are you worried about? Daniel said you chose a piece that he thought was perfect for her."

"Yeah, yeah."

"Liam. What?" Gen wiggled the baby around and patted him on the back until he let out a satisfying belch. The table in front of her was littered with a variety of baby-related implements: pacifiers, blankets, clean diapers, boxes of wipes, and other things the uses of which Liam couldn't name.

"She kicked me out," he said, feeling frustrated and maybe a little pathetic. "Said she had to work, basically told me not to let the barn door hit me in the ass."

"Well, maybe she *did* have to work."

"On Christmas Day?"

Gen carefully laid the baby down in a bassinet set up in a corner of the kitchen, watched him to see if he was going to settle, and then, satisfied, turned to Liam. A cloth draped over her shoulder was dotted with something off-white that had probably come out of the baby. She saw where he was looking and plucked the thing off of her shoulder.

"Artists are different than other people," Gen said dismissively. "They work when they feel inspired. They keep odd hours. I wouldn't worry about it."

"Huh." The scowl was still on Liam's face, and his posture suggested that he was looking for an excuse to punch somebody. Since he couldn't punch Gen or even Ryan, considering his status as a new father, there was nowhere for his feelings to go.

He picked up a teething ring, turned it over in his hands, then put it down again.

"You want me to talk to her?" Gen offered. "See if I can figure out what the problem is? If there even is one?"

He raised his eyebrows, hopeful. "Would you mind?"

"I can't imagine why she would," Ryan said, looking over his shoulder from where he was working at the sink. "It's not like she's got anything else going on right now."

"Don't listen to him," Gen said. "I'll do it."

Liam nodded a few times. "When?"

Gen made a shooing motion with her hands. "Get out of my kitchen."

Chapter Twenty-Eight

Liam tried not to think about it, and got on with the rest of his day. Christmas Day or not, there was work to do on the ranch before he could knock off early to enjoy the holiday.

He went about doing the chores that couldn't wait—feeding and watering the horses, checking on a new calf, and working with a filly they'd gotten the week before—and then went home and took a shower so he wouldn't smell like cow shit.

Trying not to think about Aria worked about as well as he'd expected: the more he didn't focus on her, the more she was persistently on his mind.

He was aware that this Christmas dinner wasn't just any Christmas dinner. Inviting a woman for a holiday meal was a big step. Of course, she'd had dinner with his family before. But that was a getting-to-know-you thing. This was different. This had symbolism. This was Liam introducing Aria as his significant other. He wasn't stupid enough to present it to Aria that way, but changing what you called the thing didn't change the thing itself.

As he stood in the hot shower, the water soothing his always hard-worked muscles, he thought about women, and relationships, and holidays.

Exactly two other women in his life had meant enough to him to be presented to the family the way he was presenting Aria. Both of them had eventually cheated on him, resulting in the dissolution of the relationship.

When women got involved with Liam, they had a tendency to discover they were happier with someone else. Was that due to a problem with him? Was it a character flaw in the women he chose? Or was it just bad luck and poor timing?

He got out of the shower and wrapped himself in a towel, still thinking about it.

Would the curse continue? Was Aria going to end up cheating on him? For her to cheat, she'd first have to admit they were in a relationship—something she could actually cheat on—and the chances of that happening seemed slim.

As he dressed for dinner—his usual jeans and flannel shirt, as the Delaney family didn't stand on ceremony—he thought about his uncle Redmond.

Redmond had been alone for as long as Liam could remember. He'd slept on a twin-size bed in a small room in the house where he'd grown up. He'd never dated, never brought a woman home, never had anyone to kiss under the mistletoe at Christmas or even to hold hands with during a walk by the creek.

What Liam hadn't known at the time was that Redmond was alone because he hadn't gone after the love of his life. He'd let her go, let her live her life with someone else. But he'd never gotten over her. He'd never moved on.

With every passing day, Liam was more certain that Aria was the love of his life, and if he let her go, he would be like Redmond, sleeping alone in the room where he'd grown up, stoically mourning what he'd lost.

When he was a kid, there was nothing he'd wanted more

than to be like his uncle. But now, that possibility—at least where love was concerned—seemed unbearably sad.

As he sat on the edge of his bed, pulling on his shoes and tying them, he knew he had to go after Aria. She was his turning point. He had two choices: He could let this pass him by and live a life that was structured, predictable, ordinary. Or he could win her over, and his life could be so much more.

He wanted what Ryan had with Gen, and what Colin had with Julia. Hell, he wanted what Drew had with Megan.

He didn't want to screw around. He didn't want to date.

He wanted love.

He wanted Aria and all she represented.

Aria had been burned so many times that she was terrified of anything that might be real. He understood that. He respected her survival instinct, which was the only thing that had kept her going until now.

But whether he respected it or not, he had to find a way to get past it.

He had to find a way to get her out of her protective shell so she could accept everything he had to give.

He went downstairs with a sense of determination and a sense of hope.

This thing with Aria was going to happen. He just had to find a way to make it happen.

Aria showed up at the Delaney house with the gifts she'd bought for Breanna's boys and Gen's baby, and a bottle of wine that she'd picked up at De-Vine on Main Street the day before. She felt jittery, and it had nothing to do with the strong coffee she'd been drinking throughout the day.

Gen had called her earlier at the guesthouse to ask whether she'd liked Liam's gift. She'd reassured Gen that she'd loved it.

But there was a lot she hadn't said.

She hadn't told Gen that when he'd given her the gift, she'd felt her composure blow apart into a million tiny fragments that could never be reassembled.

It wasn't the gift itself. It was the way the gift had made her *feel*.

She'd opened it and held it in her hands, and one simple sentence had popped into her head and had nearly escaped her mouth before she'd been able to stop it.

That sentence was, *I love you.*

She couldn't fall in love with Liam. She couldn't leave herself open that way, couldn't run the risk that he would take what she had to give and then crush her.

She'd considered skipping out on the dinner, maybe claiming illness. But she had reassured Gen on the phone that everything was fine. She could hardly now claim to have a raging case of the Ebola virus.

So, here she was, bearing a bottle of pinot noir that Rose Bachman—the wine expert at De-Vine—had assured her was a good choice. When Breanna opened the door for her, Aria smiled and made small talk as though her insides weren't fluttering with dread and nerves.

Liam wasn't in the room, thankfully, so Breanna ushered Aria in and introduced her to Colin and Julia, who hadn't been here the last time Aria had visited.

Colin was noticeably different than the other Delaney brothers—more polished and sophisticated. Based on the way he carried himself, she wasn't surprised when she learned he had once been an associate at a large law firm.

Julia, with her thick, auburn hair and pale, freckled complexion, was pretty but approachable. She was so friendly to Aria—taking her by the hand and leading her to the sofa in front of the fireplace for a getting-to-know-you chat—that Aria wondered why. Then she put two and two together and realized this was the sister of the man who'd stolen Liam's girlfriend.

The friendliness was guilt by association, no doubt. If Liam ended up happy with someone else, then Julia would be able to stop feeling bad about what her brother had done.

Not that your family's actions were your fault, or had anything to do with you. Aria knew that as well as anyone.

"Your brother is Liam's cousin, right?" Aria asked tentatively, throwing the question out there just to make sure she wasn't mistaken.

"My half brother. His biological father was Liam's uncle Redmond." Julia went through the main points of the story: how Redmond had an affair with Julia and Drew's mother decades before; how their mother had kept the truth about Drew's parentage a secret; how Redmond had left Drew a substantial part of his fortune in his will; and how Julia had met Colin when he'd come to Montana looking for Drew.

"Is Drew coming here for Christmas, then?" Aria wanted to know. If he was—if he was bringing Liam's ex to the family dinner table for the holidays—that was going to be awkward as hell.

"Oh. No." Julia's pretty face showed a hint of discomfort, a little line forming between her brows. "That's ... problematic."

"Because Drew is with Liam's ex," Aria supplied.

Julia looked relieved that Aria already knew the basics.

"Liam's been really big about it. I mean, really big. But that doesn't mean he wants to pass the turkey to his ex while she makes mooney eyes at his cousin." Julia rolled her eyes to indicate the sheer awfulness of that potential scenario.

"Does he still have feelings for her?" As she said it, Aria realized that was what she really wanted to know. This conversation wasn't about family gossip, or holiday dinner table awkwardness, or even making small talk with Liam's family. It was about this one central question.

"Yes."

Julia said it so simply and unequivocally that Aria felt her heart stutter. It wasn't what she'd wanted to hear, but there it was. "Oh."

"He's not in love with her anymore," Julia said. "I really believe that. But he cares about her. Enough that he was willing to walk away so she could be happy." Julia had a glass of wine in her hand, and she turned the stem between her fingers, looking down into the glass, as she considered what she was trying to say. "Liam has a tendency to seem like kind of a jerk when you first meet him. You know? That's how he seemed to me, anyway. But the way he handled the thing with Drew and Megan … It made me rethink things. It made me rethink him."

Competing feelings warred within Aria: jealousy about whatever emotions Liam might still harbor for Megan versus admiration for him because he'd put aside his own heartbreak for the benefit of the woman he'd loved.

She wasn't entirely comfortable with either of those feelings, because both of them meant she was in this deeper than she wanted to be.

She told herself she didn't care whether Liam had feelings for his ex, whether he was more noble than she'd realized, or whether she herself was his one best hope for finally repairing his heart.

None of that mattered because they weren't in a relationship. They were just having fun. That was all this was. That was all this would ever be.

Chapter Twenty-Nine

Liam came downstairs feeling surprisingly nervous. What did he have to be nervous about? It was just dinner with his family, for God's sake. He'd had dinner with his family thousands of times. And sometimes he even brought a woman. It wasn't unprecedented.

But it had never been Christmas dinner with *this* woman, and that made it different.

He spotted her right away amid the various family members who were standing around the living room holding drinks and making conversation. She was sitting on the sofa in front of the fireplace, listening intently to Julia.

The fact that he'd been a raging asshole to Julia when they'd first met crossed his mind. What was she saying about him? Was she telling Aria how Liam had actually punched Colin in the face over his relationship with Julia? Was she telling Aria to run like hell?

Things had been pretty good between Liam and Julia for some time now, but who was to say she didn't still hold a grudge?

But then Julia looked up and saw him as he came down the stairs, and their eyes met. The way she smiled at him—the way the smile was real and warm and reached her eyes—told him he needn't have worried.

Then Julia said something to Aria, and she looked up at him, too, and what he saw in her face was much less reassuring.

What he saw there wasn't love or even friendship. It wasn't amusement or interest or annoyance.

What he saw was fear.

He knew that if he were smart, he would take that as a warning and begin distancing himself now, before it was too late. He could go with the lie that things were just casual between them, and back away before one or both of them got badly hurt.

But he didn't want to do any of that. All he wanted to do was go to her, hold her in his arms, protect and reassure her.

He came the rest of the way down the stairs and crossed the room to where they were sitting. He put his hand on Aria's shoulder and squeezed lightly to send her the message that he was here and everything was okay.

"You get anything to drink yet?" he asked her.

"Uh … not yet."

"Sit tight, I'll get you a glass of wine." The shoulder squeeze again, his way of wordlessly communicating that she was safe with him, that he wouldn't let any harm come to her.

"Don't let her run off," he said to Julia, only partly kidding.

In the kitchen, his mother and Breanna were bustling around pulling food from the oven, chopping things, stirring other things, and arranging things on platters while Gen fed her son, a blanket discreetly draped from her shoulder down over the baby's head.

The place smelled like roast turkey, fresh rolls, and about seven kinds of pie.

"Well, there you are, boy." Sandra straightened up from where she'd been bent over checking the temperature of the bird. She closed the oven, put her hands on her hips, and scowled at him.

Sandra was wearing her usual bunny slippers and football jersey, and her graying hair was pulled back into a severe ponytail. Her face, weathered by years of hard work, was free of makeup.

"You been looking for me?" he asked, picking up a carrot stick from a cutting board and popping it into his mouth.

"If I'm looking for you, I damned well know where to find you," Sandra declared. "But that girl of yours has been here for a while, and a gentleman wouldn't make her wait."

"I'm a gentleman," Liam said, wounded.

"My dog thinks she's an antelope. Doesn't make it true," Colin said from a far corner of the kitchen, where he was opening a bottle of wine.

"Yeah? My ass thinks it's your face, and—"

"You boys get the hell out of my kitchen. Both of you," Sandra said, making a shooing gesture with both hands.

Liam grabbed two wineglasses from a cabinet, snagged the bottle of chardonnay Colin had just opened, and headed toward the door. On his way out, he paused and said, "Mom?"

She grunted in response, poking a fork into a casserole that was still steaming.

"Could you maybe … I don't know … maybe not say the *your girl* thing in front of Aria?"

"Why the hell not? She's your girl, isn't she? And if she's not, why the hell did you invite her for Christmas dinner?"

He hesitated. "The thing is … we don't really have all of that worked out yet."

She turned her full attention to him, her fists back on her hips where they so often resided. "Well, *she* might not have it all worked out yet, but I know my son, and by God, she's your girl."

He'd never been able to get anything past his mother—she read him as clearly as if he came with a booklet of instructions. He could try explaining everything to her, but he knew he didn't have to.

"Just … please?"

Her face softened a little, and she nodded. Then she lowered her voice so the others couldn't hear. "Well, now. You think she's the one, don't you?"

He thought to deny it, but again, there was no putting anything past Sandra.

"She might be."

Her face went hard again, then she turned him around with her hands on his shoulders and gave him a shove toward the door. "Then don't leave her waiting, son."

He thought he heard her voice break with emotion, but he didn't turn around.

The dinner went all right, from Liam's perspective. Everyone gathered around the big, rough-hewn farm table and ate enough food to nourish a small country. Breanna talked about her house; Colin and Julia talked about the Delaney ranch property in Montana, where they lived; Ryan and Gen took turns holding the baby while the other one ate; Breanna's boys talked about everything they'd gotten under the tree that morning; and Sandra talked about the food—whether everyone liked it, whether anyone needed more of it, and who was going to help her clean up after the making of it.

Aria didn't talk about much, which worried him. He supposed it might have been normal, since she didn't know everyone very well, and it was never easy being a guest amid such a large and tight-knit family. But he worried it was more than that. He worried there was something on her mind, and that whatever it was didn't bode well for him.

He kept refilling her wineglass in the hope that a little alcohol might relax her and drain some of the obvious tension she was feeling. But she wasn't drinking enough for that strategy to be effective.

He eyed her nervously, and he asked after her welfare. Did she have enough turkey? Did she want another roll? Was she feeling a draft where she was sitting?

His solicitous behavior began to attract the attention of his brothers, which wasn't a positive development, as his brothers tended toward teasing the crap out of him, especially in front of women.

"I guess Aria knows how to get another roll if she wants it, Liam," Ryan said, a forkful of mashed potatoes halfway to his mouth. "But if you're having trouble with it yourself, I can put one on your plate for you."

"If you're having trouble finding your ass, I can stick my foot up it for you," Liam replied conversationally.

"This is why I love my family," Colin told Aria. "The high level of discourse."

"There any more of them potatoes?" Orin wanted to know.

"Uncle Liam? Could you really kick Uncle Ryan's ass?" Michael asked.

"We don't use that kind of language at the table," Breanna told her son.

"But Uncle Liam did," Lucas pointed out helpfully.

"You bet your ... *butt* I could," Liam told Michael as though Breanna hadn't spoken. "But it would be unkind. His kid needs a dad who has all his teeth."

"Well, someday your kids are going to want a dad who's not a dick," Ryan told Liam. "But we can't all get what we want."

"Boys! By God, you'd think I raised you in a damned barn."

Sandra paused. "Come to think of it, I guess I did."

"Except me," Colin observed. "That's probably why I'm the only one who doesn't embarrass you in front of company."

"You're also the only damned one who can't rope a calf," Orin said.

"Fortunately, there wasn't much call for calf roping in law school," Colin pointed out.

To Liam, it had all the elements of a satisfying family experience: good food, sibling togetherness, and the harmless banter he'd always enjoyed with his brothers. But the tension was coming off Aria in waves.

"You okay?" he asked her in a low voice so the others wouldn't hear.

"I'm fine." She kept her gaze on her plate.

Liam had the sense he was fucking things up. He just wished to hell he knew how.

With every word Liam's family spoke, Aria could feel herself getting in deeper.

This—all of this—was exactly what she'd always wanted. The brothers playfully teasing each other, the kids chiming in and being lovingly scolded, Sandra and Orin trying to keep some kind of control over their happy but unruly brood.

This was what she'd wanted and never had, and likely never would have.

The noise and warmth and activity of a house where people felt at home, felt loved, and felt as though they belonged—how many times had she prayed for just such a thing?

It was hard enough sitting here among the things that she'd always missed. But then Ryan had mentioned Liam's children.

It had been a joke, a careless tease. But Aria couldn't help thinking of those children who would one day play in this house, sit around this dinner table. What would they look like? Would they have Liam's eyes, his lanky build, his gruff exterior and his kind, loving heart?

The thought of those imaginary children—those sweet, Liam-like children with their warm bodies and their messy hair smelling of baby shampoo—filled her with such longing that she almost swooned with it.

And then Ryan handed the baby to Liam.

Watching him cradle the boy's tiny body, the way he smiled at the infant with such warmth and love, made Aria see his future in that moment. She wanted to be in that future with everything she was, everything she had.

When it came to family—when it came to love—Aria had never gotten what she wanted. Not once in her life. Not even one time. Not ever.

Wanting something with this level of intensity, this bone-deep need, would kill her when it didn't happen. And that was the way she thought of it: *when* it didn't happen, not *if.*

She felt a heavy sickness in her gut, and her eyes started to fill with tears. She wiped them away, silently staring at her plate.

"Aria, girl, you all right?" Sandra barked at her.

She blinked hard to clear her vision.

"I just ... I'm not ..." The words wouldn't come. "Excuse me."

She got up from her seat at the table, thinking to tuck herself away in the private safety of the bathroom until she could compose herself. Instead, she left the kitchen, snatched up her jacket and her purse, and headed out the front door.

The cold smacked her skin hard as she went down the porch steps, and she hunched her shoulders up around her ears for warmth. She barely got down the steps and onto the path before she heard the front door open and Liam calling after her.

"Aria? Where are you going? What the hell?"

He didn't sound angry, just puzzled and hurt.

"I have to go." She didn't look at him, just focused on her shoes as the cold of the evening bit her skin.

"Why? Did somebody say something to you? Was it my brothers? Look, they're assholes, but they don't mean anything by it."

She shook her head, still looking at the cold ground in front of her. "No. It's not ... Your family is great."

"Then what?" He'd come all the way down the stairs and had reached her now. He was standing so close she could feel the warmth of his body from inches away. He put a hand on her shoulder, and she resisted the urge to shake it off.

"I don't belong here." She murmured the words, and at first, she wasn't sure he'd heard her.

But then his hand tightened on her arm, and she knew he had.

"You do. You do belong here." He swallowed audibly. "Aria, look at me."

Reluctantly, she raised her eyes and met his. What she saw there—the tenderness and hurt—scared her.

"You do belong here." He started to say something, then stopped. Then his expression hardened. "I know I'm not supposed to say this. I know you don't want to hear it. But goddamn it, I love you, and I'm not going to stop. Come in the house, Aria. This is where you should be. Here. With me."

She knew he didn't just mean now, tonight, for Christmas dinner. He meant forever. And she knew the truth about that: Nobody did forever. They said they would sometimes, but they never stuck.

Never.

"Liam. Let me go."

He held her arm for just a moment longer, his grip meant to reassure rather than intimidate. Then he let go and let his arm fall to his side.

"I'm sorry," she told him. "I just can't."

She turned and rushed down the path that led to the guesthouse.

Chapter Thirty

Liam didn't feel much like celebrating the holiday when he went back inside. But he had it in mind to act like everything was normal, to avoid having to answer too many questions from his family.

He knew that wasn't going to work as soon as he sat back down at the table.

"What happened? Where did she go? Is everything all right?" Gen asked, her face full of concern.

"How the hell should I know?" Liam pushed back his chair, stood up, and stalked over to the refrigerator to get a beer.

"Well, for God's sake, what did she say? Why'd she tear out of here like her damned hair was on fire?" Sandra said.

Liam, now standing a few feet from the dinner table with the beer in his hand, shrugged. "She's gone, that's all I know." He kept his voice and his posture casual, but inside, he felt like his stomach was being gnawed by some kind of angry animal.

"Liam? What do you mean, she's gone?" Julia asked.

Liam took a long swig from his beer. "You know something? I really don't fuckin' want to talk about it."

"Uncle Liam said the F word," Michael pointed out. "He's not allowed to do that at the dinner table, is he?"

Nobody answered.

Liam took his beer upstairs to his room and closed the door.

He didn't want to talk to anyone, or come back downstairs, or finish eating his dinner. All he wanted to do was lie on his bed, drink his beer, and feel sorry for himself.

He was *not* going to cry, because he was a man, for fuck's sake, and men held it together better than that. What he *was* going to do was drink. But he couldn't do much of that without leaving his room, since he hadn't thought to bring more than the one beer with him.

One nice thing about siblings was that they knew what you needed, and more often than not, they came through with it for you.

Ryan had a bottle of bourbon and two stubby glasses in his hand when he came knocking on the door, and that made it damned near impossible to turn him away.

He was sitting on Liam's desk chair pouring the bourbon when Colin came in without knocking, and without an invitation.

Breanna was no more than a couple of minutes behind him.

"I only brought two glasses," Ryan observed, passing one of the glasses to Liam, who was sitting on his bed with his back against the headboard.

"I'm on it," Colin said. He slipped out the door and came back a few minutes later with two more glasses.

Ryan poured, and everyone sat wherever they could find a spot: Breanna on the foot of the bed, Colin perched on the edge of Liam's desk.

"So, what do you need?" Colin asked, taking a sip of the bourbon. "You need us to trash-talk her, tell you she's not worth the effort?"

"No." Liam shook his head. His eyes felt hot and gritty with the effort not to cry in front of his siblings. He tossed back the one finger of bourbon that was in his glass, then held the glass out to Ryan for a refill.

"Well, good, because it would probably be bullshit," Ryan observed.

"But we'll go with that if you need us to," Breanna offered.

"Maybe just sit here for a minute," Liam said.

They all sat together, drinking, silently absorbing all that had happened. Liam reflected, not for the first time, that it was a good thing to have family.

After a while, Liam said, "All of this?" He gestured to indicate the room, the house, the meal lovingly prepared by their mother that they were even now ignoring, all of them in the room, and the entirety of all they had here. "She never had this. Not any of it." He shook his head, his jaw tight. "She never had anybody to come up to her room and check on her when her world went to shit."

They all, by silent, mutual agreement, ignored the implication that Liam's world had gone to shit. That seemed to go without saying, anyway.

"She's scared," Breanna said. "Scared to hope for more than she has."

"I get that. Fear, I mean. Hell, we're all scared of something," Colin said.

"I'm scared of fatherhood," Ryan offered. "What if I screw it up? What the hell do I know about raising a kid?" He shook his head thoughtfully and took a drink of bourbon.

"I'm scared I'm going to fuck it all up," Colin said. "The money, I mean. Handling the investments for the whole family? I mean … what if I make a mistake? What if I ruin things for everyone? Everybody's counting on me." He held out his glass to Ryan for a refill.

"I'm fuckin' terrified that she's the one, and I ruined it, and I'm never going to get her to come back." Liam swallowed hard and rubbed his face with his hand.

After a moment, they all looked at Breanna.

"The love of my life is dead," she said. "I'm not scared of anything anymore. The worst has already happened."

Half a bottle of bourbon later, Liam went downstairs to apologize to his mother for ruining the meal.

She was in the kitchen washing dishes when he found her. He nudged her aside with his shoulder and took the dishrag out of her hands.

"I'll do this." He picked up a dirty plate and began to rinse it under the tap.

"You're offering to do the dishes?" She let out a grunt. "By God, that's got to be a Christmas miracle."

"Yeah, yeah." He began to wash the dish, and the hot, soapy water was surprisingly soothing.

He handed her the clean dish, and she began to dry it. They had a dishwasher, of course, but it was already full with the pots and pans she'd used to prepare the meal. The machine swished away under the counter.

"I'm sorry," he said after a while. "About dinner."

"*Pfft.* It's just a meal. We've had thousands of 'em."

"It was Christmas dinner, and you worked hard on it. The others should have stayed, at least."

"*Hmph.* Who do you think sent 'em up there?" she barked at him.

He stopped what he was doing and raised his eyebrows in question.

"Sometimes a man needs his brothers and his sister, I

guess," Sandra said. She looked at the plate she was drying and not at Liam.

"I guess," he agreed.

They worked side by side in silence for a few minutes. Then Sandra said, "Boy, are you all right?"

He didn't know how to answer that. He didn't feel all right—he felt gutted, emptied out of all but his tough outer shell. But he was more all right than Aria, wasn't he? He had a warm, noisy home full of people who loved him. What did she have? What would she ever have, if she ran from the chance for everything good?

"I'll be okay," he said, because he would be, one way or another. Things happened, and you survived. But he wanted to do so much more than survive. And he wanted more than that for Aria, too.

He washed a casserole dish and handed it to his mother.

"She doesn't know how to be happy," he told her. "She never has been, and she just doesn't know how to do it."

She took the casserole dish from him and began to dry it. "Well, if that's the case, boy, what are you going to do about it?"

"Me?" He looked at her in surprise. "What the hell can I do?"

"Somebody doesn't know how to do something, they need somebody to show them how," she said, as though that were obvious. "You think you were born knowing how to ride a horse?" She grunted. "Hell, no. Your uncle Redmond taught you how to do it, and you practiced, and then you knew."

He wondered whether she had a point. Was happiness a skill that one could learn, like tying your shoes or doing algebra? All at once, he knew what really worried him, and he said it, for the first time.

"She needs somebody better than me to teach her. I don't

think I even know how to do it."

Sandra cackled. "Well, by God, son, you're the one the good Lord gave her. You'd better figure it out."

Chapter Thirty-One

Aria fully expected Liam to come after her, and when he didn't, she was immeasurably relieved. If he'd come after her, she would have been tempted to let him take her into his arms, to let him make promises he would never be able to keep.

Love was a fairy tale, and she didn't believe in it any more than she believed in Santa or Bigfoot.

If this felt like love, well, emotions were irrational. You couldn't trust them. You couldn't base your decisions on them.

She walked back to the guesthouse at a fast, purposeful pace. She wanted to put as much space between herself and the Delaney family as possible. Being around them made her soft, made her want things she could never have. And she couldn't be soft.

That was no way to survive.

She was cold and out of breath by the time she got back to the guesthouse. She lit the gas fire in the fireplace and sat perched on the edge of the sofa, her hands pressed between her knees.

She needed to get away from here.

Not just away from the Delaney house, but away from their property, their guesthouse—hell, away from their entire state.

He *loved* her? What made him think he was even capable of that? No one had ever loved her—not really, and not for long. What made Liam Delaney think he could manage such a thing, when everyone else had failed?

The longer she stayed here, the more damage it was going to do to both of them when the whole thing inevitably went up in flames.

She got up from the sofa, went into the bedroom, and started packing her things.

She would be out of here before morning, and Liam could get on with his life. They both could.

Liam woke up the next morning feeling groggy. Sunlight streamed in through his bedroom window, and he looked at the clock on his bedside table.

Seven a.m.

Jesus, he should have been up two hours ago. He hadn't meant to sleep late, and he was surprised he had. He was even more surprised the rest of the household had let him do it. Clearly, it was a measure of how pathetic he was. Nobody in this family cut anybody any slack when it came to getting work done. For them to let him sleep this late, they must have worried that he was damned near suicidal.

He wasn't, but he felt like a warmed-over pile of shit all the same.

Recognizing that self-pity was for lesser men than himself, Liam hauled himself out of bed and walked down the hall in his pajama pants to take a shower.

Once he was under the hot spray, he tried to put everything in perspective.

This was a setback, it wasn't the end of the world. He could go over to the barn later today and talk to her, find out exactly what had gone wrong and why. He had his ideas about why she was so afraid of having feelings for him, but his ideas probably weren't exactly right. If they could just talk it out, then he could understand her better, and that would lead them to have something even stronger than before.

This wasn't a problem. This was an opportunity. It was a chance for him to show Aria that he could be sensitive to her feelings. It was a chance to show her that he could stick.

He had a headache from drinking too much the night before, but even so, he was feeling a little bit better about things by the time he got out of the shower and toweled off. He'd long since stopped believing that things between him and women were supposed to be easy. Fuck easy. He could do this. He didn't need it to be easy.

He got dressed and went down to the kitchen to grab some coffee before going out to work. He poured himself a cup and found some aspirin in the cabinet over the coffee pot. He took two, then chased them with hot, black coffee.

Liam was holding out some hope that he might be able to get out the door and to work before his mother saw him, but that hope was dashed when she came into the kitchen a minute later, her bunny slippers on her feet and the apron she'd worn while cooking breakfast still fastened around her waist.

"Well, boy, it's about time you showed your face," she snapped at him. "Them cattle just can't wait around for you to get your beauty sleep."

She was scolding him because it was expected of her. If she'd wanted him up at five, he'd have been up at five. She'd felt sorry for him, and that was harder to take than the headache.

"I'm just getting my coffee, and then I'll be out of here," he told her.

"What, you're planning to work without breakfast? I

thought I taught you better than that, son." She scowled at him and opened the refrigerator, taking out milk, eggs, and butter.

"You don't have to cook again, Mom. I can just—"

"Now, stop yapping and sit down," she said. "The day I can't make a couple of eggs for my son is the day they wheel me out of here with a sheet over my face."

Since that matter seemed to be settled, Liam sat down while she fired up the burner under a cast iron pan and began to make scrambled eggs. While she was doing that, she popped a couple of slices of bread in the toaster and poured a glass of orange juice, which she placed in front of him.

"Somebody should have woke me up," Liam commented.

"*Hmph.* I figured you needed the sleep. You had a pretty rough night, I guess."

Liam shrugged. "I guess."

A few minutes later, he had a steaming plate of eggs in front of him, along with two thick pieces of buttered toast. He dug in, feeling hungrier than he'd thought he was.

As he ate, Sandra sat down across from him, her arms folded in front of her on the table, something on her mind.

"I guess you'd better say what you have to say, Mom," Liam told her. "If you're going to tell me I'm wasting my time with Aria, then—"

"I wasn't going to say any such thing, and I wish you'd let me speak for myself instead of wasting your time guessing," she shot back.

He waited silently for her to continue. For once, she didn't seem to have a speech ready to come fully formed from her mouth. She took a moment to gather her thoughts, and then she reached out and put one of her hands over his—a gesture that surprised him so much he blinked a few times to reorient himself.

"That girl needs you," she said finally. He started to say something, and she cut him off by holding up one finger between them.

"Now, I know you've had some relationship troubles," she went on. "I know you've had some rough times." She cleared her throat a little, and he was alarmed to realize she was trying not to cry. "You've got a big heart, son. And that's not always easy."

"Mom—"

"But if you let Aria go because you're afraid of getting that big heart of yours broken again, then you're not the man I think you are."

She seemed to be considering something, then she nodded in answer to a question only she knew.

"She's got a look about her," Sandra said. "It's a look that says she doesn't know what it's like to be able to count on someone, so she thinks it's hopeless to even try. I know that look because I saw it in my own damned mirror more than once. Now, what do you suppose would have happened if your father hadn't thought I was worth the effort?"

She squeezed his hand, stood up, and started cleaning up the mess from Liam's breakfast.

"Now, that's all of I've got to say on the matter," she told him as she stood at the sink, her back to him.

Liam felt a bit stunned at the idea of his mother as a young woman in a crisis of confidence. She'd always seemed so self-assured, so rock solid, that it was hard to imagine she'd ever been any other way.

"Mom …"

"I told you, that's all I have to say," she snapped at him. "Now, you'd better get on out of here so Ryan doesn't have to do all the damned work."

Liam had a hard time focusing on work, but he told himself to get his shit together and take care of the things that needed to get done. Ryan was kind of tiptoeing around him, as though Liam might suddenly snap and beat the crap out of one of the ranch hands.

He might have done that, but he was too distracted by thoughts of what he was going to say to Aria when he saw her.

Really, why the fuck did he have to go and say he loved her? He did, but that wasn't the point. She wasn't ready to hear it, and he goddamned well knew it. Why couldn't he have just kept his mouth shut until she was in the same place he was? She'd have gotten there eventually—he felt sure of that. But she wasn't there yet, and he'd pushed her.

Well, that was done, and it couldn't be undone. All he could do now was go to her and talk it out. He wouldn't take back what he'd said, because it was true. But he could smooth things over, reassure her that he wasn't in a rush, that he could wait for her as long as it took.

He was so focused on his strategy that he didn't hear Ryan talking to him until the man was standing in front of him, waving a hand in front of his face.

"Hello? Anybody in there?"

"What?"

"Are you planning to get some actual work done sometime today, or do I have to do enough to carry both of us?" Ryan asked.

"Ah, bite me."

They were in the stables, and Ryan leaned against the door of the stall where they'd put the new filly. He'd just finished checking the hoof where she'd thrown a shoe that morning.

"Look, if you just want to knock off and go out there to see her ..."

"I can work," Liam said.

"I guess you can," Ryan agreed. "But you're so distracted I'm afraid you're going to let a horse throw you again, and you're going to break the other damned leg. And then you really won't be any good to me."

"Very funny."

"I'm only half joking."

Liam had to admit—if only to himself—that Ryan had a point. But he'd be damned if he was going to admit to his brother that he didn't have his head in the game.

"I can work twice as hard as you could on your best goddamned day," Liam said. To prove his point, he went into the stall where his own horse was standing and started screwing around with the tack, just to look like he was doing something.

"All right." Ryan was done with the filly for now, so he turned and headed toward the door. On his way out, he turned and faced Liam. "Look. I know you don't want advice, but—"

"You're right, I don't."

"But," Ryan continued as though Liam hadn't spoken, "you'd better get your ass out to the guesthouse. Being married has taught me a little bit about women, and you don't want to wait too long to smooth things over."

"Is that right?"

"Yeah, it is. You think you're just giving her space, letting her get her head together. But every minute that passes before you go out there, she's more and more convinced that you just don't give a shit."

This came as a surprise to Liam. He raised his eyebrows, considering it. "She is?"

"She is. So, by the time you finally get out there, the fight's not going to be about whatever it was originally about. Instead, it's going to be about how you didn't even care enough to go out there and try to get her back."

This was a possibility that hadn't occurred to Liam until this moment.

"Seriously. I can handle things here," Ryan said.

On his way over there, Liam had himself halfway convinced that things weren't as bad as they'd seemed to be last night. Aria had been emotional and impulsive, and when she'd said she couldn't do this, of course she hadn't meant the relationship as a whole. She'd just meant the holiday, the family gathering, the dreaded *I love you* that had sent her into such a damned tailspin.

All he had to do was talk it through with her. Or maybe the best thing was not to talk at all. Maybe they'd skip that part and go straight to the making up.

He was feeling encouraged by that thought, until he got to the guesthouse and saw that her car wasn't there.

It was late morning; maybe she'd gone into town for something or other. Maybe she'd gone to grab a few groceries at the Cookie Crock, or to get a cup of coffee at Jitters. Maybe she was at Daniel Reed's place working on the skylight for her yurt.

He decided to wait a bit to see if she came home. If she was just out for a quick errand, he figured it shouldn't take too long.

He had a key to the guesthouse, and he took a moment to consider whether it would be an invasion of her privacy for him to go inside and wait for her there. His first instinct was to say it wouldn't, because she'd told him to just let himself in any number of times since they'd started sleeping together.

But this might be different, in her mind, after what had happened last night. She might expect him to understand that he couldn't do that anymore.

He weighed his options, then decided to go inside. She'd

never explicitly revoked his key privileges, after all.

He thought about sending her a text message, but decided it would be better to wait to see her in person.

He took his keys out of his pocket, unlocked the door, and stepped inside.

He felt the emptiness of the place before he saw it. There was an unoccupied feel to the cottage that he noticed before he even turned on the lights and saw that she'd cleaned it out.

The first thing he felt was a cold numbness that spread from his core out to his fingers and toes. The second thing he felt was a blow to the gut that made his world go swirly and dark before he steadied himself.

"What the fuck?" he said to the room, which was tidy and impersonal, stripped of all of her belongings, the way it had been before she'd come.

He walked through the living room and kitchen, and then the bedroom and bathroom, looking for any sign that she might still be staying there. Her clothes were gone. Her toiletries were missing from the bathroom counter and the medicine cabinet, the surfaces all clean and bare. There was no food in the kitchen; the refrigerator and pantry had both been emptied and wiped clean.

Feeling shaky, he left the house and went to the old barn she'd been using as her studio. He was relieved to see that the yurt was still there, but then the relief faded as he realized that it would be, wouldn't it? It wasn't like she could fit it in her car or take it on a plane.

His knees started to feel wobbly, so he sat down on the ground with his back propped up against the barn door. He dug his cell phone out of his pocket and called Gen.

"Hey, Liam," Gen answered, sounding chipper.

"Did you know Aria was gone?"

"What?"

"Did you know?"

"What do you mean, gone? Gone where?"

Gen sounded so puzzled that Liam knew it was genuine—she didn't know any more about it than he did.

"Aria moved out of the guesthouse. Either last night or this morning. The piece she was working on is still in the barn, but everything else ... She's gone."

Gen was silent for a moment or two, and then she said, "Sit tight. I'll be right there."

Chapter Thirty-Two

Liam met Gen at the guesthouse at a little after one in the afternoon. Gen, who'd always been so well-dressed when she was working, had on sweatpants and a T-shirt that had some kind of stain on the shoulder. The baby was in a carrier strapped to her chest. Her curly red hair, piled on top of her head in a messy bun, looked like it hadn't been washed in a while.

"Are you sure she's gone?" she asked before she'd even crossed the threshold into the house. "Are you sure she didn't just ... I don't know ... take a trip?"

"Come see for yourself." Liam's face was grim, his tone clipped and tight.

Gen followed him into the house and started looking around, much the way Liam had. She poked her head through doorways and into cabinets. The baby had started to make a little squeaking noise, and Gen patted his back rhythmically through the carrier.

"She's cleaned everything out," Gen said. She sounded like she could hardly believe it herself.

"She did."

"There's nothing left of hers. It looks like she scrubbed everything down. She even took out the trash." Gen poked around under the kitchen sink, where the trash can stood clean and empty.

"At least she was considerate enough to clean up before she ran like hell," Liam said. He was standing in the middle of the tiny kitchen with his arms crossed over his chest, his lips pressed into a tight line.

"Well … did you call her?"

Liam looked at Gen like she was an idiot. "Of course I called her. You think that idea never occurred to me? I called her right after I called you."

"Well?" Gen prompted him.

"She didn't answer. I texted her, and she didn't answer that, either."

"But … you said the yurt is still there?"

"Yep."

They walked out of the house and down the path to the barn, where the yurt stood silent and alone in the center of the big space.

"She's going to have to get in touch, then," Gen said. "Plus, there's a contract."

"A contract?" Liam turned to her.

"Yes. When she accepted the artist's residency, she signed a contract agreeing to produce a certain body of work that I would represent to the galleries. If she just leaves and doesn't come back, she's in breach of contract."

Liam felt his face heat up. "That's what your worried about? Your contract?"

"No, that's not what I'm worried about," Gen said, her voice gentle, trying to soothe him. "I'm just saying that she'll have to come back, or at least call me. She can't just be … gone."

"Well, she sure as hell looks gone," Liam said.

"But … what happened between the two of you? What did you say to her?" Gen lifted her hands in puzzlement, then let them fall to her sides.

"I just … I said I loved her."

"Oh."

To his horror, Liam felt his eyes fill with tears, and he blinked a few times to clear them so Gen wouldn't see.

"Oh, God, I'm sorry," Gen said. She put her hand on his arm.

He was torn between feeling grateful for that gesture of comfort and mortified that he was showing this kind of vulnerability in front of his sister-in-law. In the end, he opted for accepting the comfort.

"I'm an idiot." He rubbed his eyes with his fingers. "I knew she wasn't ready to hear it. I knew it. And I had to say it anyway. God, I'm a fuckup."

"No, you're not." She stroked his arm a little. "You're not a fuckup. It was sweet, what you said to her. She's the idiot if she can't accept what you're offering her."

"No." He shook his head, having gotten himself back under control. "No, she's just scared. She's scared shitless, and I knew that, and I pushed her too far too fast."

"Well … what are we going to do about it?"

Liam grinned despite his misery. "We?"

"Of course. You don't think I'm going to let my favorite brother-in-law lose out on true love, do you?"

Liam raised his eyebrows. "I'm your favorite?"

"Colin was my favorite last month when he helped me with my accounting for the gallery," she said. "It's your turn."

"I'm not about to turn down the help. What's the plan?" he asked.

"Let me try to call her. Then we'll see where we're at."

Gen's strategy was to keep her call to Aria completely businesslike. That seemed like the best way to get a response, Liam thought, considering it was Aria's private life—not her professional one—that had caused her to flee.

She waited a little while so her call would not come immediately after Liam's. If she called right away, Aria would know that she was contacting her on Liam's behalf.

When Gen's call went straight to voice mail just as Liam's had, the two of them reached out to Daniel Reed.

"She won't take a call from me, because she's scared. And she won't take a call from Gen, because she thinks it's really from me," Liam told Daniel as he and Gen stood in the man's studio, making their case.

"But it really is from you," Daniel said, not unreasonably.

"What's your point?" Liam said.

"Please?" Gen asked, her head tilted slightly in a way that probably got Ryan to say yes to just about anything she wanted. "She's more likely to listen to you, because you're not right in the middle of the situation."

"I'm nowhere near the situation," Daniel agreed. "I don't belong in the same zip code as the situation." He'd asked to hold the baby when they'd first arrived, and now he jiggled James in his arms to settle him.

"I know you like her," Liam said. "I figure you want what's best for her. Well, goddamn it, I'm what's best for her. I know it and she knows it. I just have to get her to admit she knows it."

"I don't see what that's got to do with me," Daniel protested.

"Look. If you help us get in touch with her, Liam won't go after her."

"What?" Liam said. "But I—"

"You won't," Gen insisted to Liam, then turned back to Daniel. "We just want to make sure she's okay. That's all."

"That's all?" Reed looked skeptical. In his arms, James waved his little hands around, his face scrunched up as though he might start to cry.

"Yes," Gen said.

They both looked at Liam, who glowered at them like he was trying to figure out whether he should rip somebody's limbs off at the joints.

"Fine," he said finally.

"Really?" Daniel said.

"I said fine, didn't I? You calling me a liar, Reed?"

"Nope. No." Daniel jiggled the baby some more. "I'm not saying that."

"Good. Now, are you going to call her, or not?"

"I'll call her," he said after a moment of thought. "But I don't know if I'm going to get any further than either of you."

"All you can do is try," Gen said. James had made good on his threat to cry, and Gen took him from Daniel and settled him in on her shoulder.

"Get your goddamned phone," Liam told Daniel.

Aria didn't pick up the phone for Daniel, either. But he left a voice mail message, and she called him back a day and a half later.

She knew he'd likely called at Liam's urging, but she needed to talk to someone, and Daniel was good at listening when she had to hash something through.

"So, what's the deal?" he asked by way of greeting when he answered the phone. His directness was one of the things she liked about him.

"The deal is ... the deal is that people need to leave me

alone." She'd arrived at her apartment in Portland less than an hour before, after two days of marathon driving, and her phone was already full of text messages and phone calls.

"Fair enough," Daniel said. "If that's what you really want."

She threw her free hand into the air, exasperated. "Why would I say that's what I want if that's not what I want?"

"Oh, I don't know," Daniel replied thoughtfully. "Generally, when somebody runs like a scared bunny after somebody says they love her, it doesn't indicate a simple desire for privacy. It indicates problematic feelings. At least, in my experience."

"Does it? And where did you get your psychology degree?"

"I filled out a form in the back of a magazine. Now that you mention it, I don't think that's how it's usually done."

Aria wanted to be mad at him, but it was hopeless. She laughed miserably and then plopped down onto the sofa in her apartment, just a few feet away from the pile of luggage she'd dropped in the corner. It was late, and the sky was dark outside her window. She'd only turned on one small lamp when she'd come in—her mood didn't call for any more light than that—and the room was full of shadows.

"I just can't handle any of this, Daniel," she told him. "Liam, the Delaneys. They're so ... and I'm so ..."

"They're so what?" Daniel asked, pressing her. "Tall? Irish? Loud?"

"No, smartass. They're so ... so perfect! They're too nice! Too well-adjusted!" It sounded stupid now that she was saying it out loud, but there it was.

Daniel launched into his counterarguments. "A, they're not perfect, and I don't think I've ever heard anyone describe Liam as 'nice' before. And B, horrors! They're well-adjusted! Obviously, that's a deal-breaker."

"Did I already mention that you're a smartass?"

"Aria." His voice was serious now. He was done joking.

"What?"

"Cut the crap. What's really going on with you? Why did you leave Cambria before your residency was done? What scared you enough to make you do that? To make you throw away everything you'd worked for?"

"Liam. Liam scared me that much." Her eyes grew hot, and a fat tear fell down her cheek. "Because people don't stay. They don't, Daniel. Not for me. And I've always dealt with that. I've always survived. But this time …"

"You don't think you'd survive," Daniel finished for her.

Her silence was all the answer she gave him.

"Are you familiar with the concept of a self-fulfilling prophecy?" he asked.

"Daniel—"

"All I'm saying is, it's not going to work out if you go out of your way to guarantee it's not going to work out."

Suddenly, she felt unspeakably tired, as though all of her muscles were made of lead. "I have to go."

"Think about what I said?"

"Sure."

She was about to tap the button to end the call when he said, "Aria?"

"What?"

"Liam's the real deal. It pains me to say that, because he can be a real shithead sometimes. But he's a good guy. If he said he loves you, it's because he does. And if anybody's going to stick, it's him."

Thinking about Liam—good-guy Liam with his big heart and his earnest spirit—made her own heart hurt so much she thought it might stop beating. She hung up the phone, turned it off, and went about the business of living without Liam Delaney.

Chapter Thirty-Three

Liam spent the next few days nursing his broken heart.

He'd talked to Daniel, and he knew that Aria had gone home because she was scared of the emotional damage Liam might do to her. But what about the emotional damage she was doing to him? What about that?

He felt sorry for himself, and he figured he had a right to it, under the circumstances. He had a right to feel what he felt, and to wallow in it a bit.

A little wallowing was fine; too much wasn't productive. Aria needed him, whether she realized it or not. For a lesser person, he might have walked away because the whole thing was too damned hard. But Aria wasn't a lesser person.

He knew what he had to do; it was time to go do it.

Ryan wasn't home when Liam went over there about a week after Christmas to ask whether he could get by on the ranch for a bit while Liam went up north to see Aria.

Gen was there with the baby, so he talked to her instead.

"Just tell him for me, will you?" Liam said as Gen walked around the living room picking up various baby-related items from the floor and every other available surface.

"Sure, I'll tell him. But what are you going to do?"

Liam shrugged. "I guess I'll figure it out when I get up

there."

"Hmm," Gen said.

"*Hmm* what?"

"I'm just thinking," she said. "You're going to need an excuse."

"An excuse?"

"A reason for you to go up there and see her. A reason she's got to let you in the front door instead of closing it in your face."

"Oh. All right." From the sound of it, Gen knew more about this kind of thing than he did, and he wasn't too proud to accept a little guidance.

"Hmm," she said again.

Gen's solution—and it was a pretty good one—was to have Liam drive the yurt and all of the related supplies up to Aria in Portland. Somebody had to do it. If it wasn't him, it would be some anonymous delivery driver. Why not accomplish a necessary errand and help Liam meet his goals in the process?

Hopefully, she'd agree to see him when he got there without putting up too much of a fuss about it. If not, he could use her yurt as a hostage.

Because of the logistics of moving something as big and potentially fragile as the yurt without damaging it, Liam wasn't able to get on his way immediately.

Gen had people she used for this sort of thing, and she called them. Since they were coming down from the Bay Area and they already had a full schedule, it took them a day or two to get there. Then, the whole process took some time: two guys in cotton gloves disassembling the yurt according to the drawings in a notebook they'd found in the barn, cataloging each piece, packing all of the various parts in protective crates, and creating large amounts of paperwork detailing what they'd done and how.

When that was finished, Gen had the guys pack everything into a rental truck Liam had gotten down in San Luis Obispo. The art handlers, who clearly left nothing to chance, strapped everything down in the back of the truck with such care that if Liam were to go careening off a cliff, the art would likely come through it undamaged even as Liam himself lay broken and bleeding in the wreckage.

With all of that done, Liam got ready to set off for Portland on a bright, clear Tuesday morning during the first week of January. He had Aria's address—provided by Gen—in his Google Maps app, he had bottled water and some snacks in the cab of the truck, and he had a bag packed with some spare clothes and his toothbrush. He hadn't packed too much, because he figured if he couldn't close the deal within a day or two of his arrival, it wasn't going to happen at all.

"Well, I guess that's it, then," he said as he stood awkwardly by the driver's side door, Gen and Sandra waiting to see him off.

"Now, you drive careful," Sandra said, reaching out to fix the collar on Liam's flannel shirt. "You get up north a ways, it rains more than it does here. A big truck like this, it might be hard to handle on slick roads."

"I know, Mom. I've driven in rain before."

"But the truck—"

"I've driven a U-Haul before." He kissed her cheek and gave her a quick hug to reassure her that he wasn't going to die in a ball of flames after a head-on collision.

"Listen, you can do this," Gen said. She wasn't talking about the truck, or about the weather. "Aria wants this. She just doesn't know how to say yes to it. You just need to … you know … give her a little nudge." Gen pantomimed the nudge, her hands pushing an invisible Aria.

"Yeah, yeah." Liam felt embarrassed to be getting the advice and concern of the two women, who both undoubtedly had other things to do. Still, it was nice, having people care about him. It was something he'd always had, something he'd taken for granted. Aria had never had love so constant that she didn't have to give it a thought.

Well, now she would, and she would just have to get used to it.

Liam climbed into the truck, fired up the engine, and got onto the road headed south to State Route 46, then east toward Highway 101. The drive was going to be long enough that he figured he'd have plenty of time to figure out what he was going to say to Aria when he got there.

Whether she would listen to him was anyone's guess.

When Aria had left Cambria in a hurry on the evening of Christmas Day, she'd regretted leaving the yurt behind. She figured she'd deal with that later.

Once she'd settled back into her apartment, she realized just how problematic that was.

How was she going to explain to Gen why she'd fled Cambria and abandoned the residency? How could she expect Gen to go to the trouble of packaging and shipping the piece, after the way she'd run away?

Aria was in breach of contract. What would that mean in practical terms? Was she going to owe Gen money? If so, how much?

And finally, there was the fact that Gen was Liam's sister-in-law. Aria wanted to cut off all contact with the Delaneys, but how could she do that when she and Gen Porter had financial and legal business between them?

All of that would have been difficult to navigate given the

best of circumstances. But these weren't the best of circumstances. In fact, the circumstances kind of sucked.

Aria felt as though she'd been lowered into a pit of sadness so deep she couldn't even see the sky from here. The sadness, she told herself, wasn't about missing Liam. It was about the chaos of everything—how she'd left her artwork behind, her residency blown, her career in shambles. And yes, maybe she felt bad about how she'd rejected him, because rejection hurt, and she never meant to hurt Liam.

But she didn't miss him. Of course not. The raw despair she was feeling had nothing to do with the absence of him beside her in bed at night, or the fact that she longed to talk to him about this or about anything, and couldn't.

She didn't need him. She didn't want him. And she sure as hell could live without him.

The fact that she had to remind herself of that several times a day, sometimes while crying, didn't mean a thing.

Aria's landlady stopped by a couple of days after she got home, mainly to check in and make sure everything was okay. Everything wasn't okay, but Aria was determined not to give that fact away.

"Oh. Jeannie." Aria opened the door to the woman standing on her doorstep. Jeannie, who was in her mid-forties, had a long braid hanging down over each of her shoulders, and she was wearing a dress with a small floral print. The two things together made her look as though twelve-year-old Laura Ingalls had suddenly gained thirty years and been transported to the twenty-first century.

"Aria, hi!" Jeannie said. "Max told me you were back, but I told him, 'No, she can't be. She's not due back in town for another six weeks.' But here you are."

"Here I am." Aria tried to sound perkier than she felt. "My

residency ended a little early."

"Well, that's odd. Isn't it? It seems odd to me."

Aria knew she should invite Jeannie in, but she wasn't up for it. What she needed was to give the woman some kind of answers to satisfy her curiosity, then get her out of here.

"Well, it's unexpected, yes. But ... I finished my project earlier than I thought I would, so ..." She hated to lie, but the truth—she'd fallen ass over end for a man and had fled in terror—didn't seem like a viable option.

"Ooh, your project!" Jeannie's eyes widened in curiosity. "What is it this time? I loved that thing you did with the surfboard and the cats...."

They hadn't been real cats, of course, because that would have had protesters from PETA on her ass, and while that would have boosted publicity for the show, it wasn't quite the effect she'd wanted.

"It's ... a surprise," Aria said. If she started talking about the yurt, she'd never get the woman to leave.

"Ah. Got it. You don't want to spoil the big unveiling."

"Something like that."

"Okay. Well, I can't wait." Jeannie's ever-present smile faded, and she peered more closely at Aria. "Say. Are you okay?"

"I'm fine." Aria tried to sound like she meant it.

"Are you sure? You seem a little ..."

"Really, I'm just tired." Even before it was out of her mouth, Aria realized her mistake.

"Oh! Well, let me go downstairs and get you some herbal tea I've got—I have it mixed specially for me. Very energizing. Then I can give you the number for my aromatherapist, and—"

Aria stopped paying attention at *aromatherapist*. She closed her eyes and leaned her head against the doorjamb, listening to the perky tones of Jeannie's voice.

Chapter Thirty-Four

It was going to take Liam a couple of days to get to Portland. He made it all the way to Eureka the first day—a drive of five hundred miles that took him almost ten hours, factoring stops for food and gas.

He stopped at a Motel 6, bought a cold six-pack at a liquor store, and drank two bottles of beer while sitting on the bed watching football. He couldn't really focus on the game—football was his mother's sport more than his—so he tried reading a book he'd brought, a John Sandford novel that he figured had enough action to provide a pleasant distraction.

The book didn't work, either—he found himself reading the same paragraph multiple times while his mind wandered to Aria.

Finally, he gave up and called Gen.

"What if this doesn't work?" he said when she answered her cell phone.

"It'll work."

"You don't know that."

"You're right. I don't." Gen blew out some air, and Liam heard it over the line like a small gust of wind. "But, Liam? If it doesn't work, you'll survive." She didn't say it like she was trying to make light of the situation and tell him that he was overreacting. She said it like she meant it. Like she was genuinely uncertain whether he knew that he would keep breathing if Aria shut him down.

"I know it," he said.

And he did. If Aria shut the door in his face and never spoke to him again, he would, in fact, survive. But survival was one thing, and living the life he wanted for himself was another. Without Aria, he could survive all right. But he needed her in his life if he were really going to live.

He hung up the phone, finished the second beer, and stared at a bad framed landscape print on the wall opposite the bed.

"Goddamn it, Aria," he said to the empty room.

Then he took a hot shower and went to bed.

When Aria had refused to take any phone calls from anybody in the Delaney family, Gen had e-mailed her. The message had been strictly business. Gen had informed her that she would consult her attorney and get back to Aria regarding the issue of breach of contract, and that she hoped they could reach a solution that would be agreeable to both of them. Then she'd told Aria that the yurt had been carefully crated and was, this moment, being driven up to her in a U-Haul truck. The truck should arrive either late afternoon Thursday or on Friday morning.

It surprised Aria that Gen, always thorough and professional, hadn't mentioned the issue of payment for the delivery. Had Gen footed the bill? Would Aria be expected to reimburse her? It would be entirely reasonable if Gen expected her to pay the bill, but she figured the cost had to be substantial, given the particular considerations of packaging and delivering a large work of art. Aria's bank account was lighter than she'd like at the moment, and this wasn't going to help.

And then there was the question of where to store the yurt. Aria had storage space in the building's parking garage, but she wasn't sure it would be big enough for the crates to fit.

She was still fretting about all of that at about four p.m. on Thursday when the doorbell rang.

A peek through the peephole didn't tell her much; whoever was out there was turned the other way, looking at the door of the apartment across the hall.

"May I help you?" she said loudly through the closed door.

"Delivery," the voice said.

Maybe he had intentionally disguised his voice. Maybe she was expecting a stranger, so that was what she thought she heard. Either way, she wasn't expecting to see Liam standing there when she swung open the door.

But there he was, looking tall and built and all man, just like he was when she'd thought of him every minute since she'd left.

"Liam. This isn't ... I can't."

She tried to close the door on him. Liam put a hand on the door and pushed, not hard enough to force his way in, just hard enough to keep her from closing him out.

"Don't you want your yurt?" he said.

The connections in her brain were crossing in complex and confusing ways, and she shook her head slightly to clear it.

"You have the yurt?"

"Yeah. I thought Gen called and said I was bringing it."

"She called and said a *delivery guy* was bringing it."

"Well ... that's me, I guess. I have the yurt in the back of a truck. What do you want me to do with it?"

She looked at him wordlessly for a moment, then said, "That's not why you're here."

He pressed his lips together tightly, then nodded. "Maybe not. But that doesn't change the fact that I've got a damned yurt in the back of a truck, and I can't just leave it there."

Gen was right; the yurt ploy worked to get him in the door. She had no choice but to take him down to the basement and show him her storage space, then stand by while he unloaded the crates from the truck and put them where she told him she wanted them.

The crates were heavy, but he had a strong back and a hand truck. A light rain was falling, but he'd worked in rain more than a few times, so he barely noticed it as he began the process of transferring the yurt from one place to another.

He had more important things to worry about than rain. For instance, there was the question of how he was going to keep Aria from going back into her apartment and closing the door on him once his work was done.

He took his time while he thought about it. When the first crate was tucked away in her storage space—a smallish area enclosed by chain link fencing—he was in no hurry to go out and get the next one.

"How are you?" he asked as the two of them stood in the basement, the glow of fluorescent lights overhead and the smell of dust and mildew in the air.

"You don't need to make small talk," she said.

"It wasn't small talk. I really want to know."

From the looks of her, she'd been better. He guessed from the shadows around her eyes that she hadn't been sleeping much. Was that because of him? He was torn between finding that to be a hopeful sign and being concerned for her welfare. The concern won out.

"I'm fine," she said.

"I don't think you are." Might as well be blunt. That was one thing he'd learned from years of living with his mother: You didn't get anywhere by pussyfooting around about what you were thinking.

"Well ... I guess you can believe what you want." She looked into his eyes for a moment, then broke contact and looked at the cement floor. "Do you think we could just go get the rest of the crates now?"

His jaw flexed, then he nodded. "Come on, then."

Aria had been stunned when she'd opened the door and found Liam standing there. Stunned—that was the only word for it. Conflicting feelings had warred within her, and she hadn't known whether to feel thrilled that he'd followed her to Portland or dismayed that seeing him was going to make it so much harder to say goodbye.

Either way, she had fully expected to tell him she didn't want to see him. She'd been ready to close the door with him on the other side.

But the yurt had complicated things. She hadn't known how she was going to retrieve it from the Delaney place, and it seemed he'd solved that problem for her. If he had the yurt in his truck, she had to accept it. What choice did she have? Leave him to drive the thing back down to Cambria?

She'd put so many hours into it, and Gen had already begun making inquiries into where she would show it.

So, she'd pulled herself together, told herself to be businesslike about it, and showed him where to unload the crates.

But now he wanted to talk about how she was, and that wasn't going to lead anywhere good, especially if she told the truth. Because the truth was that she was miserable, gutted, barely surviving.

But miserable and gutted had been her normal condition for so many years that it hardly mattered now.

As they walked back out to the truck to get the next crate, Aria couldn't help but notice how damned good Liam looked. It wasn't that he'd done anything special. He was wearing faded jeans, a flannel shirt, and a jacket that looked like it had seen countless hours of work on the ranch. His chin and cheeks were darkened by a couple of days of stubble, and his hair was mussed from where he'd run his hand through it a few minutes earlier.

But Liam didn't have to do anything special to look good to her. All he had to do was be Liam.

She wanted so much to fall into his arms and stay there for the rest of her life, until the storm ended and the skies turned clear and blue, until she forgot everything that had come before, until they both grew old and comfortable in the fact of the two of them, needing no one and nothing else, forever.

But forever was a lie. Forever was a fairy tale.

Together, they loaded the rest of the crates into the storage space. They fit, though just barely.

And now they'd come to the critical point in his visit: He was going to try to stay, and she had to make him go.

"Thank you for bringing the yurt. I really appreciate it." She held out her hand for him to shake as one of the fluorescent light bars overhead buzzed.

"You want to shake hands? You're kidding me, right?" He looked at the hand disdainfully.

"Liam—"

Then, suddenly, he took the hand and used it to pull her to him and into his arms. He kissed her, claiming her mouth with all of the urgency he felt. She stiffened, not wanting to respond to him. But her body betrayed her and she melted into him, her lips parting, her arms wrapping around him.

She couldn't let this happen. She simply could not. Because he wouldn't just hurt her when he inevitably left, as everyone always did. He would kill her. He would manage to do what everything before him had failed to accomplish: he would destroy her.

It was hard—it was so hard—but she wedged her hands in between them, put her palms against his chest, and pushed him away from her.

"No," she said. "Liam … no."

He let her go and stepped back, and ran a hand over his face.

"So, that's it, then? You don't want me?"

"I don't want … this." She made a sweeping motion with her hands to indicate the whole of what the two of them might mean.

"I don't believe that," he said. "I think you're just scared."

"I am!" It seemed absurd that she had to tell him that, as though he didn't already know it. "Of course I am! If you'd lived through what I have, if you'd—"

"Do you love me?" She could see in the set of his jaw, in the line of his mouth, that he was determined to keep control of himself, determined not to let his emotions rule him.

She wished she could do the same, but she was trembling, and her heart was pounding.

"Liam—"

"I figure you owe me an honest answer. You owe me that much."

Her vision blurred with tears. "Yes." She whispered the word so quietly she was surprised he heard it.

Liam nodded. "All right, then. I meant what I said at Christmas—I love you, Aria. And if you love me … well, I don't see why we shouldn't be together."

She wiped her eyes with her hands and took a deep, shaky breath. "I can't take the risk that it won't work. I'm not strong enough."

He stood there, still and silent. Then the muscles in his jaw flexed, and he shoved his hands into his jeans pockets.

"You know, Aria, I think that's a load of bullshit," he said.

"Damn it, Liam ..."

"I'm not finished," he said, interrupting her. "I figure I'll say what I have to say before I leave, whether you want to hear it or not."

She nodded, waiting.

"It's bullshit that you're not strong enough," he said. "To live the way you did and come out of it to be who you are today, you've got to be pretty goddamned strong. So, yeah, you're strong enough. You're just telling yourself that you're not because it's easier than putting yourself out there, taking the risk. But you know what? I'm worth it. This thing we've got? It's worth the risk."

The idea that she could just let him love her was so tempting, so alluring. But all her life, she'd dreamed of what it would be like if someone finally claimed her, if someone finally committed to belonging to her forever. First, she'd longed for a parent. Then, she'd longed for a partner, a lover, someone who could break through the walls she'd built and draw her out of the trap she'd constructed for herself.

But no one had ever come, and now she didn't believe it was possible that anyone ever would. Not even Liam. He thought he could stick—she believed that. But he didn't understand how broken she was, and he wouldn't want her when he found out.

"Maybe," she said finally. "But I still want you to go."

Liam left Aria's place feeling frustrated and hurt, but not defeated. She'd said she loved him, and that was something.

That was something big.

He wasn't naïve enough to think that love always won out. He knew that plenty of people loved each other and still hurt each other, still left each other, still broke each other into tiny pieces.

But if she didn't love him, he wouldn't have anything to build on, and he'd have no choice but to quit, go home, and nurse his broken heart.

Love wasn't always enough. But it was a key element if he was going to fight for her. Which he damned well planned to do.

Liam didn't believe in pressuring any woman to do something she didn't want to do. But this was different. Aria did want this. Hell, she needed this. She just didn't know how to let herself have it.

He planned to show her how. He just didn't know quite how to do that yet.

He drove the truck through the rainy streets of Portland and back to his motel, where he lay on the bed and looked at the ceiling, thinking about it.

She needed to know he could stick, that was all. She needed to understand what it meant to be him; Liam kept his promises and had absolute loyalty toward those he loved.

He was exactly the man she needed, and he knew it.

She would know it, too, before he was done.

After a night of restless sleep, Liam had the beginnings of a plan. The size and scope of the plan were going to make it difficult to accomplish, but the size and scope of the thing were also what was going to make it work.

The more he thought about it, the more he thought his idea was perfect. It addressed all of the longings of Aria's heart, whether she fully recognized them or not.

It also addressed some things Liam had been neglecting for himself for some time. It was a way to mature. A way to move forward.

If he did what he was planning and he still didn't manage to win her over, he would have put a lot of money and time and work into it just to be disappointed. But sometimes a man had to plunge headlong into something, no matter the consequences.

In the morning, he got into the truck, turned it in at a U-Haul place in Portland, caught a flight down to San Luis Obispo, and started doing what needed to be done to put the whole thing in motion.

Chapter Thirty-Five

For Aria, the key to getting by without Liam was convincing herself she was better off without him.

She didn't feel better off—not at all. But she told herself she was, day after day. She didn't necessarily believe it, but at least she eventually stopped arguing the point back and forth in her own mind.

That was how she got through the rest of the winter. She got through it by doing the tasks and errands and routines she always did, focusing on the minutia of her life—Was she out of paper towels? Did she need to pick up her dry cleaning?—instead of considering the bigger issues of love and contentment, and her own soul's longings.

Liam had taken to sending her letters through the mail, prompting Aria to wonder, why the mail? Why not e-mail? At first, she didn't open them, because she was afraid of what they contained. Was he angry? Was he begging her to reconsider? Was he trying to manipulate her?

But her resolve failed her on one rainy day in late January, and she read one. To her surprise, the letter was full of updates about his family and anecdotes about everything that was going on around the ranch, but there was no pressure, no bitterness. Just friendly communication from one person to another.

The letters began to come once a week. She didn't answer them, but she read them all, and after a while, she realized how much she looked forward to them.

It wasn't good, her looking forward to them. Those letters were a small wedge he was using to pry open the door to a relationship with her. Obviously, that was his intent. But it was safe as long as she didn't answer—that's what she told herself. As long as she stayed silent, up here so far away from Cambria, then how could her feelings for him hurt her?

She was still in touch with Gen, of course. They'd worked out an amicable deal for Aria to fulfill her contractual obligations. She'd transferred the yurt to her studio here in Portland and had finished it there. Gen had arranged for it to be shown at a studio in San Francisco in March, and Aria would provide Gen with a percentage of the sale, as they'd agreed.

The showing would have a performance component: Aria would live in the yurt for two weeks, and during gallery hours, she would invite visitors to come inside and sit with her. The plan was for Aria and the viewer to sit facing each other for a period of time to be determined by the visitor. Aria would sit silently, and the visitor could react to that however he or she chose.

Aria had done something similar in the past, without the yurt. She'd been surprised and gratified by how people had responded to it. They'd started out either uncomfortable or amused, but the longer they sat with her, with Aria silently looking at them in a relaxed and nonjudgmental way, the more things started to happen.

Some people began to talk about themselves, about their lives. Some stayed silent, simply looking back at her. Some felt a deep sense of relaxation. Some started to cry.

She wasn't certain what caused the emotional reaction in

people who responded that way, but she had a few theories. Maybe being silently observed made people think about themselves and about their lives. Maybe it made them deeply uncomfortable. Maybe it just made them feel seen, some for the first time in their lives.

By the middle of March, Aria and Gen had, together, arranged for the transport of the yurt to the gallery, they'd collaborated with the gallery owner on promotion for the show, and they had fine-tuned most of the details.

All that remained was for her to travel south and do the show.

Living in a yurt on an art gallery floor wasn't going to be nearly as appealing as a four-star hotel, but the discomfort, along with the opportunity for visitors to voyeuristically view her through the yurt's open door, was part of what would draw people to see her.

Her food would be brought to her, and she would have a ten-minute break every two hours to use the bathroom.

Other than that, the yurt she'd painstakingly made of refuse would be her home.

By late March, Liam's plan was most of the way to its fruition. He'd been working feverishly pretty much every moment that he wasn't performing his daily duties on the ranch. He'd hired a team of professionals, of course, and his brothers and sister were helping out here and there.

If this worked, he'd be congratulating himself on his ingenious, bold gesture for years to come. If it didn't, people would be looking at him in town, talking to each other about that poor bastard who'd done all this for a woman and had been dumped on his ass.

If that happened, at least he would know he'd tried. At least he would know he'd done everything he could.

He'd gone back and forth with himself on whether to go to her show in San Francisco. He wanted like hell to see her, just to be in her presence for a little while. The structure of the thing, as Gen had explained it, meant she would have to see him. She wouldn't have to talk to him—wouldn't even be able to, according to the rules of the deal—but she'd have to let him sit there with her as long as he wanted.

That seemed like too good an opportunity to pass up, but it would also be hard. Hard not to reach out and touch her. Hard to preserve his secret and not tell her what he'd done.

"You have to go," Gen told him a couple of days before the show was set to open. They were in the living room at the Delaney house before a family dinner, Liam with a beer in his hand, Gen with the baby snuggled up and sleeping in her arms.

"You think?"

"I do." She leaned toward him for emphasis. "It's not just a chance for you to see her. It's a chance for you to see who she is."

"I know who she is," he said. "I know her."

"You think you do, but this is her art. It's a big part of who she is as a person. You can't fully understand an artist if you don't understand their art. Believe me, Liam, because I know what I'm talking about. You have to go. You have to be there."

"Well ... I've seen the yurt. Hell, I helped her work on it." He wasn't sure why he was resisting. Was it because the idea of performance art puzzled him and made him feel dense because he didn't understand it? Or was it because he was afraid of going up there and being rejected?

"You've seen the yurt, but that's only part of it. Look." Gen put a hand on Liam's arm and squeezed lightly. "Aria's very private. She's very ... closed off. The performance part of it is how she lets people in. It's how she lets people really see her." She let go of him and sat back on the sofa. "You have to go."

He figured she was right, and anyway, just having the chance to see Aria's face, to breathe in her scent, would make it worth the trip, even if he had to crawl all the way to San Francisco.

He was scared, though, and he wasn't too big of a man to let Gen know it.

"I don't know what's going to happen when she sees me," he told her.

"Best case scenario, she remembers why she fell for you and she decides she can't stay away another minute."

That sounded too good to be true—which it was. "And the worst case scenario?"

Gen shrugged. "The two of you spend a few minutes inside a yurt made of trash, looking at each other and feeling awkward. After everything you've done for her, I figure you can manage that."

The weekend of the gallery opening, Liam drove north full of excitement and trepidation. Aria had made it clear that she didn't want to be with him, so showing up at her show could be interpreted as pushy. She hadn't answered any of his letters, so maybe he needed to just get the message already.

On the other hand, she'd told him she loved him. If Liam was choosing what to believe, he would choose that. He would choose that one moment when she'd said "yes." It had cost her something to say it, so it had to be true.

As he made his way up Highway 101 toward San Francisco, he reminded himself that a man never got anywhere by being timid about the things he wanted. A man got somewhere in life by being bold, by acting as though things were going to go his way until they actually did.

Hell, what did holding back ever get you? Redmond had held back when he'd loved someone, and he'd gotten years of loneliness and estrangement from his only son.

To hell with that. To hell with all of it.

Liam had come this far, he was by God going to go the rest of the way. If Aria turned him away when she saw him—if she refused to acknowledge him or even asked security to throw him out—then at least he would know he'd done what he could.

He'd know he'd been a man.

Chapter Thirty-Six

One nice thing about doing a show like this, Aria reflected, was that it took her mind off of Liam Delaney.

She thought about him so much that she was emotionally exhausted. But this—this period of time when she would be performing—would be about the audience and about the art, not about her. She'd have no choice but to focus on what she was doing, to the exclusion of all else.

To the exclusion, most of all, of Liam and all of her longing and regret.

That was what she told herself, though if she'd thought it out further, she'd have realized it was bullshit.

Two weeks living in a yurt inside an art gallery included nights, times when the gallery wasn't open. Then, she'd have nothing to do but think, and it was pure idiocy to imagine her thoughts would be about anything but Liam.

When the truth of that poked at her—which it did from time to time—she told herself that the Aria she'd be inside the gallery was all about performance. And she would simply perform the part of someone who wasn't preoccupied with a man.

She told herself it was working as she got herself set up inside the yurt with a mat on the floor and the various random items she needed to make herself comfortable.

She told herself it was working as the gallery opened and visitors began to stream in.

She told herself it was working as the first couple of people came into the yurt, sat with her, and then moved on.

She believed it right up until the moment when Liam folded his long body into the yurt and sat across from her, one leg tucked beneath him and the other stretched out awkwardly in front of him.

"Liam. What … You …" She was stammering, fighting competing urges to fall into his arms or flee for the exit. Her heart was pounding, and a sudden sheen of sweat covered her palms.

"*Shh.*" He put an index finger to his lips. "That's the deal, right? You're not supposed to talk?"

She'd completely forgotten that was, in fact, the deal.

Now, reminded of her role, she quieted and sat across from him, cross-legged inside her yurt, with Liam so close she could smell his soap and feel the warmth of his body. She waited, silently, to see what would happen next.

The thing about being still and quiet was that it made you think. Liam had thought quite a lot on his way up here, and before that, too. But it wasn't the same as the kind of thinking you did when you were in an enclosed space, saying nothing, sitting across from the person you'd been doing all that thinking about.

There was a process to it, a layer of phases. First, all he could think about was Aria so close to him, the way she looked, the complex mix of warmth and pain in her eyes as she locked her gaze on him.

Then, there was the self-consciousness, the wondering about what she was thinking, how she was feeling, whether she wanted him to leave.

Finally, once all of that passed, there was understanding.

Honestly, he'd thought this whole idea was stupid—the yurt itself was okay, but the thing with Aria sitting across from people and looking at them had seemed like so much New Agey bullshit.

But now, as he sat there, he started to get it. They were communicating, the two of them, without talking. They were making a connection that was different than the one they'd made before. He was seeing her—really seeing her—maybe for the first time. And he hoped she was seeing him.

And suddenly, in a sudden burst of inspiration, he understood what all of this was to her. He understood the yurt, and why she'd built it, and what it all meant in the context of her life.

She was itinerant. She was, essentially, homeless. All she had was a shell she'd built for herself out of the garbage of her belief that she could never hope for anything better.

The truth of it hit him hard, like a strong wind or a slap to the face.

She'd shown him who she was the moment she'd shown him the yurt that first day in the barn.

He wanted nothing more than to bring her out of here, out of the prison she'd built for herself, but that was no good. She had to decide to free herself. He couldn't do it for her.

When he'd come into the gallery, the owner had chatted with him a little, had told him that people were moved by the experience of sitting with Aria—that some of them even wept.

He'd thought that was crap. But now here he was, his eyes hot and filling with tears.

Gen had been right. It was good that he'd come. He hadn't known her—not really—until this moment.

•••

Sitting across from Liam without speaking, and without touching him, was one of the hardest things Aria had ever done. And it was also one of the most powerful.

He sat motionless, making eye contact with her, saying nothing, just being there, his presence strong and steady and real amid all of the artifice of this event, this place.

Time stretched on, and he didn't move, didn't look away from her.

When she'd done this kind of thing before, she'd sometimes felt inspiration about the people sitting across from her—about who they were as people, what they feared, what they dreamed.

Now, as Liam sat with her, she had an inspiration about him, something she was feeling now for the first time.

Looking at him, she knew—really knew—for the first time who and what he was. Rock solid. Steady. Reliable and sure. There was something so true and real in him, something she'd failed to notice or acknowledge before.

The inside of the yurt was dim and close, but the multi-colored skylight cast a dappled blue and green glow onto him, onto both of them, promising something better outside of this darkness.

When he finally got to his feet and left the little structure to make way for the next visitor, she knew what she had to do. She just hoped it wouldn't be too late by the time she was able to do it.

Chapter Thirty-Seven

Liam was working a couple of weeks later, building a porch railing. He'd built porch railings before, so he knew what he was doing, and he was able to let his mind wander a bit while he did what had to be done.

He was enjoying the spring weather, the sunlight streaming down on him, warming his back. He was enjoying the sound of the birds in the oak trees behind him.

He liked the work, liked the warm, tired feeling in his muscles as he hammered and sanded and hauled wood planks from one place to another. He liked the camaraderie between himself and the guys he had working with him, the banter, the kind of chatter that went on between men when there were no women around.

When his cell phone rang in his back pocket, he straightened, stretched his back, and pulled the phone out to answer it. The smell of wet grass and sawdust mingled pleasantly in the air.

He saw Gen's name on the display, and took the call.

"Hey, Gen. What's up?"

"Aria's at the house."

Liam froze. He wanted to say something, but no words were coming.

"Liam? Did you hear me? I said—"

"I heard you." He took a deep, shaky breath, then let it out. "She say why she's here?"

"She came to talk to you. Said she didn't want to call first because she didn't know what you'd say."

Liam put a hand on his belly, which was fluttering with nerves. "Well, I guess this is it, then."

"Should I bring her out there?"

"Yeah. Do it. Thanks, Gen." He hung up the phone and readied himself for whatever was to come.

"Where are we going?" Aria was sitting in the passenger seat of Gen's car, James in his car seat in the back, as they made their way along the curves of Santa Rosa Creek Road. To one side of the road, a grass-covered hill rose toward the blue sky. To the other, the creek burbled over rocks and past trees.

"I'm taking you to Liam."

"Okay, but … where?"

"Well … he didn't want me to tell you that."

"Why? Gen …"

"Just hang on. We're almost there."

Aria was so nervous she felt sick. Gen seemed equal parts tense and excited, and Aria imagined it was because she didn't know whether Aria and Liam would kiss or freeze each other out when they finally met.

The car crested a hill, and Gen turned off onto a dirt road that wound through a copse of trees and past the creek.

She pulled into a clearing in front of a pretty two-story house with a big front porch, white wood siding, dark gray trim, and the beginnings of a garden next to where the front walk would be.

The house appeared to be in the late stages of construction, with the porch railing still being built.

"Whose place is this?" Aria asked.

Gen didn't answer. She just got out of the car, so Aria had no choice but to follow.

Liam was inside the house when he heard Gen's car pull up.

"Looks like this is the moment, big guy." Liam's contractor slapped him on the back. "Good luck."

Liam swallowed hard. "Thanks. I'm going to need it."

He walked out the front door to meet Aria.

The first thought that came to Aria's mind was that Liam was helping a friend work on his house. This probably wasn't the best place for them to say what they had to say to each other, but it would have to do.

Liam stepped out onto the porch, which was still unpainted, the light wood looking fresh and smooth and spotless in the shade from the house.

"Hello, Aria," he said. She couldn't tell what was in his tone. Was it nerves? Relief? Regret?

"Liam. Can we talk?"

"We can. But first, I want to show you around some." He motioned for her to come up onto the porch, and then he ushered her in the front door.

Confused, she asked, "Is this a friend's place?"

"Not quite."

He didn't elaborate. Instead, he launched into a tour.

"Here's the front room. Big enough to have people over, if you're interested in that sort of thing, but small enough to feel cozy. At least, I think so." He moved on, and she followed him. "The kitchen's got an extra-large refrigerator like they've got in professional kitchens. Six burners on the stove. I'm not sure why that's important, but Ryan's friend Jackson says it is, so ..."

He led her through a tour of the pantry, various closets, four bedrooms, bathrooms equipped with double sinks, glass-tiled showers, deep soaking tubs. In the main rooms, oak floors gleamed in warm honey tones. Fireplaces—one in the living room and one in the master bedroom—promised warmth on the chilliest nights.

"So? What do you think?" Liam asked when they'd made the full circuit and were back in the living room in front of the big stone fireplace. His tone was neutral, but she could see that his hands were shaking slightly.

"It's beautiful. Whose is it?"

"It's yours," he said.

Once the words were out, there was no taking them back. Liam waited to see how she would respond. He wasn't much of a praying man, but he was praying now.

"It's … what?" She looked a little pale, and her voice was barely above a whisper.

"I built this. Me and a contractor and a crew of guys. For you. For the two of us, I mean." He shoved his hands into his pockets to keep them from trembling. "I wanted … I needed to do something to show you that I'm in it forever. You've never had a home—not a real one—and I figure that's one thing I can give you. If you want it. If you want me." He cleared his throat and ran a hand through his hair. "This can be your home. I can be your home. If you'll let me."

Tears sprang to her eyes, and she blinked to clear them. "You did this for me?"

"For you. For us. Yeah."

She looked around at the walls, the crown molding, the gleaming floors. "I can't believe you did all of this for me."

He looked at her, his face showing nothing. "Well. The

question is … do you want it? Do you want me?"

She nodded, the tears spilling onto her cheeks. Her throat was thick with emotion. "Yes. Oh, God. Yes."

She stepped toward him, and he met her in the space between them, pulling her into his strong, warm arms.

"You're home, Aria." He stroked her hair with his hand. "You're home."

If they had been alone, he'd have made love to her right there on the floor. But Gen was there with the baby, and so was the contractor, along with a crew of guys who were finishing up the last of the construction. So he had to make do with kissing her long and hard, with his hands holding her face to his.

"I came here to ask you to take me back," she said when they were pressed together, his body hard against hers, his arms around her. "I didn't know if you'd say yes. I didn't know if it was too late."

"No such thing as too late," Liam said. "Not with you and me. You could have come back in ten years, and I'd have been waiting."

"Liam … there are a lot of things that are broken in me."

He nodded. "That may be true, but we can fix them." He grinned. "I've got a hell of a contractor."

She didn't know if things would work between them, or if he'd break her heart into a thousand shattered pieces. But she knew she needed to be with him, no matter the risk.

She would give him her broken pieces and see what he could do with them.

"It's time to come out of the yurt," he said, stroking her hair.

"It is," she answered.

It was time, finally, to come home.

Go to www.lindaseed.com to sign up for Linda's twice-monthly newsletter and get information about new releases, exclusive content, giveaways, and more.

Made in the USA
Columbia, SC
14 August 2020